BO(
THE SOU]

Nancy Bowser

ISBN-13: 978-1507631935

Cover Design by Connie Stoffel

Unless otherwise stated, quoted Scripture is taken from the New King James Version (NKJV®). Copyright © 1982 by Thomas Nelson. Used by permission. All rights reserved.

Revised Standard Version of the Bible (RSV®), copyright © 1946, 1952, and 1971 National Council of the Churches of Christ in the United States of America. Used by permission. All rights reserved.

Note: This is a work of fiction. Names, characters, places, businesses and events are either the products of the author's imagination or are used in a fictitious manner.

DEDICATION

To the God of love, and all power, grace and mercy.
May Yours be the dominion for ever and ever.
Amen.

To the Lord Jesus Christ.
May all honor, power and glory be to Him who is victorious and has
overcome.

To the Holy Spirit.
May your intercession on behalf of the people be blessed.

To the Bride of Christ.
May you return to your first Love.
May the God of peace sanctify you completely;
And may your whole spirit, soul, and body be preserved blameless at
the coming of our Lord Jesus Christ.
May you be sober and alert, aware of the signs of the times.
May the Lord Jesus Christ lead you into hope, healing and freedom
so that you will be prepared to stand for Him and
against the evil in these last days.
And after you have suffered a little while, may the God of all grace,
who has called you to his eternal glory in Christ, restore, establish, and
strengthen you.

To abuse victims,
To those who have suffered severe trauma,
To those who are seeking to be free from bondage of any kind,
To those in need of healing.
May you fully know hope, healing and freedom through Jesus Christ.
May you persevere in His presence, power and perspective.
May you overcome with the blood of the Lamb and by the word of
your testimony.

To those who have no comprehension of these things.
May you have a new understanding of and compassion for those who
have.

May you be blessed,
Nancy Bowser
2015

CONTENTS

ACKNOWLEDGEMENTS

I want to thank my husband,
children and parents
for walking through life with me and loving
unconditionally.

I also want to thank my husband
for his love, patience, support and helpful guidance as I
worked on this book,
along with my dear intercessor friends
who encouraged me in this endeavor with their
prayers and faithful support.

AUTHOR'S NOTE

There are some, in reading this manuscript (Book One and Two), who would say I'm eccentric and have a vivid imagination bordering on crazy. Some would say that DID, dissociative identity disorder (alias MPD or multiple personality disorder, which is the splitting of the mind as a defense mechanism to escape the pain of reality), does not exist; and some would say that it is not DID, but demons.

Some will think I've gone too far and will close the book in fear or disbelief at the descriptions of Satanic Ritual Abuse and the disclosure of the plans and purposes of the Occult, Free Masons and Illuminati along with others who are working to usher in the New World Order, a sign of the end times.

Some will think the words here are just fiction. And then there are those who know the truth, have lived it themselves in one way or another; some who know the validity, the power, the hope, healing and freedom that comes from the healing power of Jesus Christ and His blood; of integration of the spirit, soul and body as it works together in unity with the Spirit of Truth; and some who are searching for this very thing.

Some believe in the reality of the spiritual world, of the two kingdoms at war with one another, one of light and love, the other of darkness and death, of angels and demons, both fighting since the beginning of time as we know it, for the souls of mankind. Some recognize the reality of the spiritual, but don't believe that it affects Christians; and others (especially Christians) know from experience the strongholds of power that Satan wields over those who either knowingly or unknowingly enter into his dominion of darkness and the bondage that entraps and seeks to destroy them. Some of these have experienced deliverance as they surrendered to God and worked through the process of dismantling Satan's rights to rule in their lives.

These two kingdoms or spiritual realms are much more closely related than many would like to believe, for the one was born of the Other. In the beginning was the Word, and the Word was with God and the Word was God.

I've heard it said that it is the other way around, that the one that came after, the one of demons and darkness and death, is the most ancient of all religions. And I suppose if it is religion rather than relationship one is speaking of, then, yes it would be the oldest. However, it was God who, in love, created Lucifer and his minions, the very ones who chose to leave the relationship in search of power and authority of their own.

Satan is not a creator, just a copycat. Everything in Satan's kingdom is a replica of the real thing. All of Satan's works are tricks of deception, a distortion and perversion of God's supernatural power, and as the day of the Lord grows closer, it seems as if he's pulling all his tricks out of his bag.

In general, we don't see God doing supernatural things much any more. Why is that? There are many differing doctrines concerning this question, but it really comes down to the fact that God is supernatural and the inventor of supernatural works. His nature and character haven't changed just because some copycat devil is out there frightening people with stolen tricks.

It seems to me that many Christians have become afraid that all supernatural activity is demonic, and they take great care not to fall under the lies of deceiving spirits and doctrines of demons as 1 Timothy 4:1 warns. However, they have gone to such an extreme in trying to protect themselves that they have voided out the voice of the Holy Spirit along with His gifts, and have created a systematic theology through which they have every trap that they were trying to avoid!

On the other hand, there are those who have gone to the extreme of wanting the gifts and power of the

Holy Spirit without studying and applying the sound doctrine of Jesus Christ found in scripture. When there is a lack of knowledge of the truth and it is coupled with desiring the gifts from a place of selfish ambition rather than from an intimate love for God, it is very easy for deceiving spirits to gain a place. This desire for power without love is manipulation and control, the definition of witchcraft itself.

Is our fear so great that we have hindered God from doing supernatural things? Have we asked God to stop being God? Has our love for Jesus grown so cold that we have replaced it with worship of self? Have we as a church asked God to be who we want Him to be rather than embracing who He really is? Have our consciences become so seared by the perversion around us that we are blinded and deafened to truth and unaware that God has been displaced in our lives, homes and churches?

Have we allowed lies, deception, fear, doubt, unbelief and disbelief to hinder God from doing what He does? From anointing us to be and do what He created us for? Have we so freely given these gifts and abilities over to the enemy who is using them for his own destructive purposes?

In these seemingly hopeless days of evil, our youth are so hungry for the supernatural and true move of God that they have fallen prey to the alluring deceptions of Hollywood's version of vampires and werewolves as their heroes. They are seeking out and embracing the enticements of the occult like lambs to the slaughter. If God's people don't fill the shoes, Satan's people are eagerly waiting to do just that.

I believe that God is calling out and waiting for His people to take up His mantle and to begin walking in the gifts of the Spirit. I put to you Christians, isn't it time for us to take back the gifts and abilities that God created us, His people, to have? To stop allowing Satan to distort and pervert them and cause us to be afraid of them or to enticed and led astray by them? To crucify our flesh, pick up our cross and follow Jesus?

We would do so much damage to the enemy, and would bring so much hope, healing and freedom to the world if we would take back the gifts, keys, weapons and tools that God has given to us, and learn to use them effectively in these last days!

It is time for us to stop walking in fear and to begin walking in faith! To start listening to His voice, to take up His authority and power that brings His Kingdom here to earth. It is time that we put an end to Satan's lies in this area of the church, for if we don't, in essence we have already opened ourselves up to deceiving spirits and bondage that leads to destruction.

While it's true that this work is fiction, words without experience have no power behind them. I can only write what I know, what I have learned through years of discipleship and Christian counseling.

Jesus is my Soul Redeemer. He redeemed me the moment I first confessed my sins and asked Him to be my Savior; and He continues to be my Soul Redeemer as I choose Him and His ways every day. I want God to be God in every area of my life. I need Him! I need His eyes to see, ears to hear, heart to love, and power to live. I need all the supernatural gifts, abilities and help from my heavenly Father that He sees fit to pour out on me and in me and around me.

I am committed to studying His Word, listening for His voice, surrendering my right to rule and obeying in faith as I stand on the promises of His Word, firmly rooted and grounded in His Love. I am committed to fighting the battles in the spiritual realm that the Holy Spirit leads me into, and to running this race with perseverance.

My prayer is that I will love the Lord my God with with all my soul, with all my strength and nd; and that I will love others as I love 27); and from this place, I will preach and of Jesus Christ, heal the sick, cleanse the lepers, raise the dead and cast out demons. Freely I have received, and freely I want to give (Matthew 10:7-8).

I hope you will join with me in reading the story of those who have received salvation and committed their lives to fulfilling this awesome journey of trusting and obeying our Soul Redeemer.

It may be that you will begin to see glimpses of truth that challenge your belief systems; that will shake the sleeping into wakefulness, and the dead into life. And I hope that the reader will bear in mind that I am not writing against anything except Satan's deceptions. I am writing for something, and that is for hope, healing and freedom in and through Jesus Christ as His bride is being prepared to enter into the end times on this earth. I am writing for the glory, honor and praise of our Great God.

PROLOGUE

"I have come as light into the world, that whoever believes in me may not remain in darkness." (Jesus: John 12:46, RSV)

I **was enthralled** as I sat quietly listening to the appalling tale that was unfolding before me as the beautiful, older woman of God recounted the story of her life. It was a tale woven with horror and peace, of torture and healing, of despair and joy. I had heard bits and pieces of it before and I had yearned to understand this peace that characterized her life and radiated from her in spite of all the unspeakable things she had been through.

It was with this in mind that I had asked if I could come and interview her. I was so glad that I had brought my digital recorder. Hours had passed since she had begun speaking, and as her story came to an end, she leaned over close to me and took hold of my hand. Her eyes took on a far away look and she passionately proclaimed in a voice barely above a whisper, "They are out there waiting.... Thousands upon thousands of them...hopelessly waiting...."

It was as if she had gone someplace inside her mind that I couldn't follow. I gently asked, "Who is waiting?"

The question seemed to remind her of my presence, and she slowly brought her eyes back to focus on mine as she answered, "Those who are being taken away to death. Satan is the thief and has stolen parts of the souls of many unsuspecting people, even Christians. They are hopelessly bound and are being led to the slaughter. My heart sorrows for those whom I understand so well, and I cry out with the Lord's heart, *'Whom shall I send, and who will go for* 'Where are His hands upon this earth? Where are His is His heart of compassion for those who are 1emy? Where is the church, the body of 1ed, and then continued. "I don't think Jesus is the Overcomer who triumphs

10

victoriously, but He uses His people. They must be told!" In that instant, the story of The Soul Redeemer seemed to be downloaded into my mind.

It's not just her story. It belongs to countless others around the world; many experiences all pooled into one book. It's fiction, and yet it's based on truth. And so it's my prayer that as this book is read, that the reader would not get lost in some of the difficult details, but that the God of peace would guard your hearts and minds in Christ Jesus and would help you to know the truth.

My reason in writing this book is to call the church, the bride, the body of Christ to action in preparation for the coming storm of the end times; to bring the darkness into light; the secrets out into the open; that Satan would lose his ability to hide; that his schemes would be laid open and bare before the world; that God's power, might and complete victory would be made known; and that God's people would have an awareness of the need.... After all, Jesus came to destroy the work of the devil, to heal the broken hearted and to set the captives free. We, His people are to do the works that He did, and even greater....

*A*nd now for the story...

It was in the days when God had awoken the watchers, the seers, the intercessors, upon the face of the whole earth because the days were evil. The signs of the times pointed to the end of days, and YHWH was calling His own people together to pray, to usher in the end of time on the earth as we know it.

It was the time when God was pouring out His Spirit upon all flesh, and His presence and power were manifested in the abundant usage of every spiritual gift. It was a time when many of God's people were prophesying, dreaming dreams and seeing visions as God was indeed raising up an army that was being trained and equipped for the battles that had begun raging against the principalities and powers in the heavenly places, battles that crushed the enemy under the feet of those obedient to Christ; battles that would only increase in intensity as the intercessors gained momentum and unity.

And it was the time when Satan had his own plans, plans for the annihilation of all Christians and the building up of his own kingdom on the earth, the New World Order.

Every intercessor had a story. Every intercessor had witnessed and experienced the miraculous healing, delivering power of God Almighty in their own lives. This is the story of just one of those intercessors.

CHAPTER 1
BATTLE-AX

"You are My battle-ax and weapons of war." Jeremiah 51:20

P resent day.....

N icole stood facing the two men and knew she was in trouble. She found her voice and said "I am just leaving, so if you'll excuse me...."

"No problem lady," Victor said, but his expression and body language said otherwise. The two men glanced at each other with an air of camaraderie, and then they turned their attention back to Nicole.

The second replied, "Yeah, sure. We just want to have a little fun with you; then we'll let you go." Without taking his hungry eyes off of Nicole's body, he added, "I don't think he'd mind her showing up with a few bruises in places that won't show, do you Victor?"

She saw no way of escape, and Nicole's emotions suddenly changed from fear to anger. "God, I thought you were with me! I thought you would protect me. Where are you? Where are your angels?" her spirit cried out. The words of Isaiah 63:15 rang through her mind. *"Where are Your zeal and Your strength, The yearning of Your heart and Your mercies toward me? Are they restrained?"*

Nicole began to sense what seemed like a circle of protection surrounding her, and then she heard a familiar voice answer as power and authority began to pulse and resonate throughout her spirit, soul, and body. *"Remember, Nicole. You have the Sword; use it."*

Had there been a witness to the events that followed, the question would surely have arisen. How was it possible that this petite, inconsequential woman had become such a warrior?

PART 1
BLOODLINE

CHAPTER 2
BLOODLINES

The year was 1889...

The baby was a boy. The two dark angels hovered outside the house, as close to the room where the newborn slept safely in his mother's arms as possible. Their fear became reality as a third, larger, darker angel appeared.

"I thought you had this under control," the newcomer hissed.

The others both tried to make excuses simultaneously as to the reason they had failed to end this pregnancy, but were interrupted by the unexpected understanding of the third demon.

"We have all misjudged the extent of His power over this bloodline. The high counsel has already heard of your incompetence, and has called a meeting to discuss options. I am to stay here and watch for any opportunity that might present itself for me to creep in and steal the life," explained the Spirit of Death. He knew the chances of that happening were minimal because the love of the parents for their "God" was strong, and their prayers had built hedges of protection around themselves and their home. Even now, while they were sleeping, the brightness of the shining angels protecting them caused Death to need his blinders, and he was outside the house! At this point, he was relying on his senses to detect any point of weakness in the light, a chink in the armor through which he might be able to take advantage... He continued, "The two of you are to appear in court as soon as possible."

The relief that had come through the understanding words of the dark angel a moment before quickly vanished as they contemplated their fate in the hands of the high counsel. There was nothing they could do but obey, and as they swooped up and away, they conversed together, consoling one another. After all, they had worked together many times before and had been quite successful. That was why they had been assigned this important case! They were not mere peons in the dark kingdom. They were important spirits! Not at the top of ranking demons, but certainly not at the bottom either! Surely they would not be punished too severely, for after all, everyone experiences failure from time to time....

This was the line of communication between them until they came close to their destination and fear began to overtake them once again. Their true nature of pride, preservation of self at all costs began to emerge; their consoling tones quickly ended and became a blame game as Infirmity assigned the responsibility of their failure to his companion, Miscarriage, and vise versa. By the time they reached the court house, they were close to combat mode.

"Order in the court!" shouted the acting judge. As the disciplinarian wolf-type spirits that were surrounding the room cracked their legendary whips, Infirmity and Miscarriage grew quiet and hung their ugly, misshapen heads in shame and fear.

The judge continued. "Because of the failure of these two incompetent nincompoops, our job now is to discuss options, not to punish them...although we hold the right to do so at a later time." Infirmity braved a glance around the room and witnessed the vile expressions of the demons looking back at them. He noted the look of anticipation as some were hungrily licking their lips at the mere thought of punishment, of violence, and he was grateful when the judge turned the focus of the meeting back onto the problem of the family by saying, "As much as we'd all enjoy a mutilation right now, we need the input and information this team has gained through their watchfulness of and interaction with the people in this case."

The courtroom erupted in loud exclamations of disappointment, and the judge beat his gavel on the podium and the whips cracked, quickly restoring order.

"Court is now in session! Let's begin."

It was established that this family had been under surveillance for generations. The baby boy was the concern at this moment, as were any other children that would be born to Sophia and Hans. The mother's bloodlines had strong ties with the Illuminati and the occult, however, Sophia had rebelled and gone rogue. The father's family had been Christians for several generations, but because of curses of emotional distance, isolation, and spirits of hindrances toward spiritual growth assigned to hide and protect those curses, his family had been kept in check, until now. Their spirits may have belonged to the High King and they may have been morally righteous, but there had been no real relationship with their Maker. No evidence of the One called the Holy Spirit. Sophia was the problem. She loved her Savior and this love had been the reason that Death had tried for years to steal her life. Her life was clearly guarded by the Holy One, and because of this and the many holy angels surrounding her, he was never able to get anywhere close enough to inflict his sting. It had finally come down to stopping her bloodline from continuing, and so Infirmity and later Miscarriage had been assigned to her. She was never supposed to be able to conceive a child or carry it to term if the unexpected happened and conception did occur.

As the appointed speaker who had been recounting the family heritage summed up his research by declaring that it was Love that seemed to be the root of the problem, the whole court erupted into a frenzy of hisses and curses. Many began spitting up what looked like green puss out of their mouths, snouts or beaks at the mention of that despicable word, "*Love*". The court room that had smelled badly before now reeked with a stench that was worse than an infected human limb full of gang green when lanced.

When the ranting and raging and stomping in the room subsided and order was reestablished, the high court began searching through the generational bloodlines with hatred, a motivation that triggered a renewed vigor and determination to find any open door, no matter how small, that might allow them to reroute the current course of this family.

Evaluating the father's side revealed more possibilities. In fact there was a building of excitement in the room at discoveries of open doors. Several generations before, there had been a shaman, a medium in the family, a woman actually. Her specific ruling spirits of Defilement, Witchcraft, and Seduction had been eradicated from the next generation, however, when her son had come in contact with some Christians and had converted to their faith. The court's hope became founded in the fact that the bones of Defilement and his minions were still in place in the bloodline because of a curse the shaman had strategically positioned in them before she died. These curses blocked the Holy Spirit's seal from complete closure in that family's bloodlines, and held the door open in wait. Before her death, the shaman had made a blood sacrifice of a ram, the emblem and representation of Satan himself, and then mixed it with a stolen bit of her son's blood. In this way, the bloodlines of Satanism had been held open, waiting for the opportunity to become reestablished in hopes of cutting off the abhorred spiritual blood line of Christ.

The court room exploded with shouts of enthusiasm and anticipation! Breakthrough was eminent, and now was the time for planning. It would take patience and careful strategizing in order to mask the deception and stay hidden long enough to avoid exposure and risk of discovery. Sophia was a watchman and had the Gift of Discernment. She was an intercessor and was connected with the heart and mind of the High King. She would not be easy to fool.

To Infirmity and Miscarriage it seemed that the interrogation process would never end as they were questioned thoroughly regarding everything they could think of concerning Sophia and Hans that could possibly be of any help. The high counsel came up with many plans, but none seemed to be the right one; that is, one that they could all agree on and that they could all foresee having the desired results. When the dissension in the court became uncontrollable, it was with much dread that the acting judge shouted the ultimatum he had been trying to avoid. He would call upon the presence of one higher in rank to come and decide upon their course of action.

At this proclamation, the room grew silent. The seeker, scanner and eavesdropping spirits had done their job; for it was evident that IS was near before he was seen. The temperature seemed to drop and the air filled with the tangible presence of evil that inspired dread even in the hearts of the Spirits of Fear. Awe and terror took on an image as IS slithered into the court room full of power and confidence.

There was none standing upon the arrival of IS. [*A note to the reader: IS is pronounced as the letter I and then the letter S*]. His presence commanded reverence, complete respect and immediate obedience. All bowed down before him, and no one dared to even glance at him. When he spoke, it was barely above a hissing whisper. *"What is so difficult about killing a baby and its mother?"* He spread his wings wide, floated up into the air and wrapped his wings around his snake-like, reptile looking body, his true form. When he uncovered his body and retracted his wings, he descended onto the floor in the form of a man, a very delicious looking, beautifully handsome man, with slicked back black hair, dressed in black pants, shirt and boots. There was something that caused one to evaluate the striking beauty of his face, for while it was obvious that it was predominately masculine, there were also some feminine traits that were not as evident except upon further inspection. Over his shoulders, covering his clothes was a huge purple mantle or cape. He could take any shape he chose, and had many disguises, but this was his favorite.

IS began pacing the length of the court room, taking note of all present. Miscarriage had never been in such close proximity to one so high up before. IS stopped directly in front of him and repeated the question a little

19

more loudly this time. "What is so difficult about killing a baby and its mother?"

Miscarriage did the only thing he could think of, and that was to blame the stronger of the two. "Your honor," he blubbered, "It was Infirmity's fault. He was supposed to make her so sick that she would either die herself or be unable to conceive."

"It is not my fault!" Infirmity said as he kicked Miscarriage. "It was that woman! She..."

"ENOUGH!" The powerful roar emanated from IS, who, without touching either one of them, picked them both up by the scruff of their necks and threw them across the room. Every one was still bowing with their heads touching the ground, and no one gave in to the temptation of watching the display of violence. Infirmity and Miscarriage landed hard on their heads and stayed right where they landed, fearing that any sign of movement might bring on more attention of the negative kind.

IS sauntered purposely over to the empty chair that had previously been occupied by the acting judge, and sat down. After a moment or two, he said, "At ease. We have work to do. Tell me why this case has drawn so much attention; and I want all the information relevant to this case." The rest of the high court slowly rose, took their places and were surprisingly quiet through the remainder of the meeting as the judge spoke for them, giving IS the information he asked for. He was careful to explain that the relationship between the mother and the High King was very strong; that her prayers were effective; that it had been prophesied that the boy's life or those in his future bloodline, if not stopped, would lead many to freedom which would result in many losses of those they held in captivity.

IS contemplated all he had heard, then more to himself than anyone else he recalled, "I remember Lord Satan mentioning this very family. He had just come from one of his visits to heaven where he had been summoned...."

He was quiet a moment, then stood and said, "I need more understanding of this case." IS closed his eyes as he went into a trance like state, then projected himself toward the high place, the favorite earthly dwelling of his master. He arrived just as Satan was ready to begin his walk to and fro upon the earth.

IS bowed low. "My master."

"What is it that brings you here, IS? Rise and walk with me," the Adversary said as he quickly pushed the huge ball and chain that was his constant companion out of the way.

IS averted his eyes as his master rearranged his "jewelry," as he had been known to call the tool of imprisonment that had been assigned him by the Creator. No one dared call attention to it, for no one dared provoke the wrath of one who desired to be and pretended to be all powerful, all knowing and in all places at once, yet who lived with this daily reminder that he was not. "Your highness, I am working on a case that I believe you are familiar with. You had overheard a prophecy in one of your visits to...." And he pointed upward.

Impatiently Satan replied, "Yes, yes, I know what you are referring to. I remember it well. It is interesting that you should bring this up because I was just recently thinking about that case." He stopped walking and his dark eyes took on a faraway look. "I had been summoned, you know." He smirked, "Every time I pass through the great hall into the High King's throne room I take much pleasure in spreading a stench of defilement. I know they can smell me coming a mile away!" He resumed his stroll. "At any rate, I remember that day especially well because as the door of the throne room opened and I entered in, I caught a snippet of a prophecy over the very family you are working on. This was surprising to me since they are usually very guarded about the words they say in my hearing. It was that prophecy that led me to station Death over that home."

After a short pause, he continued. "I didn't let on that I had heard anything, and when I came before the King and He looked me in the eyes, I knew that He knew that I had heard. *'Satan, this will change nothing, you know,'* He said. *'My blood runs strong and My love runs deep within this bloodline.'* I added that my seed ran just as deep. He went on to say, *'You can not change or stop My plans from bringing freedom to those you have taken captive. As time grows short, I am raising up a daughter within this very bloodline that will love Me so much that through her obedience to Me, **I will crush you under her feet**.'* I was aware of course, that every time a Christian obeys the King, I am trampled on and bruised, so to speak, by Jehovah God; but, hearing it mentioned in context of a specific person in a specific bloodline let me know that this was a case to add to my 'watch list.'"

He again stopped walking as the emotions of that day rose up within him. He had not replied out loud, and yet the Lord had known his prideful, rebellious thoughts. Thinking about that meeting now began to reawaken the murderous rage within him. IS was not easily intimidated; however as he watched the change in his master's countenance, he began to wonder if he had made a mistake in coming. Satan's body was shaking. "He is wrong you know! I will stop this nonsense! I will not be crushed! I have my plans and I will do the crushing!" He had blown up like a red hot balloon and what began as an angry growl erupted into a violent roar that filled the earth, shaking it to the core in a devastating earthquake, and killing twenty people in Kumamoto, Japan.

IS was blown backward and knocked to the ground. When all was quiet and he dared look toward his master, he was shocked to see how calm he was.

Satan was standing serenely with his hands behind his back as he looked out over the land. "What is being done about this matter?" Satan asked.

IS slowly stood to his feet but kept the distance between them as he answered. "We are working on a plan at this moment. I left the court room and came to you seeking for a more clear understanding of this case. I believe that I have acquired what I came for, your highness."

"IS."

"Yes my master?"

"Do not fail me. I perceive that if not stopped, this bloodline may have negative effects on our strategy concerning The Great Plan."

IS bowed low again. "I understand, my lord, and we will not fail you."

And with that said, IS propelled himself back into the courtroom where the demons were in the process of picking themselves up off the floor and blasphemous words flowed freely around the room, for the earthquake had been experienced in the spiritual as well as the physical. IS had only been absent for a rift in time, but already, a plan had begun to form within his mind.

He took his seat behind the bench and banged the gavel gaining attention. When all was quiet, he began to explain the new plan of action that would take years to accomplish, but that he was certain would prove to be successful. The new plan would take advantage of the shaman's curse and reintroduce witchcraft and the occult back into the bloodline. He explained that though the goat had died, the parasites that had been feeding on it were alive and well, in hibernation until they were needed. He said that they were comparable to seeds awaiting their time of germination; only these were spirits awaiting their time of action. That time was now. They had the capability to infest and infect those who were weak and vulnerable, ignorant of their presence, complacent or who disbelieved in the relevance of the prince's power in the heavenly places. Once they had been given an assignment and had infected the subject, they would begin to grow in strength and power.

IS assigned parts of the plan to each one in the high counsel, and left it to them to assign specific jobs to certain demons.

Just before leaving the court room, IS turned back toward the judge and asked, "Just for the record, what is the baby's name?"

"David."

With a crooked smile of knowing, he said, "Of course," and strode back out the way he had come. Once, years back in the history of the world, there had been another boy named David whose bloodline had been the strongest, most protected bloodline that IS had ever encountered. It had been predetermined that the boy would be a king, and the prophecy surrounding his lineage had been that an even greater King would be born to him. IS hated recounting the memories of his greatest failure, the failure to stop the prophecy from becoming reality. Even though this new bloodline reeked with similarities of the other, he refused to beat himself up. He comforted himself with the commitment that this time, *he would not fail.*

CHAPTER 3
THE STING

Nine years later....1898...

David loved the Lord, and he loved his mother. She was dying, and he felt as if his heart had been pulled from his body and thrown down upon the stone floor, causing it to shatter into a million pieces. His mother lay silently on the bed in which he had been born. Her skin was pale and her breathing was shallow. His father had told him to go outside and play, but he could not. The pain and loneliness of his soul was worse when she was out of his sight, and so he hid behind the open door watching his father bathe her beautiful face and bare arms with cool water as he tried to bring the fever under control.

David jumped when all of a sudden his mother sat upright in bed! She began to call out for David, for *him*; but the unexpected change frightened him almost as much as the thought of losing her. Hans tried to console her. He was able to help her lie back down, but she insisted as strongly as she could in her weakened condition that she wanted David. Finally his father called out to him to come, and David cautiously stepped out from behind the door into the room. Sophia seemed to grow calm and she smiled when she saw him. She reached for him. He took the hand she held out, and shyly stepped closer as he listened to her last words.

"Don't be afraid my little Davy boy. In a little bit I am going to go live with Jesus in heaven. Do you remember how we read that Jesus is preparing a special place for us to live in someday? Do you remember how we dreamed about what that place would look like? Soon I will get to see if we were right. You will be sad Davy, because you will miss me. But when you feel very sad, I want you to remember you are not alone because Jesus is with you. Remember that I love you and will always love you and will wait for the day when Jesus says that it is time for you come and join me. Do you understand what I am saying David?"

David could not speak because there was a very large lump in his throat, but he nodded his head, yes.

Sophia was noticeably weakening, yet continued on with great purpose. "And David, there is something I have to tell you, and I need you to listen very closely to me, ok?" He again nodded. "Davy, never forget that Jesus loves you and has a plan for your life. Look for Him everyday and listen. Talk to Him. Love Him with your whole heart…There are those who want to…"

Davy stepped closer to his mother because she was speaking barely above a whisper when she stopped talking altogether. She seemed to see something above his head, then her eyes closed, she drew a deep breath, and her whole body that had been tense with pain, relaxed. Panic began to steal his mind. "Mother?"

David looked up at his father and knew by the expression on his face that his mother had left for her new home. Neither he nor his father had been aware of the glory light surrounding the bed where Sophia lay. Nor were they aware of the dark angel that had been hovering in the shadows waiting for the breath to leave his mother's body. Neither one was aware of the spiritual encounter taking place as Sophia's spirit and soul, her real self, was raised out up and out of her physical body.

Sophia had been in mid sentence, trying to tell David something very important when a very bright light had overcome her and lifted her up. She looked around and was able to see into a realm that before this moment, she had only minimally perceived and imagined! The light in the room was so beautiful! She knew that that the shining ones surrounding her were angels, welcoming her into their world, drawing her up and away from the body that had been so full of pain just a moment ago. Sophia felt a sense of freedom and release and joy beyond anything she could have ever imagined!

And then she looked down. She could see her body lying on the bed; she could see Davy, close to her, holding her hand, and Hans kneeling at her side. And she could suddenly see the dark ones in the room as well. She wanted to warn Hans and David! This was what she had been trying to say when she was raised up, but had been unable to finish. She had discerned the danger before. But seeing it as she did now caused her anxiety because she was afraid for her son and unable to do anything about it. Sophia could sense the great emotional pain, and was powerless to protect them from either the pain or the threat.

She realized that the angels were leading her further away from the things of the world, and her distress over the impending danger to her son was so great that the largest angel called out for them to stop. Even though the angels were speaking in their angelic language, she was able to understand their words.

"Cantor, why are we dillydallying?" asked one of the angels. "Distress and Anxiety are not a part of our Kingdom! We must take her quickly."

The shining one called Cantor spoke to her. "Sophia, you can not go back, and there is nothing that you can do for them now. But we will allow you to watch for a moment more so that you will know how much God loves David, and that He will be with this boy. As you know, David will have his own battles to face, choices to make. You have done well with this one. Your prayers have been heard and answered for him and your bloodline. Now you must entrust him to our loving Father."

The world stopped fading as she drew closer again to her bedroom and the scene became clear. As they watched, neither Hans nor David sensed the evil presence as the demon now stepped forward, masked and cloaked as Grief. It drew close to David, stretched it's claw-like hand out, and reaching through his little chest, he grabbed hold of David's heart. This Spirit of Grief would have overtaken him completely had an angel of Light not stepped between it and the boy. Grief had been unprepared for this

27

interference and growled as he began to push it away with his one free claw, only to realize that it was much larger, much stronger than itself. It thought about letting go and running to escape discipline from this enemy, but decided to stand its ground and see what would happen. He had encountered glory light angels before, and while they were to be greatly feared and avoided when possible, he was also thinking that if he bungled up this job, there would be all hell to pay. So he waited a moment longer, taking his chances with the angel. When the angel didn't do anything except continue to stand between him and the boy, Grief decided to keep this job and do his best to fulfill his assignment. He had established a stronghold, and now he would wait for another opportunity to completely overtake his target.

CHAPTER 4
SOPHIA'S JOURNEY

Cantor lovingly wrapped his wings around Sophia and said, "It's time." She became aware that she was hearing the loveliest song, and that the angels were singing praises to their Great King. She rested her head on Cantor's large shoulder and gave up the struggles of the world as peace overcame all else. She was aware that she was being carried and that they were moving with what seemed like lightning speed. She opened her eyes and saw that all was dark around them, but she was not afraid. The angels traveling with them had continued to sing, and the song got louder and more beautiful.

Then their movement and the singing stopped. In the quietness she almost startled when Cantor called out loudly, "I am Cantor of the King's servants. With me is Sophia, daughter of the King, dressed in robes of righteousness and covered in the blood of Jesus Christ, God's Son. We bid you open!"

Immediately it was like a portal opened and blinding light streamed into the dark place. As soon as the portal opened, Cantor still carrying her, and the others with them, dashed into the light and she heard the portal close behind them. It was so bright that Sophia was unable to see. She felt safe; she felt joy and peace; but it was the love she began to sense that was the most amazing thing she had ever experienced. It seemed to be tangible and was emanating from everywhere touching every part of her! It was like this love was the very air she was breathing! She took in a deep breath and realized that she didn't need to exhale. This love was filling her up, sinking deep into every fiber of her being.

Sophia was aware that they were moving once again, although not so fast this time. "Cantor, I can't see anything. I want to see where we are."

Cantor laughed with delight and answered, "You will see soon enough my Sophia! We are on our way to the throne room so that you can be welcomed by the King Himself. And that is when He will clothe you in your new body. Yes you will see very soon, and then you will see forever."

This was sounding very enticing to Sophia. "Well, when I get my new body will you put me down? Or are you to carry me forever?"

Cantor chuckled, but when he answered her, his voice took on a serious tone. "My little Sophia, always so eager to experience all that the Master has for you. I have carried you for a long time, in ways you never realized, all through your life. Now when I carry you into the throne room and place you at the Son's feet, that will be the last time you will need me to carry you. In your new body, there is no sin, no sorrow, no sickness. You will be complete in Christ, and He in you. That will be the moment of celebrating your new life in the place He has prepared just for you."

As Cantor spoke, Sophia was beginning to realize just who he was. "It was you, wasn't it! You are my guardian angel who has watched over me throughout my life!" Cantor just held her a little closer and wrapped his wings around her a little tighter. Sophia now recognized the comfort of his wings. If she had been able to cry, tears of joy and gratitude would have run like rivers down her face. As it was, these emotions coursed through her soul and she said, "There are no words to express my gratitude, Cantor. Thank you."

It was Cantor's turn to respond with thanksgiving. "Little Sophia, you have blessed me many times over as you chose to love and worship our Lord and King."

"Cantor, doesn't your name mean singing? I've heard you sing, and you do have a lovely voice."

Joyous laughter erupted from Cantor as Sophia said this. "Yes it can have to do with singing. I am named Cantor because I carry your prayers to heaven with singing as you and I worship the Son. You are an intercessor, and I am your Cantor."

They must have reached their destination for Cantor stopped. Sophia sensed another angelic being close to them. She could feel Cantor bowing even as he cradled her in his arms, and then he announced, "I am Cantor and have brought Sophia to see the King."

She heard the rustling of pages and then the voice said, "Welcome Sophia, daughter of the King. Your name is written in the Lamb's Book Of Life. You are welcome to enter into the throne room of God."

CHAPTER 5
DAVID

David released his hand from his mother's, and ran from the room in an effort to escape his broken heart. Unaware of the two spirits that moved with him, David ran out the front door into the corn field and did not know that an even bigger dark angel had followed him out the door, and then stopped to speak with another of its kind.

"It is done," Death said to Infirmity.

When David reached the middle of the field, he fell to the ground and began to sob. Grief was doing his best to twist the boy's heart and cause as much pain as he could, but his enemy continued to stand between them, making it difficult to keep a firm grip and was shielding David from some of the pain. Grief was beginning to think that he might need some help, and decided to call for backup. While he was unable to get close enough to do too much damage, his two comrades, Rejection and Abandonment would be able to approach from the front and whisper lies into the boy's mind.

They arrived within seconds of the call, and quickly assessed the situation. Rejection and Abandonment both began to fill David's hurting, vulnerable mind with thoughts that undermined his mother's love for him and that tried to make him feel worthless, or like he had done something wrong and that her death was his fault.

When David had cried until he could cry no more, he fell asleep in the middle of the field. After waking some time later, he was not sure if he had dreamed that his mother had come to him and comforted him, or if it had really happened. Regardless, David was reassured of her love for him and of God's love and purpose in his life. He didn't know how long he lay there in the corn field, but when he finally got up and started walking back toward the house, he believed that somehow he would be ok.

The angel known as Peace winked at David's guardian, Perseverance, then leaped up into the air on his way to another case. Grief wasn't the only one who had called for backup.

After a few months, Hans began to realize that his grief seemed stronger than others in his community who had lost wives. His relationship with Sophia had always been unique and different in a good way. Their spirits and souls had truly been one as their love for one another was a reflection of their love for God and His love for them. Hans was completely unaware that Grief had also grabbed a hold of his heart and was holding him captive to pain and torment as it stirred up his own emotions and then magnified them at least fifty fold. Depression had crept in as well and was isolating him and his son. These two demons were working together, slowly shredding their hearts in pain, gradually leading them toward the next step in their plan for the destruction of this bloodline.

Hans' friends who wanted to be helpful began advising him to move on, telling him that he needed to marry again; that even though he would never forget Sophia, she would want him to be happy, to keep living. He doubted that he would ever be happy again, but it was true that Sophia had enjoyed life, even on the darkest of days. And it seemed like the grief that he and David shared was tearing them apart rather than drawing them closer. David had always been so close to Sophia. Maybe the men were right. Maybe he did need a wife, and more importantly, maybe David needed a mother. Maybe marriage was the answer.

Even though David had a knowing that he would be ok, he was also sinking deeper into a pit of grief that he could not seem to pull himself out of. He was actually considering how he might be able to go and join his mother. And then his father did something unthinkable. He brought home a new wife.

Nicole wasn't so bad to look at, and in fact she was quite pretty. But David did not like her eyes. They were dark eyes. It wasn't their color that was dark, but it was the dark feeling he felt when he looked into them that made him shudder from the inside out. He avoided her as much as possible, and it seemed like his father did too. Nicole fixed them food, cleaned the house, did their laundry...all the things his mother had done. And yet nothing was the same. Every time David looked at her, the grief and pain in his young heart seemed to grow. Her presence was not only an unwelcome intrusion, but it was also a reminder of his mother's absence.

It wasn't long after Nicole arrived that the nightmares began. Things too unspeakable to put into words kept him from confiding in his father. Several times David came close to crying out for his daddy, but shame outweighed the terror and he bore the torment of the dreams in silence.

Two years later, a baby sister was born. David fell in love with her from the moment she looked into his eyes. She became the one good thing in his life, a gift he felt that God had given to help sustain him. Even the nightmares seemed to stop with her arrival, and for the first time since his mother died, David felt at stirring of hope.

One afternoon when Donna was three months old, Nicole told David that they were taking Donna to a baby dedication. David was not to tell his father about it. She said it was to be a secret and that he would be severely punished if he told.

They arrived at a neighbor's farmhouse and descended into their basement. Fear clutched at David's heart as never before. He sensed great evil! Something inside him told him to run. He turned to go back up the steps and was met with resistance by a man he did not recognize. He was told to stand by the wall and to keep silent. He watched in horror as the people began dancing in a frenzy, chanting, calling up evil spirits, and then as

Donna's clothes were removed from her tiny body, she began to cry. He screamed and tried to reach her, but they came and made him drink something bitter. His mind began to reel; he staggered and fell to the floor.

He was aware of chaos in the room as they proceeded with their ritual. And then everything got quiet. A moment later he heard a man's voice say, "We have a problem. She is not the one who is to be the carrier."

And then Nicole's voice answered in disbelief, "What's this you are saying? Of course she is! It was prophesied that my child would be the one! Here she is. I have no other and never will."

Others began questioning, "If not Donna, then who?"

Someone said, "We must pray and ask our lord."

The room broke out in loud wails and cries, and David heard words spoken in languages he could not understand. When the room became quiet again, David struggled to open his eyes to see what was happening. The first man who had spoken said, "It is to be him."

David's heart sank deeper into a pit of despair. They had pointed at him, and even though he wasn't sure what that meant, he knew it wasn't going to be good. The one thought that gave him some relief was that maybe now they would leave his sister alone. He wanted to get up and grab Donna and run, but was still unable to move his body, and his eyes refused to stay open for more than just a passing moment.

David jumped in alarm and reopened his eyes when a loud voice roared out "NO!" The shout had come from Nicole, but it didn't sound like her voice. And her face was contorted in such a way that she had become hardly recognizable. It was as if all the darkness that David had seen in her eyes had taken over her whole face, and she began to scream vile words such as he had never heard before. Nicole, or the thing controlling her, finally yelled out in disbelief, "That's impossible! He is not my son!"

The leader argued, "Of course he is your son. You entered into a marriage covenant with his father. He is legally under your authority through your union with Hans. All that is left to do is to mix your blood with his, and then the bloodline will be complete and transference will be possible."

Another voice that David did not recognize brought up another issue. "There is something else we must consider. We have been working these last two years to establish strongholds in this boy, but we can not ignore the fact that the Spirit of the High King is strong in him." He continued, "Are you certain that he is the one? It doesn't make sense that Lord IS would choose one such as him."

"I must admit," said the leader, "that I do not fully understand. But our obedience in this matter is of utmost importance. We will fulfill the desire of our lord and master Satan, and I know this is his command. Are there any who would question my discernment in this matter? Are there any who wish to directly challenge the will of Satan? If so, speak now or forever hold your peace."

David could feel the tension and the fear in the room. He waited to see if anyone would take the challenge, but the room was draped in silence so thick that David opened his eyes for another brief second hoping to see that he was at home in his own bed and had been having a nightmare. He quickly closed them again with great disappointment. No one spoke up, and even Nicole was quiet.

The effect of the drug was making him very sleepy, and in the quietness of the moment as David's mind began to drift off, he became aware of another Presence, one that reminded him of the comfort he had felt long ago when he was being cradled in his mother's arms. This Presence spread a mantle of peace over him and spoke words that were like healing ointment to his broken soul.

"I will never leave you, David. When you walk through the valley of the shadow of death, fear no evil for I will be with you. I will protect you. Do not fear, for I have redeemed you; I have summoned you by name; you are mine. When you pass through the waters, I will be with you; and when you pass

through the rivers, they will not sweep over you. When you walk
through the fire, you will not be burned; the flames will not set
you ablaze. For I am the LORD *your God, the Holy One of Israel,*
your Savior. Trust in the Lord with all your heart, and lean not
on your own understanding. In all your ways acknowledge Me,
and I will make your paths straight. Call to Me and I will answer
you. Because you have set your love upon Me, therefore I will
deliver you; I will set you on high, because you have known My
name. You shall call upon Me, and I will answer you; I will be
with you in trouble; I will deliver you and honor you. With long
life I will satisfy you, and show you My salvation."
(Paraphrases from Joshua 1:5; Psalm 23:4; Isaiah:43:1-3;
Proverbs 3:5-6; Jeremiah 33:3; Psalm 91:14-16)

These were words his mother had read to him from
the Bible. She believed them, and in that moment he
committed with his whole heart that he would too, no
matter what. David's spirit cried out to Jesus, and YHWH
heard the call and answered him.

The Comforter continued. "I will be faithful to you
David. Love me with your whole heart, soul, mind and strength
and I will restore your soul and those of your children and
grandchildren. Through your faithfulness, all of your children
will love and serve me There will be a fierce battle for their souls
Many will be taken captive by the enemy, but I will be faithful
and will bring them out and will restore them and redeem the
years the locust has eaten. I am the redeemer and healer. My love
always wins, David, and it will be that one of your grandchildren
will overcome and destroy the seeds the enemy has planted in
your bloodline that continually sprout up and try to overcome
My seed. She will be a fierce warrior in My Kingdom and will
love Me as your mother loved Me and will have the gifts of
wisdom and discernment concerning spiritual things, also as
your mother did. Through her the generational curses will be
reversed as she learns how to apply the blood of the Lamb and to
ignite the fire of the Holy Spirit.

Your mind will not remember what I have said to you,
but your spirit will; so when you begin to doubt My love for you,
don't trust your feelings; rather practice believing the Truth of

37

My Word and obeying the voice of My Spirit. I love you David, My son."

God did not stop the ritual. He would not interfere with the will of even evil men. But He would do as He had promised David. He would protect him in this valley of the shadow of death; this fire and this flood. His love would cover this multitude of sins being committed against him and his bloodline, and He would be faithful to David for many generations! He knew even the tiniest details in Satan's plans for the destruction of this family. There was nothing hidden in the darkness that He could not see. He had plans too, plans for good and not for evil, to provide David and this family with hope, healing and freedom in their future. He alone was God and He would not fail David this day or ever, for He had come to heal the brokenhearted, to proclaim freedom to the captives, to comfort all who mourn, to give them beauty instead of ashes, the oil of joy instead of mourning, and a garment of praise instead of a spirit of heaviness and despair. He would forgive their sins and heal their land so that they would be called oaks of righteousness, a planting of the LORD for the display of His splendor; and all would know that He alone was God. He would help them rebuild the ancient ruins and restore the places long devastated; they would renew the ruined cities that had been devastated for generations. Jesus had come to destroy the work of the devil. It had been accomplished and would come to pass in David's bloodline. (Promises found in 1 Peter 4:8; Matthew 10:26; Jeremiah 29:11-14; Isaiah 61:1-4; 2 Chronicles 7:14; 1 John 3:8)

David was jolted out of his reverie by a sharp pain on the fourth finger of his left hand, his ring finger. Someone had cut it with a sharp knife, and it was bleeding. He heard them chanting again and remembered what they had said to Nicole about mixing their blood. Then someone lifted him up and he was being carried to the center of the room where they placed him in a circle on the floor. The voice of the leader called for order, and all grew quiet. He called for Nicole to come forward and to stand before him. Then talking to Nicole, he explained that David's spirit did not belong to them, but because he was a child, he was under the spiritual authority of his parents. She was being recognized as his mother so that she could give legal rights, permission to them so that they would be able to impart the spirits to David that he was to carry, and was solemnly asked, "Do you, Nicole, mother of David, give us spiritual authority over your son?" David heard Nicole take a deep breath before she replied, then with resignation in her voice she said, "Yes, I do."

He felt utterly betrayed, hopeless and alone. He was aware of noises and chaos; of words spoken in the strange language; of people touching him, violating him in ways that made him want to cry and scream out; of dark beings hovering. But he could not move or respond. He could not make sense of it, and then gratefully he drifted off into unconsciousness.

David woke the next morning in his bed. His mind began to clear and to replay this latest nightmare in his head. It was similar to the others, but there was something different this time. His sister had been involved, and in wanting to protect her, he had remembered more of the details. He started to get up and felt a momentary wave of dizziness and other strange feelings he was unable to identify. A terrifying thought came to him, and as he contemplated it, he realized the truth. These were not nightmares. They were reality.

The enormity of this revelation, the shock and revulsion of it all seemed too much for him to bear. In great sorrow and despair, he dropped back onto the bed and began to moan a deep wail that came up from the depths of his being. He was too overcome with grief and shame to consider that his step mother might hear him, but she did not. She had gone out into the field before sun up and had not yet returned. David's moans became great sobs, and he did not know how long he wept into his mattress. But when the tears slowed and finally stopped, there was a quietness in his soul that was strangely comforting.

It was in that quiet place he heard what sounded like his mother's voice reminding him of her words before she left him. "Davy, never forget that Jesus loves you and has a plan for your life. Look for Him everyday and listen. Talk to Him. Love Him with your whole heart."

David sat up looking around him. "Mother?"

There was no audible answer, yet he sensed a peace that he hadn't known since his mother left. He dropped to his knees beside his bed and began to pray like his mother had taught him. She had said to talk to God like he talked to her, and he realized that he hadn't done that in a long time. "Dear Jesus, I remember what my mother told me about You. I'm sorry I haven't been looking for you or listening to you. I'm sorry I haven't been loving You with my whole heart. I kind of forgot about You. I'm really sorry, God. Will You forgive me?" David stopped and listened for a minute but didn't hear anything. "Well God, I need help. I'm in trouble here and I don't know what to do. Please help me. I will love You with my whole heart, and I'll talk to You every day from now on. But I don't want to go back to that wicked place. So please help me!" As David continued to kneel beside the bed, he didn't receive any quick answers; but Grief that had gripped his heart since his mother died, was forced to release its hold on him. Of course David only knew that he felt better and that he had hope, and even a measure of peace.

Grief, the demon, was in pain; several kinds of pain actually. The holy angels that had removed his claws from David's emotions were placing chains around his arms so that he was unable to use them or even lift them up; and they were moving him somewhere that seemed to be growing colder...he hated cold; and he was hungry! Lately he had been experiencing insatiable cravings for parasites, especially fleas and ticks.

David began to wonder what he was to do now. He began to make plans while he did his morning chores. He saw no help in telling his father, and felt that it would only make things worse. Hans' grief had not improved even with marriage. The emotional isolation that surrounded his heart as a means of protection, though false protection, clouded his mind and it seemed that he had shut David out of his life. He could not turn to the community for he did not know who he could trust. There was one word that began as a still, small voice in his mind and continued to grow into a roaring thought...*Run.*

PART 2
AWAKENING

CHAPTER 6
GENERATIONS

The 1960's...

At a very young age, Nicole was aware of the emotional distance between herself and her grandfather. Granny was sweet and lovable, but granddad seemed to avoid contact with her except for the quick goodbye hug he bestowed on her as she was leaving his home. And that hug only happened because her parents told her to hug him goodbye.

His rejection of her became more apparent when the whole family was gathered at Granny and Granddad's for a holiday, and she watched as he wholeheartedly hugged each cousin as they walked out the door. In all of her almost four years, he had never hugged her that way, had never playfully tickled her face with his whiskers as he did with the others. Nicole backed away from the door, from him. Mother called her to come forward for her hug, but fear held her back. His eyes were kind enough, but she could sense his reluctance, his disgust at the thought of touching her. She would have run out the door past him if it had been possible, but Mother took her hand and led her to him. Granddad dutifully picked her up and quickly gave her a squeeze, then set her down. There was no jolly laughter and kind word spoken to her as there had been with the other cousins. What was wrong with her that he didn't seem to want to touch her? It was a great relief when she stepped into Granny's comforting, loving arms. Granny's hugs always seemed to make her feel better.

As David hugged each grandchild, a memory flashed through his mind; a memory of God's promise of faithfulness to him, his children and grandchildren if he would choose to love God with his whole heart. He heard the words being repeated in his mind as if it were

43

yesterday..."*Through your faithfulness, all of your children will love and serve Me... it will be that one of your grandchildren will overcome and destroy the seeds the enemy has planted in your bloodline that continually sprout up and try to overcome My seed. She will be a fierce warrior in My Kingdom and will love Me as your mother loved Me...*"

David pictured the prophet Samuel in the Bible as he lined up Jesse's sons and was searching God's heart to discover which one of them was to be anointed as Israel's king. As he hugged the first 6 children, he questioned the Lord, "Is it this one Lord?" But the Lord was silent.

Then David looked at Nicole. She had backed up against the wall as far away from him as she could. Fear was written in her eyes, and fear welled up in his own heart as those distant memories of another Nicole invaded his mind. The poor child. He knew with his mind that she was innocent, but his heart had not been able to process the truth, and it was his heart that always seemed to win.

David's wife loved the name, Nicole, but he had forbidden her to use that name or even mention it; however, his daughter had named her girl Nicole. He had nearly begged her not to, but she had wanted to please her mother. And now every time he saw the girl, he was tormented with memories.

This day as he dutifully picked Nicole up and hurriedly gave her a squeeze, David's heart jumped within him. He nearly dropped her in revulsion. "Not her Lord! Certainly not her!"

But the Lord replied, "*Why not her, David? I am in the business of healing and restoration, and it is time for Me to heal the pain in your heart that feeds the bitterness of your soul. This is an open door for the enemy, and it must be closed. For many years I have set a guard over this vulnerable place in your heart, David. But it is time for this well of defilement to be cleansed. Will you allow me access to this painful place? For you see, this is not only a breach in your life, but it is a gaping hole in your family line that Satan will take full advantage of in leading his armies into your bloodline. As we speak they are already in place*

44

waiting for the moment when I remove My guard from your heart. Will they find a gap through which they can enter? Or will they find a solid, impenetrable wall?"

God had David's attention now. He wanted to pass on a Godly heritage and certainly didn't wish evil on any of his children or grandchildren; not even Nicole. As the company left, David went outside to the small carriage house behind their home that had become his sanctuary. "God, what do I do? I've carried this pain, this bitterness so long, I don't know if I can be rid of it."

"I will cleanse and heal you David if you will surrender to Me. You must understand that your granddaughter Nicole is not your step mother. Her name means Victory of the People. Nicole, your step mother was on the other side, seeking victory for those in the rebellion. My little Nicole has been chosen to seek victory for My people. She carries the mark of a leader and a warrior and will have to choose which side she will serve. Pray for her David, for the battle for her soul will be fierce.

But first, forgive your step mother because the earnest prayer of a righteous man makes tremendous power available. And then prayerfully embrace this little one. Pray that My Spirit will be strong in her. Pray that the encounters with the enemy that are sure to come, will send her into My arms just as it did with you, rather than to tear her from Me. The enemy sees the mark on her as well, and she will need your prayers as she encounters fierce battle for her own soul; for the victory of your bloodline, and for many others that she will lead into spiritual freedom."

David knelt at his work bench and surrendered all the pain in his heart to the One, the only One who could truly bear it, and indeed had already done just that through His blood sacrifice on the cross. Tears ran down wrinkled, old cheeks and into his beard as he allowed Jesus to bring all the memories of abuse to his mind, and then in obedience to God, chose to forgive his step mother, Nicole, for each and every one of them. Strength, honor and glory shone upon David's spirit, soul and body as the wound was healed and the Spirit's seal was set upon his heart.

The demons were restless. They didn't know what was happening, but they knew something big was taking place or about to, and they were drooling in anticipation at the thought of charging into David's bloodline and spreading their defilement and destruction. They watched in eagerness as the large guardian who had been standing in front of the gap with His sword drawn throughout David's lifetime, suddenly looked up, sheathed his sword, and disappeared. It was time for them to feast! But as they began charging toward what they thought would be an opening, those in the front lines stopped as quickly as they had begun, causing a massive pileup of demons colliding one on top of another. The air was thick with curses and foul language, confusion and chaos. Bringing order to this bunch was no easy matter, but finally things calmed down enough for their leader to examine the situation. It would be a dark day for this troop, for the breach had been repaired...and not just repaired, but had been made like brand new. There was no way through to the bloodline from this angle. As the news spread throughout the ranks, violence and fighting broke out as the hungry demons turned their rage and bloodlust onto one another.

On the other side, a full blown victory celebration was in progress with singing and music and dancing! Not only had David allowed the healing wings to work a miracle in his own life, but he was praying for little Nicole! His prayers were already being answered for some of the mightiest angels had been assigned to her and were being dispatched at that very moment.

CHAPTER 7
BEGINNINGS

It was not long after the family holiday that the greatest battle for Nicole's life began. *Actually it had begun on the day she was born as Lord IS, who had closely been watching David's bloodline, encountered the holy angel, Cantor, at her birth. For IS, Cantor's presence was confirmation that this was the one that carried the mark of God's plan for the destruction of Satan's purposes in David's bloodline.*

The two angels, one dark, one light, looked at each other with understanding in their eyes. There was no need for words, for the two who had known each other as friends long ago before the world was created and before the war had divided them, now understood the plans and purposes of the other. Cantor held no bitterness toward IS, for there was no bitterness in the Kingdom of Love. However, he could not help but feel the sadness that still pricked his heart upon seeing the one he had once called brother, but who had chosen to reject YHWH and to align himself with the Adversary. He nodded at his opponent in recognition...recognition of him personally, recognition of their conflicting purposes in being there, and recognition of the battle they were facing. If IS felt any nostalgia, he did not let it show. His eyes remained dark and fierce. Yet he nodded in return at Cantor, a nod that declared, "Let the battle begin."

The two warriors were well matched in knowledge, strength and purpose. Incubus Succubus was as perverted and unholy as Cantor was holy and righteous. They were both high ranking officials in opposite, warring kingdoms. Both were equally and totally committed to serving their masters, and both had access to armies under them who would respond upon command.

The admonition God had given David to pray for his granddaughter was the precursor to the next phase of Nicole's life as the heat of the battle was increased beyond measure. IS felt an urgency to step up his plan. He had decided that one bloodline was not enough to carry the responsibility of this important case, and was very pleased to find upon examination that the father's side would be able to not only help, but would most likely seal the deal.

He was not of her blood, but had married into the family. He was a Freemason, Grand Master of the 33rd degree in the Scottish Rite, which meant that he was the head of all the lodges in his region. Masons were a secret society and it was not commonly known, even to those in the lower degrees, that they were Satan worshippers and connected with the Illuminati. Having served a term in the US Senate, Marcus had become familiar with those high ranking government officials (of which there were many) who were also involved themselves in the same agenda and pursuits connected with what they referred to as the New World Order. After leaving office, he had continued his involvement in this more secret side of his political associations.

Because Marcus was a master of the highest degree within the Masons, he was also master/chief of the Satanic covens in his district. Marcus was quite familiar with IS, for on many occasions during satanic rituals, Marcus would allow and even invite this principality to use his body to accomplish his purposes. So when IS came to Marcus and presented his plan, he readily agreed to help. IS warned Marcus to be on his guard and explained that in David's bloodline, Nicole had been chosen to be the host for IS himself as the times were pointing toward the fulfillment of the Great Plan. However, their arch enemy had chosen her as well to be set apart in *that* Kingdom for His purposes. Marcus loved a challenge.

It was not too great a surprise when Marcus received a phone call from Capital Hill the following morning. "Marcus, I had a visitor last night. I know that he has given you a very important assignment and I want to know specifically what he told you."

Marcus sighed. He wished that for once they would just trust him. "Well sir, I know that she is the chosen one and that I am to prepare her for the role she will be assuming. I already have a plan in place and am working on the details even as we speak."

"Very good, Marcus," came the reply. "I'm assuming that you understand fully the importance of this assignment. Her DNA has been prepared specifically for this position over generations and we can't risk failure at this late date."

"Yes sir, I understand the magnitude and ramification of this specific assignment. I can assure you that I will personally see to it that all the bases are covered. I won't fail you or the brotherhood, sir," Marcus replied.

The voice on the other end of the line responded, "See that you don't." After a slight pause, he continued. "I'm assuming that you were also informed of the *Other's* interest in her as well."

"Yes sir, I do understand that side of the issue and I'm sure I can work around that."

"Very well, carry on Marcus."

"I will sir. Good day."

Marcus was Nicole's great uncle on her father's side. He was married to her grandfather's sister, and it just so happened that they lived within his jurisdiction. He initiated his preparations by suggesting to his wife that they invite her grand nephew's family over for dinner. They were relatively new to the area, and he explained that he would enjoy having family around. That was the beginning of Nicole's introduction to Marcus, and he made sure that she loved to come to his house. They had TV and a swimming pool. He made sure that he paid just the right amount of attention to her so that she would feel comfortable with him, yet not so much that anyone would suspect him of foul play. He made sure that his teenage daughter was available to babysit Nicole at their house, then conveniently arranged for his wife and daughter to have to leave while she was there, volunteering to babysit until they got back.

He discovered that Nicole would be an easy target because she already had great dissociative abilities as well as a premature sense of spiritual insight. He would have no problem setting up barriers in her mind to block her memories of his time with her in their home, and later at the ritual. She was also at exactly the right age, four years old...Old enough to understand certain things, but young enough to be able to mold her mind, to create programming so that she could be controlled. Most four year old minds were blank slates and they were spiritually vulnerable as well, which made it easy to layer in demons that would work with the programming to accomplish their purposes. In Nicole's case, she had been dedicated to their God by her parents as a baby which made it a bit more complicated. The dedication by the parents, her spiritual covering, had essentially claimed her for their side until her age of accountability when she would be responsible for making the choice herself. But Marcus understood the power of the human will and was experienced in understanding ways of working around that small problem.

It wasn't difficult to locate a woman in the occult and assign her the job of winning the trust of Nicole's parents so that she was allowed the privilege of spending a day alone with her. The plan worked out more easily than Marcus had imagined. While he groomed and prepared Nicole mentally, emotionally and physically, Carol was faithfully attending church with Nicole's family. After about a month, she deceptively played her hand, asking if she might spend the day with Nicole, taking her shopping and such since she didn't have a child of her own. Nicole's parents had no idea that this was a bogus shopping trip or a dangerous situation for their daughter, and were delighted that they could share Nicole with this woman. Nicole was excited because she had been dreaming of pink high heeled shoes she had seen in the toy section at the local department store, but until now, had no hope of ever owning them. In Nicole's way of thinking, if this woman wanted to take her shopping, she would be sure to let her know exactly what they were shopping for!

And then the day came. Nicole was full of hopeful expectations. She excitedly chattered about the shoes she wanted as they drove along, and was unsure what to think about Carol's sudden silence and emotional distance. When they pulled up at a large apartment building instead of a department store, Carol explained that shopping would have to wait until later. They went inside and descended into the basement. Nicole became uneasy and pressed in close to Carol, who pushed her away. Another woman came and knelt down in front of Nicole and began to talk nicely to her, comforting her. The nice woman gave her some Kool-Aid to drink, but soon after that, Nicole began to feel very strange. She suddenly didn't care about pink high heels and she began to cry, asking if she could please go home now.

A man called a doctor took her into a room to "examine" her. He laid her on a bed and her body seemed to go to sleep. She could hear him, but was unable to respond to anything the doctor told her to do. Nicole was aware of another man standing in the doorway. She could hear the doctor talking to him, and there was something familiar about his voice. *Uncle Marcus?* Was he here to help her? She tried to call out to him but couldn't. Nicole heard the doctor say, "She'll be ok, but we won't be able to do anything with her when she's like this. She has no tolerance for drugs." The other man responded that they would just have to wait for another day then. Uncle Marcus' voice was strangely comforting and disquieting at the same time. Why didn't he acknowledge her and help her?

Marcus was frustrated with this turn of events. The gravity of this case was weighing heavily on him and he was ready to have this assignment over and done with. And then there was the frustration of working with the inferior, less experienced covens that irritated him. He preferred to worship his master with others of his own rank and caliber, and rarely involved himself directly with those in the lower echelons.

Nicole must have slept, for some time later she awakened as the nice lady was shaking her, telling her that it was time to wake up. Nicole opened her eyes and sat up with help. Her body felt very heavy. The lady gave her some water to drink and some bread. Nicole had to go to the bathroom, and the lady told her where to go. She looked up at the narrow, dirty stair case, and as she began the climb, she felt more and more uncomfortable. Looking back at the lady, she asked if she would come with her, but the lady told her that she would be fine. Nicole reached the top of the stairs and turned to the left. The bathroom door was slightly open, and in the dim light, she saw it was small and dirty. She was afraid to go in, but because of her need, she pushed the door open wider and entered. Upon entering, Nicole gasped in disbelief as she gazed upon a tiny, naked, dead baby in the wastebasket. At first she thought it was a doll, but she reached down and picked it up. It was soft and looked broken. It was not a doll.

She dropped the baby and screamed for help. She could no longer control her bladder and wet her panties. She began descending the steep staircase as quickly as she could in her panicked state. The people in the room were just standing there, staring at her in eerie silence as she cried and begged them to help the baby. The doctor man tightly took hold of her arms. It hurt and Nicole began to frantically thrash about trying to escape his grip, but he held her more tightly confining her arms and legs until in exhaustion, she calmed down.

In a quiet but authoritative voice the doctor said, "Nicole, the baby is dead. You are not to tell anybody about the baby or anything else you have seen or heard here today, or that you were even here. In fact, you will not even remember that you were here. You see, we killed that baby, and we will kill your family if you tell. Do you understand?"

Nicole's dissociative abilities readily kicked in, and the memories of the baby and the emotions associated with it were immediately filed away behind thick walls in her mind; and yet the importance that she was not to tell stayed with her in her subconscious. They made sure that any memories of the day were buried as well, especially those concerning Marcus.

They placed the suggestion of shame in her mind for wetting her underpants, then gave her clean ones. She heard the doctor tell Carol to take her shopping after all; that it would pave the way for her to gain other days with Nicole. Nicole got her pink high heels, but somehow, they did not bring her the joy she thought they would.

Nicole didn't know how she knew, but she did know that she needed help. She couldn't explain why, and she knew that even if she could, she would not because that would be bad. But she felt desperate for help. That is when something unexpected happened that neither Marcus nor IS had anticipated. Nicole remembered her daddy had told her that God could help people, so she told her daddy that she wanted Jesus to come into her heart. He asked her if she knew what that meant, and she said that she did, that she needed Jesus to help her. He asked what she needed help with, and she replied that she just needed help. So he led her in a prayer, asking Jesus to come into her heart, to live inside her, to help her.

The following week when Nicole's mommy told her that Carol was going to pick her up again for the day, Nicole begged not to have to go. But Mommy and Daddy thought that it was a very nice thing to share their daughter with this thoughtful woman and didn't understand her plea. Nicole couldn't explain because she felt that she had to protect her parents from the bad people, and she finally accepted the fact that she would be going with Carol again.

This time, Marcus arranged for the ritual to be in a place of higher privilege. In some ways, he was honored that he had been contacted by several members of the Illuminati. They had heard about this serious case and desired to be a part of it. The fact that the child would be given no drugs had added to the novelty of the situation, for few would be able to survive mentally and emotionally under such duress. But Marcus thought that it was probably the rumors of a prophecy in connection with Nicole that had drawn their attention.

From the moment Nicole entered the room, her dissociation kicked in, and she was no longer Nicole, but Little Nicki. The goal was to inseminate Nicole with the spiritual seeds of IS that would grow to be sexual immorality, defilement, evil passions and desires, anarchy and rebellion against the High One and any under His authority, and ultimately, the destruction of them. Nicole had been marked as a leader and a warrior, and after being raised within the despised church and gaining respect as one of their leaders, in the fullness of her time when the seeds were mature, she would host IS himself, and would lead a rebellion within the Christian community, recruiting members from among their own, wreaking spiritual, emotional, mental and physical havoc and destruction in her wake. Nicole would be one of many who had been targeted, trained and planted with the purpose of destroying God's Kingdom, aborting His coming rule and reign on earth, and ushering in the rule of their true lord, Satan.

But of course, she would need to be united in unholy matrimony with Satan and his kingdom, so they set about preparing her with unholy communion and unholy baptism. These words were familiar to Nicki, and even though she didn't have a clear understanding of those things, she did know this was bad. After baptizing her in urine and feces, they explained that flesh and blood were necessary for her communion.

Nicki heard two things. She heard classical music, and she heard the baby crying. She turned and saw the tiny little thing lying naked and alone on a table. Maternal instincts kicked in and she started towards the table to comfort the frightened baby. As she reached down to pick it up, a hand stopped her. She could not see the person to whom the hand belonged, and she was unable to recognize the voice that whispered closely in her ear telling her to pick up the large knife that was on the table next to the baby. The table which stood on top of a large circle with a star inside of it was now surrounded by the people, mostly women, a few men and the doctor. There was total silence in the room except for the music and the cries of the baby. Nicki was beginning to be greatly fearful for the baby and she refused to pick up the knife. She closed her eyes and clenched her fists tightly. The man behind her took her right hand and forced her hand to open; forced her to pick up the knife; placed both of her hands around the handle and held them tightly there with his own hands wrapped around hers, then lifted them up in the air and as he brought them down forcefully upon the baby's heart, he shouted, "In the name of Satan!" The cries stopped suddenly.

The voice of the man behind her whispered into her ear again, but she was barely able to comprehend his words. He was praising her for providing the blood and the flesh; welcoming her into their sect for she was one with them now. All Nicki knew was that she had done a terrible thing! She had killed a baby! When the man released her, she fell into a heap on the floor. Tears of remorse and shame silently flowed from the depths of her soul, and there was none to comfort her. They left her on the floor for several minutes, and then someone picked her up and set her on a table.

The music played on. It was now time for communion. The blood had been drained. They set the dead baby on the table next to Nicole. The body was cut and they offered her a piece of flesh. She refused it. In an angry voice, a man asked if she would rather have her meat cooked. There happened to be a fire in the room, in the fireplace. They threw the baby into the fire. Nicki knew the baby was dead, and yet the effect that that act had upon her was devastating. The smell of burning flesh permeated her nostrils and wouldn't leave. It wasn't in the fire very long. They pulled it out...The poor blackened baby. He cut into the flesh again, a small piece, and forced it into Nicole's mouth. The feel of it in her mouth caused Nicki to wretch and she threw up. She was severely reprimanded. Another piece was forced down her throat, and somehow, she was able to keep it down. And then she was offered a cup from which she drank the warm, red liquid.

The climate in the room began to change immediately after the unholy communion. The music grew louder as the people started dancing and chanting things she didn't understand in words, but in her spirit she knew they were bad. She didn't see the dark angels, but the people were calling them and she knew they were there. She could sense the evil in the room growing by the second. She was searching for help, and felt abandoned by Jesus. This was a wicked place, and she knew that He would not be in a place like this. The truth was that Cantor had never left her side, but he was prevented from interfering or from comforting Nicole with anything other than a thin shield of peace that was able to block some of the evil impact upon her soul. He was cloaked and not even the other demons knew of his presence. He had learned not to question YHWH, for His ways were of the highest, and Cantor trusted Him implicitly. But that didn't make it easy for him to bear the pain with this precious one.

It was time for the wedding ceremony to begin. No amount of words could describe the terror of the next hours as sexual appetites consumed the people and sacrifices were made. Through unholy sex, soul ties were created, invisibly linking people together, allowing unclean spirits or demons to gain power and to transfer between people; and they were purposefully being assigned to Nicole.

Blood sacrifices, especially human, call forth the most powerful of demons, principalities and powers. When Nicki saw Carrie enter the room, she wasn't sure if she was relieved to have someone who might be a friend, or sad for the little girl who was also stuck in this terrible nightmare. She looked to be about Nicki's age, and even though they had not known one another before that very moment, an instant connection was made between the two little girls; the kind that happens when two people share an experience of the most desperate kind, each knowing that the other understands like no one else ever could.

Nicki felt Carrie's hand clasp hers, and they stood together as a man looked at them and slowly declared words that became branded on Nicki's soul, "One must die, so one can live. Carrie, you are the chosen one." And they picked her up and laid her on the table that was still placed in the center of the circle and the star. After strapping her down, they stationed Nicole near Carrie's face, and Carrie turned and looked deeply into Nicki's eyes. Nicki watched in amazement as somehow, the initial look of fear on Carrie's face dissipated and Love began to radiate from her eyes into Nicki's. What Nicki did not know was that it was the Love in her own eyes that had been transferred to Carrie and had dispelled the fear, then was being transferred back to her. They did not understand at that time that God's original plan and intention had been to create people with the ability to form soul ties so that His Spirit could be passed between people. It was Satan's perversion and defilement of this gift that was being practiced within the occult.

This time, the doctor raised the knife and was holding it high above Carrie's neck when Carrie was redeemed. Nicki didn't know that was the word for it, but that is what she witnessed. Carrie's attention suddenly switched from Nicki to something else above her. Nicki turned her head to see what Carrie was looking at, and it seemed as if time froze as she watched beautiful, white angels swoop down into the room and lift Carrie's spirit from her body. For a moment it was like she was seeing two Carries. One was still lying on the table looking up, and the other Carrie was sitting up as two angels, one on each side of her began lifting her out of her body. At first, Carrie looked surprised, then Nicki saw her smile in joy and delight, and then disappear along with the beautiful shining ones.

The demons were used to such intervention. They had come to terms with their inability to stop such thievery, and had become content with taking the life from the body even if they failed to secure the spirit and the soul of their sacrifice.

At that very moment, time returned to normal and the blade above Carrie's neck came down hard, separating her head from her body. Nicki closed her eyes as blood sprayed over her face and body. She couldn't run from it, for she was being held in place. The chanting that had been going on in the background grew loud and they began to chant in English so that she could understand their words, and remember their words. "Red, red, Carrie's dead; yonder rolls her severed head."

As the life blood left Carrie's body, Nicole was aware of many dark angels moving from the people in the room to Carrie's body; through Carrie's blood; and then moving toward her. They were so terrible to look at that she closed her eyes. She wasn't aware that they had been unable to penetrate her body, soul or spirit as planned, for as they approached her, they saw that she was already dripping with Another's blood, covered completely, shielded by righteousness and sealed with the Holy Spirit. They didn't dare touch her, and began to frantically fly around the room, screaming in frustrated pain as their heightened, lustful desires of new prey went unfulfilled.

Apparently however, no one else saw or noticed the tormented evil spirits. The doctor was continuing his training speech. "One must die so one can live. Carrie died so that you can live, Nicole. You are to live for a purpose; to serve your lord and master Satan." The chanting in the room grew louder and what seemed like chaos broke out in the room. The people began to jump around and dance in a frenzy as the frustrated demons returned to occupy their previous carriers, trying to satisfy some of their bloodlust and insatiable desires. Having been summoned, new dark angels were also arriving, joining in all the pandemonium.

Two entities wearing purple capes with hoods that covered their heads entered the room. Nicole thought one was a man, but the other must be a giant, for his head almost touched the ceiling! Immediately the room grew quiet and everyone dropped to their knees with their heads bowed low. After a moment the smaller of the two said, "Well done." The people replied, "Welcome Grand Master. We are here to do your will." Marcus had been in attendance earlier in the ritual to make sure that things were done according to his specifications, for this case was far too important to leave it up to anyone else; and there was too much at stake for him personally as well. His entrance at this point was the grand entrance of the most important part of the ritual, for he was ushering in Lord IS himself, and some semblance of pomp and circumstance was required. After the greeting, Marcus commanded preparation for the great event to continue.

They all rose up and reverently began to move about. Nicole was afraid of the giant, but no one else seemed to notice his presence, and this gave her some comfort. They dressed her in a small, white bridal gown. The others donned black capes with hoods that were lined in red, and the look Nicole saw in their eyes as they watched her made her tremble. She began to feel like a fly caught in a spider's web, for they had the look of a predator waiting in anticipation for his meal to be delivered to him. After looking intently around the room and then observing Nicole for several moments, the giant approached the man and whispered something into his ear.

The man in the purple cape slowly approached Nicki. He picked her up by the arms and looked into her eyes. She steadily looked back into his. Then in rage he screamed, "NOOOOOO!!! It can't be!" And he nearly dropped her. He began to pace back and forth talking to himself or to an unseen force, and then he stopped and said, "Call her. We can't proceed until we have legal rights. This one has been redeemed by Another's blood and her spirit belongs to Him, sealed tight!" As he said this, he spat on the ground. Then he turned to the doctor and said, "Well don't just stand there wasting time! Go do something with this mess! This thing has just become a whole lot more complicated!"

Nicole was taken into another room. The music had stopped. The wedding dress was removed. She was dressed in boy's clothes, placed on a stool and given a baseball cap and glove. The doctor began programming her mind. Her spirit may have been sealed, but her soul, her mind, will and emotions, were still open to manipulation and control. By the time Nicole stepped down from the stool, a part of her mind now believed that she was a little boy named Willie. His job was to watch for opportune moments to try to get Nicole to kill herself, and two dark angels had been assigned to help him: Suicide and Death.

Back in the big room, they began to work on breaking Nicole's will down. She was stripped of all clothing and forced into a large black bag which they zipped tight. Nicole hated darkness, as did Nicki. To be locked inside a dark place like that was horrible, but the dead, cold, stinky body also occupying the space beside her sent her into a deeper level of dissociation. She was utterly helpless and was in a state of hopelessness too deep for tears. Time stopped for Nicki. She had no idea how long she lay perfectly still in that body bag, but when they opened the bag and brought her out, their purpose for her was accomplished. Her will had been broken, and was now bendable to theirs.

The white gown was once again placed on her, and she was put inside the circle on the bottom point of the inverted pentagram or star. The man in the purple cape was standing on the outside line of the circle to the side of Nicole, and everyone else was standing around the outside of them. The room had grown quiet, except for the music that was playing once again. The man said, "Bring her here." The air inside the room took on an electrifying quality as the newcomer stepped forward. All eyes watched her approach and a few stepped aside to let her pass. Someone grabbed her and stopped her progress while murmuring broke out. The man demanded silence. He was quiet a moment, then said, "In spite of the Other Presence we are encountering, we will proceed. This is our territory and He will not interfere."

The woman was pushed forward until she was standing on the edge of the circle. Nicki looked past the hood and gazed into a familiar face. Hope welled up within her! She would have run to her mother, but was being held back. "Mommy!" She called out as she reached for her.

In controlled rage, the man addressed the woman. "What have you done? Last week she was ours and now we are all compromised because you allowed her spirit to be turned?" Nicki looked at the woman who was her mother, but at this moment, she looked like someone else. She watched as her mother fell to her knees and bowed her head in respect and shame and said that she hadn't known about the turning of Nicole's spirit, and was very sorry. The man answered, "There's nothing to be done about it now, so we'll proceed, however, this negligence will not go unpunished. And as Nicole grows up, you will have much to do to prove your allegiance to us. There will be markers set in place that you will be held responsible for. Are you willing to continue with this assignment?" Mother answered, "Yes," as she was yanked to her feet. And then the man's stance became rigid, and in a powerful voice he asked, "As Nicole's spiritual covering and authority, who

61

gives this girl in unholy matrimony to Satan?" In answer to the question, Nicole's mother said, "I do."

Nicki's soul cried out, NO MOMMY, NO MOMMA, NO! But her body remained silent and still as the pain of betrayal, rejection, abandonment and complete despair overwhelmed the already broken little girl. In response to this enormous burden, she collapsed onto the floor and curled up into as tight a ball as possible, then did the only thing she knew to do. She buried the pain of it all so deep down inside that it would likely never be able to be retrieved.

The woman was told to seal her vow, and so she removed the white wedding dress from Nicole's body, and while Nicki lay naked and vulnerable on the floor, the mother covered her daughter with a robe that was red and cold, still damp with Carrie's blood. She said, "Under the covering of the blood, I seal my vow. Flesh of my flesh and bone of my bone is being given in unholy matrimony to Satan."

Nicki became aware that the chanting in unholy tongues had resumed. She was made to stand up again, still covered by the bloody robe. Nicole's mother was led out of the room. As the man in the purple robe moved forward and stood just inside the line of the circle in anticipation, Nicki heard her mother scream in pain. She would have bolted at that moment if the robed man had not stopped her, for she realized that no matter what her mother had done to her, she was as much a victim as herself. She vowed that from then on, she would do everything she could to protect her mother.

When she realized that she could not escape, Nicki looked up at the man. His eyes were closed but his hands were raised like he was waiting for someone to put something in his arms. As the chanting grew louder and the people were growing restless and dancing about, they began removing their clothes, and Nicki closed her eyes against the horrible deeds going one in front of her. But when she felt the ground under her begin to shake, she opened her eyes, and jumped to the side of the circle next to the man. She watched in terror as the floor in the middle of the star and circle had opened, and that the most hideous, evil spirits were rising out of the pit. The giant moved into the circle and removed his cape. As it fell to the floor, he began to transform from a beautiful looking man into a giant snake-like creature with large wings. He was no longer beautiful and was indeed terrifying! Nicole would have run, but again was being restrained.

The spirits that had come out of the pit began swirling around the creature, and one by one they entered his body through every opening they could find. The creature seemed to grow as he feasted on those entering his body. As he turned and looked into Nicole's eyes, the robe was removed from her and his snake like tongue emerged and extended itself far enough to encircle her body, hungrily tasting every part of it.

When the last demon had merged with its host, the man in the purple cape stepped into the center of the circle where a moment ago there had been a hole, a portal from the depths of hell to the earth, and bowed low before the creature. He said, "I welcome you my Lord IS. I am yours to do with as you see fit." At this declaration, a mighty hissing sound came from the creature as it slithered up into the man.

The purple robe was then removed from the man, who no longer looked exactly like a man. He took Nicole's hand and led her into the center of the circle as well, then laid her down on the cold floor. As his naked body came close and hovered over Nicki, for a split second she recognized her Uncle Marcus, and in the next second, Marcus was gone and the most vile, evil, grotesque dark angel covered Nicole's body with his own. In a low seducing tone it hissingly proclaimed, "In the name of our lord and master Satan, I, Lord Incubus Succubus take and do wed Nicole in unholy matrimony, to be joined together with her until death." Nicki saw what appeared to be part man and part woman on the same contorted face of the creature. Just before she felt that she was being crushed to death, sexual desires apart from Nicki's control were being stimulated and manipulated within her. She knew it was bad and tried to resist, but was unable to defend herself against this torment.

Nicki must have fainted for after a brief moment of sexual pleasure mixed with terror and then physical torture and searing pain as the monster penetrated her body with his own, she was not aware of anything else until she woke up clothed in her own dress, lying on a bed in a quiet room. The doctor smiled at her and came and sat down on the bed next to her. Nicki was glad for any measure of comfort and welcomed his friendly embrace. He picked her up and sat her on his lap. He told her that she didn't need to be afraid, but that there was something he needed to do that might hurt just a little bit. He sat her back on the stool where Willie had been created, and explained that she would not remember anything about that day, the people or what had happened there; but he was going to give her a mark that would last forever, claiming the vows that had been made. He took her left hand and held her ring finger apart from the others, then with a large knife, he quickly ran the sharp blade over the soft skin on the inside of it twice. He said, "This shows that you have been wed to Satan. But Nicole, you must not speak of this to anyone. If your parents ask you what happened to your finger, you must not tell them the truth." He put a band-aid on the bleeding wound and kissed it.

The doctor worked for a while more, splitting off several other parts of Nicole's mind and assigning demons to those parts as protection from her memories for the sake of the coven, Marcus, and her mother. She would be completely unaware that her mind had been programmed to activate those parts of herself if she ever got close to remembering anything about the ritual; nor would she be aware of the demons that had been layered into those parts who would do their best to help each part fulfill its job or purpose.

When the doctor was confident that memories had been properly dealt with, Carol put Nicole in the car and drove her home. Nicole didn't remember anything about the day, but there was a very odd smell that was stuck in her nose. She didn't know what it was, but she didn't like it. She was also concerned about the band-aid on her finger because she couldn't remember what had happened to it. Carol told her that she had gotten it stuck in the car door. She also told Nicole that when her parents asked what they had done that day, she should tell them that they had been window shopping but had not bought anything. Nicole's little mind was working hard, trying to remember about the smell, about the finger. She felt like they were right there on the tip of her thoughts but she just couldn't quite reach them.

Nicole was so tired that when she got home, she voluntarily took a nap! Mother woke her up some time later. "Come on Nicole sweetie. Wake up. We are going to Peggy's house for dinner."

Nicole loved Peggy. She was a teenager and was very intriguing to the little girl. But there was something bothering Nicole. As she woke up, the smell was still stuck in her nose. "Mommy, what's that smell?" she asked.

"I don't smell anything dear," Mother said. "What does it smell like?"

"I don't know. It's just a bad smell," Nicole answered.

It was such a strong, overwhelming odor, and it followed Nicole through the whole car ride to Peggy's and was the one disappointment of the evening. Peggy didn't smell it either. She knew this because she asked Peggy if she smelled it, and she said no. There was another thing that disturbed her about the smell. It was the feeling that she should know what that smell was, but every time she thought she was beginning to remember something that would help her to identify it, the thought was gone like a vapor in the wind while the smell remained.

IS was laughing. Of all the things that had happened that day, Nicole's body was remembering the smell of burning flesh. Well good. Let that beautiful stench torment her. He loved torment! He was fairly certain that the memories were buried deep enough that the body memory would not trigger any other memories, and he believed that it would dissipate soon. In fact he decided that every once in a while, he would use the smell in years to come as a little token of torturing remembrance....

But Jesus had not forgotten His own precious jewel. He would come to Nicole at night in dreams. Sometimes He would hold her, and sometimes He pushed her back and forth on a swing. He would pour His love into her while she slept, and in the morning, her spirit would be refreshed. Nicole knew that Jesus was real and that He loved her. She loved Him in return and no one would ever guess the secrets that were buried behind the bright smile of the little girl.

CHAPTER 8
INSIDE MY MIND

"How lovely is your tabernacle, O LORD of hosts!
My soul longs, yes, even faints for the courts of the LORD;
My heart and my flesh cry out for the living God.
For a day in your courts is better than a thousand.
I would rather be a doorkeeper in the house of my God
Than dwell in the tents of wickedness."
Psalm 84:1,2,10

Not so distant past...

As Nicole grew, the war between the two kingdoms had raged inside her, each competing for dominance. On the one hand, she was ruled by fear, depression, and suicidal thoughts even as a young girl. But on the other, Love continued to hold her and to press through the darkness of her soul. At times, the voice of the enemy shouted death so strongly that it was nearly impossible to resist. And on the few occasions when she gave in to that voice, because of Nicole's heart of love for Jesus, angels of God stepped in and delivered her.

While the voice of the enemy was obnoxious and relentless, the whisper of the One who had overcome sin and death held infinitely more power and pull on Nicole's heart. Her love for Jesus and desire to obey Him became her key of victory.

As an adult, when Nicole thought back over her life, her memories were in snap shots with a little bit of video footage. Lapses in memory didn't disturb her because she was used to that happening. When she was 12 years old, she remembered questioning some feelings, dreams and pictures she saw inside her mind. She was quite surprised when she heard a voice answer back, telling her things she didn't want to hear. When she cried out against these things, the voice said, "It's ok. Go to sleep." She did and when she woke up, everything inside her mind was quiet once again.

Then there was the strange decision that she made when she was fifteen. She was in class and there was a guest speaker talking about child abuse. It was the first time she had ever heard it spoken of, and as he revealed the fact that most abuse victims become abusers themselves, Nicole's spirit had seemed to rise within her. And that was when she made the conscious decision that she would not become an abuser; that this cycle would break and end with her. It was a strange decision because she had no reason to make a commitment such as this. She had no memory of abuse of any kind. However, she was aware that this was one of the most important choices that she would ever make in her lifetime without understanding why.

Nicole didn't know anything about demons, but she knew they were real and that she was terrified of them. She didn't know anything about astral projection, but there were times when she would feel like there was a man standing beside or behind her and would even smell his body odor; but when she would turn, there was no one there. It would be many years before she would come to understand that Uncle Marcus' spirit had been near her on those occasions even though she hadn't seen him. Long after his death, the demons that had been passed from him to his successor upon his death would continue to monitor her life through this unfamiliar human spirit.

The Lord had been keeping a constant eye on Nicole, and at just the right time in her life when she had grown into adulthood, married, and had three young boys, He called together a counsel of angels on Nicole's behalf. They were all great in power. The Lord's desire was to set Nicole free to become the warrior He had created her to be, and to break the generational curses from being passed down any further in her bloodline. Even though He knew that this was the desire of her heart as well, it would cause spiritual, mental, emotional and physical conflicts within her. The risk was great. He knew that the revealing of truth had the ability to destroy Nicole if she chose to reject it; for in rejecting the truth, she would be walking away from His protection, and toward the ones set against her that were hiding in the dark recesses of her mind. And He knew that if she chose to accept the truth, the intensity of the war for her body and soul would escalate to new heights and depths; that extra care would be necessary for nurturing the wounded places of her soul and for protection in every area of her life.

In the physical realm, the Lord knew that Nicole would need a special friend, a sister in Christ who would be able to encourage her in Truth, and so he introduced Lynn. The two ladies became fast friends. Lynn had been through some of the same things and therefore would be able to comfort her and help guide her through this healing part of her journey. God also knew that Nicole would need a safe place deep within herself where she could meet with Him, and so it was that He began to prepare a place just for her inside her mind. A tabernacle, a place of meeting.

And then He began to waken the sleeping parts of her soul that were buried deep inside her mind. The battle had begun, and the demons that had been layered in were being activated. But there was a heavenly host in place as well....

RUN

Nicole was awakening from what seemed to be a very long sleep. It was a very strange sensation, for while her body was functioning like normal as she went about her daily routine, she was simultaneously experiencing things deep inside her mind. She felt as if she were in two places at once, living two lives, one inside of her mind that no one but God and herself were able to experience, and one outside where she was a wife and mother.

On the morning of the awakening inside her mind, she heard music that seemed to be coming from within her, yet was all around her, and she slowly opened her eyes to

69

identify its source. She wasn't sure where she was or how she had gotten there, but she found herself looking into the most beautiful and kind eyes she had ever seen. In a fraction of a second, Nicole's spirit assessed the woman who appeared old, and yet young; who was familiar and yet unknown. She was dressed in a white robe that completely covered her except for the skin on her face which was wrinkled, but smooth. Nicole knew that her name was Joy and instantly trusted her.

When the woman saw that Nicole's eyes had opened and were looking at her, she smiled in great joy and sat down on the edge of her bed. In looking around Nicole saw that she was lying in a small bed in a large room along with many other people lying in beds like hers, some awake, some asleep, but all were attended by those dressed in white robes like the one beside her. She started to sit up and found that she was very weak. Joy gently helped her lay back down, then leaned over and began whispering words into Nicole's ear. Some she understood and some she did not, but the effect over her spirit was peace. Nicole realized that the music she was hearing was the affect of so many voices whispering truth, healing words, and that as their voices came together, surprisingly there was no chaos, just complete unity and harmony.

"Little Nicki, you have been very sick, but by the power of Jesus blood, He has healed you. Praise God! He came to *heal the brokenhearted, to proclaim liberty to the captives, the opening of the prison to those who are bound; to proclaim the acceptable year of the LORD, and the day of vengeance of our God; to comfort all who mourn, to console those who mourn in Zion, to give them beauty for ashes, the oil of joy for mourning, the garment of praise for the spirit of heaviness; that they may be called trees of righteousness, the planting of the LORD, that He may be glorified (Isaiah 61:1-3). Because* you fear His name, The Sun of Righteousness has arisen with healing in His wings *(Malachi 4:2). The joy of the Lord is your strength. Make a joyful shout to God, all the earth! Sing out the honor of His name; Make His praise glorious. Say to God, "How awesome are Your works! Through the greatness of Your power Your enemies shall submit themselves to You. All the earth shall worship You and sing praises to You; They shall sing praises to Your name. Come and see the works of God; He is awesome in His doing toward the sons of men...He rules by His power forever; Do not let the rebellious exalt themselves. ...Oh, bless our God, you peoples! And make the voice of His praise to be heard, who keeps our soul among the living, and does not allow our feet to be moved. For You, O God, have tested us; You have refined us as silver is refined. You brought us into the net; You laid affliction on our backs...But You brought us out to rich fulfillment.... I will declare what He has done for my soul...Blessed be God, Who has not turned away my prayer, Nor His mercy from me!"* (Psalm 66)

As the woman continued to speak, Nicole seemed to gain strength. "Nicki, Jesus came to destroy the work of the devil in your life (1 John 3:8) and as you choose to humble yourself before Him and *cast all your cares upon Him, He cares for you and will take care of you. Be sober, be vigilant; because your adversary the devil walks about like a roaring lion, seeking whom he may devour. Resist him, steadfast in the faith, knowing that the same sufferings are experienced by your brotherhood in the world. But may the God of all grace, who called us to His eternal glory by Christ Jesus, after you have suffered a while, perfect, establish, strengthen, and settle you. To Him be the glory and the dominion forever and ever. Amen"* (1 Peter 5:6-11).

Then the woman gently sat Nicole up in the bed, took hold of her face in her hands, looked deeply into her eyes, and said, "My Little Nicki, my beloved, my job is done. It is time for you to go. There will be much for you to learn, and there is much you will not understand for a very long time. But there is One who is with you, and He will never let you go."

Nicole was suddenly very much afraid at the thought of being alone without her companion. She realized that she had been relying on this woman for what must have been a long while. "Can't you come with me?" Joy pulled Nicole into her arms and held her there for several moments, transferring peace into her spirit. And then she spoke something into Nicole's spirit that began as a faint whisper but grew louder and louder until she could no longer resist. Run. Run Nicole, run! Run my little one! RUN!

Nicole jumped up out of the bed, surprised at the strength in her body. She looked at the woman, who smiled and blew her a kiss. "Run Nicole. Have no fear. When you are afraid, trust in Him, and He will keep you in perfect peace when you fix your mind on Him. Now go! Run!"

Nicole began to run, slowly at first, then more quickly. She started in the direction the woman had pointed out until she came to what appeared to be an elevator of sorts. She looked back and saw the woman standing beside what had been her bed, watching her. The woman raised her hand in one last goodbye as Nicole turned and stepped through the doors into the unknown.

THE TABERNACLE

After the strange encounter inside her mind, Nicole began experiencing very disturbing feelings, dreams and pictures that made no sense at all. She tried to ignore them, but when they began taking over her mind and emotions even during her waking hours, she became worried. She was afraid to tell anyone about them because she thought she was going crazy and thought that they would put her in a mental institution. She knew enough to know that if that happened, they would drug her, and drugs held an especially frightening place in her mind.

Nicole decided to talk to Lynn about what was happening and take the chance that she would have her committed. But Lynn told her that she was fine, that she wasn't crazy; that Jesus was just getting ready to do some important work in her. It wasn't the best news because Nicole wasn't sure that she wanted any work done. But she agreed that she did want to be whoever Jesus created her to be, so Lynn told her not to read anything except the Bible, and began giving her homework looking up scriptures that taught her what God said about everything she was feeling, remembering and dealing with. Every time Nicole called Lynn in a panic, she always pointed her right back to the Truth of God's Word.

One morning as Nicole opened her Bible for her daily time with God, inside her mind and spirit she suddenly found herself outside in a very busy, noisy, dirty, chaotic place. She oddly felt as if she were two different people. She was aware of her existence as Nicole, but she also felt as if she were a little girl. The little girl wasn't at all sure where she was or even how she had gotten there. There were people everywhere, and animals. Business was being conducted in stalls, and there was much buying and selling going on as if it were an outside market place of sorts. Nicole had the distinct impression that she was in Israel during Bible times. No one noticed her, and everyone seemed to know what they were about except for her.

She realized that she was standing near a door in a wall, and cautiously lifted the latch, opening the door a few inches. As she drew close to peer inside, a wave of indescribable peace washed over her. It was such a welcome contrast to the chaos around her that she found herself wanting nothing more than to be inside this place of peace. She saw no one in the building, and without waiting another second, she silently slipped inside. She stood quietly taking in her surroundings. It was a large, beautiful room, furnished with a rocking chair that stood beside a fire place in one corner; a table that was sitting near a closed door on the other side of the room; and in the middle of the room were seven large, gold, lamp stands that were on either side of a rather large stone structure that resembled an altar.

The girl was afraid that at any moment someone would find her here and tell her that she had to leave. She could not imagine ever leaving this place, especially if it meant that she would have to go back into the world outside the door. She decided that she would rather hide here forever than to go back out that door, so she ducked under the table and sat very still.

For the next three days, inside Nicole's mind, the girl rested under the table while Nicole went about her normal routine of life, also aware that somehow, a part of her was in a safe place that she imagined was something like the tabernacle described in scripture.

On the first day, the girl experienced a moment of panic as the door next to the table opened and a Man in a long white robe entered the room, closing the door behind Him. She held her breath in hopes that He would not see her there, and she watched Him as He carried a large black bag over to the altar, set it down and poured red liquid all over it. He raised both arms up toward the sky and breathed out a large breathy sigh. Fire came from somewhere and He watched it until the bag was completely burned up. Then He began polishing the lamp stands while singing a song in a language she did not know, but that was strangely familiar and comforting to her. After He was finished, He scooped up the ashes, placed them carefully in a small golden box that was inlaid with jewels, and carried it with Him as He walked past her hiding place and back through the door from which He had entered.

The next day was the same, except that this day, the black bag He carried to the altar was much smaller. On the third day, the black bag was even larger than the first one. And each day when He placed the bag on the altar, He covered it with the red liquid and went through the same routine. The girl had become comfortable in her hiding place and was very surprised when, on the third day as the Man came close to the table, instead of opening the door and going back into the other room, He stopped and knelt down and looked at her with the most beautiful eyes she had ever seen.

His face was kind and He smiled and said, *"Hello Little Nicki. I thought it was time for Me to welcome you to My home. I want you to know that you do not have to leave, and no one is going to tell you to go. On the contrary, I have waited a long time for you to come to Me and find My rest. I am so very glad you are here now and I hope that you will choose to remain here with Me. You are welcome to stay under the table as long as you like, and you are free to explore and enjoy the riches of My Kingdom when you are ready to."* With that, He stood back up and disappeared behind the door as He had done every other day.

The words of the Man were like liquid love that filled up her being and drove out all her fear. Yes, she would stay, and she would learn about this Man and His home. It would become her home now.

Nicole had come to realize that the things the girl was experiencing were somehow connected to her. Since the girl had entered the Tabernacle, peace had come over her own spirit and the plaguing images and fears had stopped tormenting her.

Several weeks went by, and the girl was learning the songs the Man sang as He burned the black bundles and polished the lamps. She noticed that there were days when there were several bundles; and others when there were none. On those days, it seemed that the Man was especially quiet and spent extra time and care polishing the lamp stands. She asked Him once about the bags and their contents, but He did not reply. His eyes just took on a faraway look, and an expression of the greatest love imaginable overcame His face. It seemed as if He was remembering something of great value, and then He smiled. In the evenings, He would come and light a fire, sit in the rocking chair while she reclined at His feet, and He would tell her many wonderful, exciting things. The Words He spoke came to life as they worked their way from her mind into her heart. She was content for the first time in her life.

And then one day, as the Man was ready to go back through the door after His daily routine, He stopped and called to her to follow Him. She couldn't explain it, but she was instantly filled with dread! She had not felt anything like this before in this place of peace, and it frightened her. She had never questioned what was behind that door before, or what the Man did there. The fear paralyzed her, and she realized that she didn't want to know. The Man looked at her with some disappointment, but quietly said if she wasn't ready, that they would wait for another day.

The girl took no comfort in that. Another day! She didn't understand why she ever had to look inside that door! She moaned in distress as she asked herself why the Man had to destroy her peace! Why He couldn't just let her be happy!

The next day and the next, the Man asked her to join Him, and each day, the girl withdrew further from the dreaded door. And it wasn't just the door that she was avoiding; it was the Man as well. She no longer sat near Him in the evenings by the fire because she was afraid that He would try to talk to her about the room beyond the door. Isolation, fear, anger and rebellion were fast becoming her companions in this place where she had once lived in such contentment and love with the Man. There was no peace now.

It was a bit of a surprise, when upon waking up many days later to find that she had slept beside the *other* door; the one that she had been so desperately eager to come through in order to enter this place of peace. It was an even bigger shock to realize that she had begun to think about going out through that same door, back into the place of chaos and filth.

Despair overcame her as she realized that she had no hope of peace left in this place as long as the Man insisted that she look inside the dreaded door. She remembered the chaos beyond this door, but began to wonder if perhaps there might be another place such as this one out there where she could have peace without demands. The longer she stood by the door leading to the outside world, the greater her longing to return to it became. She began to remember with fondness some of the things she had experienced out there; to deceptively believe that it wasn't really as bad as she remembered; and she began to think that the answer to her quest for peace could be found out there after all.

Nicole was also experiencing fear and despair. She had begun to relate with Little Nicki, and more and more their feelings were becoming connected. She found that she was in the tabernacle too, and that she was just as afraid of the room as Nicki. Her desire to run out the door was as intense as the girl's. The two stood together contemplating their options when the roof suddenly lifted off the room and a violent wind swept through. Instead of turning and running out the door to escape the danger of being carried away in the wind, both girls cried out in fear for Jesus, the Man whom they loved.

And suddenly, He was there beside them. Little Nicki ran into His open arms and began to cry. He quietly said, *"Peace, be still."* And it was. The ceiling fell back into place and Jesus picked up Little Nicki, then reached out and took Nicole's hand in His.

Jesus led them over to the rocking chair in front of the fire, and still holding Nicki, He sat down and began to rock with Nicole sitting at His feet. For a long time they sat quietly enjoying the peace after the storm and the Presence of the Man, His love and safety. Finally He asked, *"Do you still want to leave?"*

Nicole and the girl answered together slowly, "We don't think we ever really wanted to leave; we just don't want to go inside the room. Why do You insist that we go there?"

"My beautiful girls," He replied, *"Do you remember when you asked Me about the bundles that I carry out of that room and burn?"* They nodded and He continued. *"It is time for Me to answer your question, but you can not know the answer until you are willing to face your fear and look into that room."* He paused for a moment then asked, *"Do you know how much I love you? Do you realize that in your fear you have run from My love? It has caused you to doubt Me and has placed*

you in a very vulnerable position. You are safe when you are in My love, but love requires surrender, trust and obedience. I know that this fear wants to cause you to run away from My love so that you will be enticed and ensnared by your enemy. He does not want you to continue to live in My Presence, to listen to My Words, or to look into the room, because when you do, you will begin to know truth, and truth will set you free. You will overcome the hold the enemy has on you and you will become strong and no longer defenseless against him."

Both understood His words. They thought about what they wanted and realized that more than anything, they wanted to be close to Him. They realized that the peace they so strongly desired was connected to Him because He was Peace, and that they were the ones who had isolated themselves from peace through their rebellion. Nicole trembled when she thought about how close they had come to walking back out into the world where her spirit knew there was no peace.

Little Nicki buried her face in the Man's strong shoulder as she asked, "Oh please forgive me for not trusting You; for being angry and rebelling against You! I am afraid of the room, but I will choose to trust You. I know that I can't live apart from You any more!"

Jesus smiled and looked lovingly at Nicole. "And what about you Nicole? Are you willing to face what lies behind the door? Will you trust Me and allow Me to help you overcome this fear so that we will not be separated again? Will you believe that I want only what is best for you, and that the plans I have are for good and not for evil, to give you a future and a hope?"

Nicole knew that this was a pivotal moment in her life. She somehow knew that Little Nicki could not enter the room without her; that if she refused to face what was behind it, she would be walking away from her relationship with Jesus and would be entering into that world of fear, confusion, chaos and terror with no heavenly help. She knew that she would be signing her own death sentence of mental illness.

"Jesus, am I crazy? I have to know!" Nicole cried out.

Then Jesus laughed. It was the laugh of an indulgent Father. *"The world may very well label you crazy, My Little Nicki, just as they do Me. But I can promise you that if you will trust Me, I will lead you into an abundant, fulfilling life of love, joy, peace, patience, kindness, goodness, gentleness, faithfulness and self control. Does that sound crazy to you?"*

Nicole was deep in thought. Jesus had called *her* Little Nicki, and she suddenly realized something else. There were no longer two of her, just the one. She was Little Nicki, and she was Nicole, one and the same. Integrated. That was the word that filled her mind, and she wasn't sure she liked this new arrangement. She wasn't sure that she wanted to be Little Nicki because Little Nicki knew things she didn't want to know.

Jesus of course knew very well what was happening in Nicole's mind. *"Nicole, you are one with Little Nicki, however, the integration is not quite complete. You now have understanding that she is a part of your mind that was split off to conceal memories and emotions you were unable to deal with. Integration will be complete once you come to a place of knowing and accepting her memories and emotions as your own."*

Jesus saw that Nicole was struggling to accept this fact. Then He continued. *"It is time for you to make a choice. You can walk in the way of truth and light which is to accept Little Nicki and all she has carried for you; or you can refuse to accept her which is the same as choosing darkness. I can protect you if you choose truth. You must either allow Me to reveal these things and help you overcome them, or you may continue in the darkness of dissociation. But I warn you, if you choose the darkness, it will consume you because the time of My protection over the things hidden in the darkness of your mind is coming to an end."*

Little Nicki also understood the change that had occurred within Nicole. She was experiencing feelings of immense relief! She felt as though for the first time in her life, her job of protecting Nicole and blocking memories from her mind would be easier, for with integration and protection from Jesus, certainly Nicole would be able to share in holding onto the weight of the past. With great anticipation that came from carrying a much too large of a burden for much too long of a time, she began to share a particular memory.

This was more than Nicole was ready to handle, and she began to feel as if she were drowning in pain. Jesus immediately spoke to Nicole and told her that she needed to take control and stay in control. That she needed to talk to Little Nicki and let her know that she would indeed relieve her of her job, and would accept the memories that she carried, but that Jesus would be the One to help her know what Nicole was ready for and what she was not. Jesus asked for the keys of their memories, and they both readily agreed to allow Him to bring them up in His time and way. Nicole's pain stopped and He lifted the exhausted girl up and carried her through another door that she had not noticed before, just off to the side of the fire place. He laid her on a little bed that was just her size, and covered her with a cozy blanket. Then He sat down beside her in another rocking chair and began to play a song on the harmonica while He rocked. Nicole closed her eyes and peace washed over her like a song. As she drifted off to sleep, she was sure that she heard angels singing a Reba Rambo song, "*Sweet Jesus Peace, Water so free, flowing from Him to you and to me. Sweet Jesus Peace, Fountain we need, flowing from Him, to you and to me.*"[1]

In the morning, Nicole woke with renewed purpose. She rose up out of the little bed and went in search of Jesus. When she found Him, she ran to Him and fell at His feet. "Jesus, there is no other way I can live. I need You and I want You more than anything! I choose to surrender to You and to trust and obey You even when I'm afraid and don't like it. I do believe You know what I need. I certainly don't. I feel like I don't know anything anymore! It seems like my world as I have known it has just been demolished and I feel so helpless. Without You to guide and protect me, there is no life. So please Jesus, help me!"

Jesus reached down and pulled Nicole into a loving embrace, then laughed delightedly and said, *"Well, there's no time like now to face your fears."* He released her, then turned and began to walk toward the door. Nicole stood and watched Him open the door and stand beside it as He had so many times before, waiting for her to follow Him. This time, the fear of separation from the One she loved outweighed her fear of the unknown, and she began her journey toward the open door.

THE HEALING ROOM

Nicole approached the door slowly and saw that there was a short flight of stairs. As they descended, she was unprepared for what she saw. It was like a hospital room with many people lying in beds. "What is this place?" she asked.

"This is My healing room, the place where I care for My people, those who have chosen to believe in Me, but who are too weak, sick, wounded or vulnerable to function in the world," He answered. *"Some are here for a short time, while others are here much longer, and then there are some who will never be ready to leave My care until they enter the place I am preparing for them in heaven even now."*

Jesus stepped inside the door and Nicole suddenly knew that she needed to follow Him into this place. As she entered, He turned her attention to a boy who was sitting in a wheel chair with a look of great concentration and determination on his face. *"This boy was badly damaged many years ago. Last week, he laid his unbelief at the foot of the cross and has been practicing faith since that time. I'm so very glad that you chose to join Me today, for such a time as this!"*

At that very moment, the boy pushed himself up out of his chair and stood on his own two feet! And as his feet touched the floor and he took his first step, the boy was instantly transformed into a man! The room became filled with joyous activity! Healing angels and ministering angels joined hands as they floated upwards and swirled around the room rejoicing. Nicole was also aware of some others holding huge blazing swords of fire that were standing in the corners of the room. They were smiling even though they had not entered into the celebration with dancing. Jesus noticed her curiosity and explained that they were warrior angels, watching over and guarding those in the healing room. As she glanced back over at the boy who had matured in the course of a second, Jesus said, *"A part of his mind and his emotions have been stuck in the trauma of his experience. Through facing the pain of it and then renouncing unbelief and choosing faith, he has been released and is now free to be the man of God he was created to be."*

Nicole continued looking around the healing room and pondered all of the things she was seeing, then she quietly, almost fearfully asked, "I was in this room, wasn't I?"

"Yes you were, for quite some time; since you were four years old, actually. My holy servants cared lovingly for you day and night. They read you My Words and sang you My songs that fed your spirit and helped you to gain strength. Then came the day when you were ready to be released. Not long after that, you found your way to the door and entered my Kingdom of Love," He responded.

Nicole realized that the songs she had heard Jesus sing in the tabernacle were familiar because she had heard them sung over her countless times in this room. It was then that she noticed a very large cross at the end of the room. It was not pretty to look at, and yet she was unable to take her eyes off of it. Even though she didn't fully understand, the beauty of what it stood for began to draw her further into the room, closer to it. Jesus walked beside her and began to explain that when she had chosen to give her life to Him, He had taken her sin and removed it as far away from her as the east is from the west. He told her that she was completely cleansed and forgiven, but that her soul (her mind, will and emotions) still carried the wounds and the pain of the past; that she still believed some of the lies the enemy had planted in her thinking.

As they approached the cross, Jesus explained to her that the black bundles she had seen Him carry to the altar were the things that His people had chosen to release and had laid down at the foot of the cross; things that they had been trusting in and relying on apart from Him. For some, it was choosing to exchange anger and bitterness for forgiveness; for others, it was choosing the way of humility, surrender and obedience over selfish ambitions and pride. Still others chose to release physical suffering for joy. The number of potential problems was endless, He told her, but the results were always the same. When people chose to hear the truth of His Word and chose to release those things to Him that had been hindering their relationship with Him, He was then able to break the bondages of the enemy and bring healing to the wounded places of their body, soul and spirit.

Jesus was quiet for a moment and then He gently said, "Nicole, I have begun an awakening process in you and have brought you into this healing room for a purpose. There are defensive walls inside your mind that I have allowed to be there for a period of time as a means of protection. But now it is time to begin breaking down those walls because they have become a hindrance rather than a help. As long as there is division in your mind, there are dark places. This will be a very long hard process, but it is time for Me to begin to reveal the truth and to dispel the darkness and the power of the enemy that is hiding in there, for you see, he is manipulating you with his vile and destructive patterns of thought and behavior. We can't combat this and overcome unless you know the truth. Nicole, will you trust Me? Are you willing to allow me to do this for you? For us?"

Nicole pondered all that she had seen and heard. She replied, "Jesus, I hear what You are saying and I don't fully understand it. But I do trust You and I want to be the person You created me to be. So, Yes, I will allow You to do whatever You need to in me."

As she spoke words of surrender, it seemed as if she could see Jesus taking a key out of His heart and unlocking something inside her mind. She felt Little Nicki hug her and say, "I'm so sorry that you have to know these things that will hurt you so much." And instantly some of the memories of a Satanic Ritual and her mother's involvement made their way into Nicole's consciousness. The pain of the memories was so intense that she doubled over and dropped to the floor, gasping for breath.

In the outside world, Nicole had been trying to take a nap, but the events going on in the inside of her mind were preventing her from sleep. She was fully aware of Little Nicki and her memories now, and she was experiencing them physically just as she was inside her mind. Her body had stiffened in terror and stress, and she began gasping for breath. Jake was awakened from his sleep when Nicole screamed and then began a mournful wailing and crying that continued for several hours. He was unable to understand what was wrong, but he patiently held his wife and prayed for her through the next couple of hours as memories and emotions that had been buried for 30 years began to surface. She was experiencing body memories as well, physical feelings and smells attached to the memories and emotions which had all been tucked away by Little Nicki. She had done a very good job of hiding them from Nicole in order to keep her protected from the pain.

Inside the healing room in Nicole's mind, at least a dozen large angels had surrounded her. Knowing her pain and sorrow, Jesus knelt down beside her and prayed for her in His Spirit as only He knew how to do. He understood a broken heart more than anyone, and even though He knew that He could and would heal this one, He also knew that it would be a process. Little Nicki had been unable to cry or to express any of the feelings and emotions tied to the trauma of the ritual so many years before, and it was time for those emotions to begin to surface so that He could begin to heal His beloved's broken heart and replace the sorrow with joy, hope, healing and freedom.

"*Nicole, will you give your emotions to Me?*" Jesus asked.

Because of the pain, again she wasn't sure what He meant, but she said, "Yes, Lord. Take them."

Immediately Jesus showed her a visual of what was happening. Her emotions were in a large pot hanging over a fire. They were all tangled together, but she could see some of the individual emotions rising to the top as they swirled around. She saw anger, rejection, abandonment, self-pity, pain, and on and on. And she saw a demon with an impish face standing next to the pot, feeding the flames. He had a large poker stick in his hand, and every little bit, he would stick it into the pot and poke around as he stirred. The effect was a magnification of whichever emotion was being poked as well as a constant state of chaos and confusion.

"Jesus, help me! What does this mean?" she cried out.

"*I created you with emotions,*" He replied. "*Good as well as bad, and they are neither right nor wrong. The good bring pleasure joy and peace, a reminder of My love and Kingdom treasure. The bad are to be indicators that something is not right so that you will bring them to Me and allow Me to reveal the troubled spots so they can be fixed. However, Satan assigns his demons to watch for open doors, and if you do not guard your heart, he will take your emotions captive and then torment you with them.*"

"I feel so overwhelmed. What do you want me to do?" Nicole asked.

"*In the past as you have listened to lies in your mind about feelings, you have given permission and rights to this demon, whose function is to keep you in a state of constant emotional pain. Will you renounce those lies and give Me permission to remove the demon that is feeding the flames so that hope and healing can take place?*"

85

"Yes! All that," she agreed.

"*Alright my little one, however, I want you to understand that one of Satan's biggest tricks is to assign many demons to hover and watch for emotional entry points. Once this demon is gone, you must be on guard for there are others with poker sticks, waiting for the opportunity to heat up your emotions, to prick them and stir you up, hoping that through an emotional reaction rather than a godly response, they will be able to gain a stronghold.*

Jesus went on to explain that she must not allow her emotions to rule her life or her decisions. "*When you are in constant communication with me, I will be your Guide rather than your feelings, and you will be safe.*"

After several hours, inside and outside her mind, Nicole lay exhausted emotionally, mentally and physically. She felt as if she had been through the biggest fight of her life, and even her body hurt. But something was different. When her tears had subsided, inside her mind Nicole was aware of someone singing, and it was a new song, a song she had never heard before. She lay quietly listening to praises of Almighty God, great in Power and awesome in Love. Cantor sang of peace no matter the circumstances and of victory through the Blood of the Lamb of God. It magnified Jesus of Nazareth, her Healer/Deliverer, it spoke of the power of His shed blood and gave praise to the Spirit who was the Comforter and Guide that would lead her into all truth, hope, healing and freedom. Jesus leaned forward and whispered into her ear, "*Nicole, this is your song, the new song of your new life.*"

Nicole was very grateful that it was not one of hopelessness and despair, but even though the power of the pain had been washed away, she realized that in its place was sorrow. Sorrow for what she had been through as the truth concerning her life came into the light of consciousness; the type of sorrow one experiences in times of great loss. And she told Jesus this. "Lord, thank you for the song, but I am so very sad. I don't think I'll ever be able to sing again."

Jesus lovingly stroked her cheek and said, *"Nicole, you are grieving. That is good even if it doesn't feel like it. You will be sad for a short while, but then My joy will break through this night, and your mourning will be turned into dancing. You will see the reality of this song and it will become yours in every way very soon. As you begin to comprehend these things, you will go through the grieving process many times and will experience other things such as fear, doubt and anger, but just call out to Me when these things come upon you, and I will show you My truth and walk with you through those times. I will always lead you through to victory. I am the One who overcomes, and as you are in Me, you will overcome as well. So don't worry My little one. All is well and in time, My time, your life will sing this very song."*

It was all too fresh for Nicole to comprehend, and she was very tired. Jesus picked her up off the floor and laid her down on a little cot nearby. As Nicole slept peacefully in the healing room, outside of her mind her body also gave way to sleep. And just as she drifted off, she was sure that if she had opened her eyes she would have seen several angels who were singing peace over her.

LIFE WITH LITTLE NICKI

When Nicole woke after her nap, it was dark outside. She remembered what had happened, and heard Little Nicki speak to her. "Are you going to get us some supper now? Cause I'm reaaaalllly hungry!"

It frightened Nicole because she had been aware of Little Nicki when they were together in the tabernacle, but this Little Nicki was right there in her life! She could actually hear her voice and it really sounded like another person who was inside her head! It felt very weird and frightening. She picked up the phone and called Lynn.

After explaining what was happening, she asked, "Am I crazy?"

To her surprise, Lynn replied, "No sweetie. Jesus is bringing things out into the open that have been buried deep within you. You need to call out to Him and ask Him what He wants you to know."

Nicole's heart was encouraged, and with a confidence she hadn't felt before, after hanging up, she immediately yelled, "JESUS!" She saw Him in her mind and asked, "What is happening to me? Little Nicki is in me and she's talking to me!"

Jesus sat down on a chair like He might need to be there awhile. Nicole could now see Little Nicki, sucking her thumb and cuddling a blanket. She went over to Jesus and climbed up on His lap, and they both just sat looking at her with sweet smiles on their faces.

"Jesus! What am I supposed to do about this?!" Nicole asked in frustration.

With great patience, Jesus began to explain. *"Nicole, Little Nicki is a part of you that has not been able to grow and mature. She needs you to love her and to teach her the things she needs to know about Me, about you, about life in general. She needs a new job, and so as she matures, she will learn to use her gifts and abilities, and over time as you work together, what appears to be the two of you will become so perfectly blended together, that you will think and function as one whole, healthy person. You will be the woman I created you to be, doing the things I destined for you to do. In the meantime, even though you know that she is really you, you will need to treat her like you would any other little girl in your care, teaching and training her."*

Nicole sighed. "Does it have to be like this Jesus? Why can't You just take her and train her? You'd do a much better job at that than me. I don't even really like little girls."

Understanding her fear of little girls, Jesus said, *"Nicole, Nicole, Nicole. I can't take her from you. She is you! You can choose to reject her, to push her back deep down inside a dark place in your mind. But if you choose to reject her now, you will be rejecting yourself and the plans I have for you, as well as opening a door for Satan to gain an advantage over you. Your healing and freedom depend on the light of truth ruling in your innermost being."* Jesus replied.

"This is like the choice I had to make in the Tabernacle isn't it?" Nicole mused. "You know that I want to please You Jesus. So, ok, You win; I will surrender to You and Your plan. But I want You to know that I think this is really weird, and if I end up in a psych ward, it will be Your fault!"

Jesus laughed, whispered something in Little Nicki's ear, and the two of them smiled conspiratorially at one another. Then Little Nicki climbed down off of Jesus' lap and ran to Nicole with her arms raised up, wanting Nicole to pick her up and hold her. Nicole looked helplessly over at Jesus, but He just smiled and nodded His head. So she reached down and picked up Little Nicki, her four year old self. Weird.

For several days, as Nicole went about her every day life, inside her mind she was carrying Little Nicki and answering tons of questions. It seemed that Little Nicki had as inquisitive a mind as any child that age.

Living with Little Nicki was bringing healing to both of them. Little Nicki was freed from the responsibilities that were no longer hers even though she still held many of the memories and much of the emotional pain. Jesus told her that Nicole wasn't quite ready to handle everything at once and that it would be a process for them, but He now carried the weight of the pain so that Little Nicki was free to experience joy like she never had before. And He was telling Little Nicki when to give certain memories and feelings over to Nicole.

Healing for Nicole wasn't quite as easy or joyous as it was for Little Nicki. As Little Nicki slowly released memories and emotions to Nicole, she had to face truth about her life that had been hidden, and experience very difficult emotions. As she began remembering specific things about the ritual and realized what a counterfeiter

Satan was, Jesus taught her to use the power of truth to stop the things in her mind that just kept going round like a never ending video.

One day she began hearing chanting that just kept repeating itself over and over to the point she felt that it was beginning to take over her mind. In desperation she called Lynn.

"What are you hearing them say? Lynn asked.

"I keep hearing Red, Red, Carrie's dead; Yonder rolls her severed head. Am I crazy now?"

Lynn calmly replied, "Not even close. Next time you hear the voices just say, 'Red, Red, Jesus bled on Satan's head, and now he's dead!'"

That worked! Satan didn't want to hear that, and after repeating it a few times, the chanting stopped altogether.

Questions began flooding her mind, and confusion and anger emerged. Nicole knew that her mother loved her! But she didn't understand how a mother could abandon her daughter and give her to the devil. She was beginning to see puzzle pieces of her life fit together as memories continued to surface; some that had been buried, and some that she had known about but that had never made sense to her before. Nicole spent more and more time studying God's Word and talking to Him than she ever had before. She knew that she could not handle any of this on her own and was desperate for help. Divine help. She was learning to rely on Jesus as never before, and He was teaching her a process of dealing with these memories that would bring her through the pain as they surfaced, and on into victory as the power they had held over her lost their place in the light of truth.

As Nicole would experience new memories or feelings, she was learning several key steps:

1. Call out to Jesus immediately to come help her and to reveal truth to her. She did not want to fall into a trap of false memories.

2. When Jesus would confirm that the memory was real, she would have to choose to accept it, which was often much more difficult than it seemed it should be.

3. She would then tell the memory to her safe person, which was either Jake or Lynn. It always amazed her at how the power of the enemy seemed to break when she would speak the things out loud that she had been so afraid to think about, let alone to say.

4. She learned that pain was not always a bad thing and was in fact a part of the healing process. She was learning to distinguish between her own pain that she had buried deep within her and the pain of torment that the demons inflicted. She learned that experiencing the pain of the memory was critical if there was going to be complete healing and freedom from it, for in denying the pain, she was denying the truth of what had happened; and denial was an open door for the enemy. But she had spent a life time of hiding from the pain and she found that she was terrified of reliving the pain of the memories. So she would remind herself and Jesus that He held the keys to her memories and emotions, and that she could trust Him. She determined that she would allow Him to open the door to every pain in His time and way, allowing Him to bring the memory and its pain to the surface of her mind and emotions. She found that when He would bring something up, there would be intense pain as she seemed to relive the moment of its initial impact, then it would be gone! The pain that she had buried and that had been torturing her for 30 years, was gone in an instant! There just seemed to be so much there, that it began to feel as if she would never stop reliving painful things. So when Lynn suggested that she should maximize every victory God had in store for her and to minimize the power of the memory, she discovered another weapon in her arsenal. When she focused on the victory rather than feelings of defeat, the fear of pain seemed to vanish and boldness took its place.

5. Confessing her part to God was very important. Even if she had not done anything wrong at the time, over

time, she had allowed the event to harden her heart, to defile her with bitterness, and she had almost always believed the lies the enemy had shot at her.

6. Nicole learned about renouncing the lies and the demons attached to them.

7. She learned to search out the truth in God's Word, then to believe the truth and act on it instead of the lie that she had previously been reacting to, regardless of her feelings.

8. She learned to forgive and to accept forgiveness.

9. She began to understand soul ties and the need to ask God to break those ungodly connections with people that had been formed in sin. She experienced the freedom that came from cutting off access of her soul (mind, will and emotions) from those of the person on the other side of the soul tie, along with destroying lines of transportation that demons would use for transferring back and forth between people, causing confusion and chaos.

Nicole was doing fairly well in practicing her lessons; however the anger she had for her mother was greater than all the anger she had for all the others who had done even greater physical harm to her, against her. Her anger was rooted deeply in the pain of rejection and abandonment, and unbeknownst to her at the time, huge demons of Rejection and Abandonment had attached themselves to her own feelings and were continually stirring up the pain and tormenting her with anger, rage and hatred. She couldn't seem to get past the fact that her mother was the one who should have protected her, and she just couldn't seem to forgive her.

One morning as she was doing the dishes, Nicole shouted out to God, "Why don't You just strike her dead?" And before she was done in the kitchen she had her answer. A very clear audible voice next to her said, "*I'm going to strike you dead.*" Nicole had heard the voices of her enemies and was learning to distinguish between them and Jesus. This was definitely God. She dropped to her knees,

92

and asked, "Why God? I haven't done anything wrong! I am trying to do everything right!" And God in His wisdom and mercy replied, "Nicole, I love your mother as much as I love you. It has nothing to do with what either of you have or have not done. Come away with me Nicole, to the healing room. I have more to show you."

BACK TO THE HEALING ROOM

It was becoming second nature for Nicole to move back and forth between the two realities, to live in them simultaneously. This time, she was not afraid to follow Jesus into the healing room, but she admitted that she was a little nervous about what would happen there.

She looked around once again in awe of the Presence of the Lord and the worship that permeated this place. All of a sudden, her eyes grew big and her heart began to pound. Jesus stepped up beside her and took a hold of her arm. "It's my mother isn't it?" Nicole whispered. Jesus silently nodded. Conflicting emotions began coursing through her heart.

Nicole knew in that moment what she needed to do. Jesus had brought her back to this room because even though she had been learning the lessons, she had been avoiding the biggest pain of the past, the pain of betrayal, rejection and abandonment by the one who should have loved her most and done all to protect her. It was time to surrender her bitterness.

Seeing her mother laying motionlessly on a little bed with a very bright angel singing over her did strange things to Nicole's heart as well as Little Nicki's. The hard shell of bitterness began to melt away, and she began to feel compassion for her. Little Nicki realized that she was relieved to see that she was in a safe place. She remembered that no matter what her mother had done, she loved her and she had worked hard all her life to protect her from anyone else ever finding out the truth.

Jesus said, "*Nicole, your mother belongs to Me just as her father did before her.*" And then He seemed to grow and grow until He was as tall as the highest point in the ceiling. His voice seemed to boom within her. *"She is mine and I will let no one speak against her!"* And then He returned to His normal size and Little Nicki suddenly knew that Jesus was protecting her mother and that she didn't have to hold onto that job any longer.

"Will she ever be well enough to leave this place, Jesus?" Nicole asked quietly.

In answer to this question, Jesus asked one of her. *"Nicole, do you believe that I love your mother?"*

As she pondered this question, she watched the beautiful shining one sitting beside her mother as she tenderly reached down to brush a stray hair out of her eyes, then lovingly touched her cheek before picking up a golden book sitting nearby. As the angel began to read to her mother words of truth, Nicole knew the answer. "Yes Jesus, I do believe that You love her."

Jesus asked Nicole another very strange question. *"Do you remember Isaac in the Bible? What is it that he accomplished in his life?"* Nicole responded that she couldn't think of anything other than that he was the father of Jacob and Esau. Jesus smiled and said, *"Nicole, his job was to be the carrier of the one who would become the father of Israel, Jacob. He may not have seemed to accomplish much in your eyes, but he was faithful to me and he passed on the godly seed to his son. Your mother carried you and passed down the godly seed in your family line to you. She is not perfect, but she has accomplished her job and I will redeem the things that are out of place in My Kingdom."*

Then He asked a third question. *"Will you entrust your mother to Me and not worry about whether she stays or goes?"* She knew what He was asking of her. She had been thinking that no one would believe the things she had been through, and that if her mother would acknowledge the truth, she, Nicole would be vindicated. Jesus was gently reminding her that neither justification nor gaining understanding from others was important. Could she accept that?

Once again the cross seemed to call out to Nicole, and once again she knelt down beside it and answered Jesus' question as honestly as she was able to in that moment. "Jesus, I trust You and will choose to leave my mother in Your care. I choose to surrender my will and my past to Your care as well, and if my mother is never able to make any of it better, I will accept that. Please forgive me for all the anger, bitterness and unforgiveness I've been holding onto. I do choose to forgive my mother. I understand now that she is sick and wounded, maybe more so than I was. I am thankful that You are caring for her, and I do want what's best for her. You are the only One who will know if and when she can handle the truth and deal with her own past. I choose to believe that You will redeem all the bad things in my life and that You will guide and direct my future."

Then Jesus knelt down beside her and asked, *"Little Nicki, do you trust Me?"* Little Nicki knew exactly what He meant. She took a deep breath and looked into the loving eyes of her Father and said, *"Yes I do. I choose to forgive Mother too. From now on I will trust You to protect me."*

Jesus then reached into Little Nicki's head and said, *"For the word of God is living and powerful, and sharper than any two-edged sword, piercing even to the division of soul and spirit, and of joints and marrow, and is a discerner of the thoughts and intents of the heart"* (Hebrews 4:12).

As Jesus spoke that last word, she was suddenly transported to a room that was full of boxes stacked floor to ceiling on shelves. Just when Nicole thought that things would get better, they got worse. At least it felt worse! On the floor was a box with a girl standing inside of it. As Nicole looked at her, the girl stepped out of the box and began to grow in size until she was as big as Nicole. She was dressed all in black and wore a black leather jacket. She looked about seventeen years old and on one hand she wore brass knuckles, in the other hand she carried a switchblade. Through eyes that were hardened with anger and hatred, she looked around and asked, "What is this place? A new kind of prison?"

BAD

Oh, this was bad. Nicole looked over helplessly at Jesus who was just standing there grinning like a proud Papa who couldn't wait to introduce his most precious daughter to the world! *No help there!* She turned away from the newcomer and whispered to Jesus, "What am I supposed to do now? She looks like she wants to eat me!"

"*Nicole,*" Jesus answered, "*I have brought this girl out at this time because she is the part of you that has born and carried your hurt and anger against your mother. All the anger, bitterness and rage you have experienced have been her feelings. You did right to confess these feelings and to forgive your mother, but the forgiveness can not be complete until every part of you has chosen to forgive and has been forgiven. You must choose to accept her as a part of you or not. If you choose to accept her, healing and freedom will come to you. But again I warn you that if you choose not to accept her and help her, you…*"

Nicole broke into His words and finished them for Him. "I know, I know… If I choose to reject her, I will be rejecting myself and the plans You have for me, as well as opening a door for Satan to gain an advantage over me. But it looks to me like he's already got one!" With a very big sigh and with an even bigger knot in her stomach, Nicole turned and faced the girl with the wicked smile.

"Hi, I'm Nicole…what's your name?"

"I know who you are. I hate you! I hate your life, I hate your husband, and I hate your God!"

"Ok then!" Nicole turned and began walking towards the door into the tabernacle. She needed to be in the Presence of the Lord more than ever before. She sarcastically remarked, "Well Lord, that went well, don't You think?"

Jesus answered, "*Nicole, you must stay in control. This one is strong, but all is not what it seems. You will begin to experience her feelings, and you must remember that no matter how you feel, you must not let her control you or she will take you to some very dark places. You must stay in control. I will help you and there will be times when you must call Lynn. I have placed her here at this time to help guide you when you aren't sure what to do."*

Nicole turned back to the girl and said, "Look. It doesn't matter what you think or how you feel about any of this. The fact is, you are stuck with me for now, and I'm the one in control here. So you will come with me. Now." Then she turned back towards the door and entered into the Lord's Presence. She breathed a sigh of relief when she saw that the girl was following her, even though reluctantly.

Her name was Bad. Her boyfriend was a large reptilian-looking demon that wore black leathers and rode a Harley. Nicole saw him in the alley sitting on his bike waiting for her to join him one day when she looked out the window. She told him to leave in Jesus' name, and he did. That made Bad mad, but then everything seemed to make her mad. At first, Nicole could sense more than feel Bad's feelings, which was a good thing because life with Bad was very difficult. She cussed and smoked and loved sex. But not with Jake. She hated Jake and did not want him to touch her which made life very difficult for Jake and Nicole.

Nicole learned that as a teenager, Bad had gotten her body into trouble a few times, and so Jesus had locked her up inside the box, a prison of sorts, in Nicole's mind and had set an angel protector/guard over her so that she was unable to come out and take over Nicole's body. Now that she was let out of her prison box, she was intent on wreaking havoc in Nicole's life. She was so full of rage that she was bent on pushing life to the point of death. Nicole had to be careful when she was driving because Bad would want her to drive fast and furious. When Nicole left the house Bad would hound her to go buy cigarettes. At first it seemed crazy, but every day that passed, Bad's feelings and attitudes were wearing Nicole down. The thing that finally pushed her to say "enough" was when she, herself, couldn't stand for Jake to touch her. That did it.

Nicole grabbed Bad by the arm and pulled her into the tabernacle. Then she yelled out, "JESUS!" as loud as she could. Jesus came into the room and greeted the girls. When Nicole explained that she couldn't take it anymore, Jesus asked Bad if she would join Him in His garden for a walk.

Reluctantly Bad followed Him out a side door. Dawn was just breaking and the sky was brilliant in color as the world prepared for the coming day. The garden was full of ancient olive trees and others she didn't recognize. The sun was shining, and it was like morning on a warm spring day. The dew was just beginning to go into hiding until evening, and the air smelled fresh and fragrant. They walked silently along a wooded path just wide enough for the two of them. The beauty and serenity of the garden had a calming effect on Bad and she actually began to feel a measure of peace.

As they rounded a bend they came upon four black puppies playing in the path while their mother lay nearby taking a nap. Bad forgot that she was bad and knelt down to greet the puppies who were jumping up on her, all wanting her attention at once. As she reached out to touch the puppies, she realized that her hands were full, and she had to make a choice. Put down the weapons so she could pick up a puppy, or hold onto her weapons and reject the puppies.

Knowing full well Bad's dilemma and recognizing the crack in her hardened shell, Jesus asked if she would like Him to hold the weapons for her while she played with the puppies. He reassured her that if she wanted them back that He would give them to her. The temptation to play with the puppies won, and Bad removed the brass knuckles and handed them and the switchblade over to Jesus. She reached down and picked up the shyest of the puppies, and as she held it close, it nuzzled its head against her neck and lay very still. She stood still soaking in the puppies love and acceptance.

When Jesus said that it was time for them to head back, Bad felt real disappointment. Jesus asked her if she would like to keep the puppy, and Bad's face lit up, and then turned dark and she answered. "I can't take care of a puppy because I have to hold onto my weapons."

Jesus said, "*Hum, that is a dilemma. I understand that you need protection. What if I could give you weapons and a suit of armor that would allow your hands to be free to hold the puppy, but would offer you full protection; better protection than the weapons you have now? Would you be interested?*"

Now Jesus really had Bad's attention, but she was skeptical. "I don't know. I'd have to see them. And what's the catch? I mean, nothin's free."

They reached the door leading back into the tabernacle, and Bad stopped, put the puppy down and reached out to retrieve her weapons. Jesus gave them back to her, opened the door and all three, Bad, Jesus and the puppy, entered. The puppy followed Bad right at her heels and made her smile.

Nicole had been waiting near the altar, praying, and was surprised to see a smile on Bad's face. She had never seen her smile a content or happy smile before, and she was greatly relieved! One visit with Jesus was already changing her. Nicole could barely refrain from shouting, Hallelujah! But thought she better be careful not to spoil anything, so she determined to just sit and wait.

Jesus led Bad over to the altar near Nicole and then disappeared. A moment later He returned with a suit of armor. He explained to Nicole that Bad might be willing to exchange her weapons for His, and so He was going to let her try on the armor.

Once again Bad laid down the weapons in her hands, then ran her fingers against the coat of armor that Jesus had brought in. Just the touch of it against the skin on her hands was like nothing she had ever experienced before. It radiated strength and power, life and love, and Bad knew in that moment that she wanted this kind of protection; that she needed it.

After a moment, Jesus spoke and said, "*Bad, I would like you to have this armor more than anything else in the whole world. But there is something about it that you must know. The strength and power that you feel in this armor is My strength and power because it is an extension of Me. I Am the helmet of salvation. I Am the breastplate, and it is righteousness. I Am the belt of truth. I Am the protection for your feet which is Peace. I Am the protector for those who choose Me. I Am the shield and defender of the weak, and My Word is the Sword that destroys the enemy. I have chosen you and love you with a love beyond your greatest comprehension, but you can not have the armor unless you choose Me.*"

Bad removed her hand from the armor and stood quietly thinking, then she asked, "What does this mean, to choose You?"

Jesus smiled and replied, "*I am so glad you asked that! It means that you would have to give Me all the things you have been relying on for protection, and that they would be destroyed because they are really weapons of false protection. It would mean that you would allow Me to wash you in My blood and to cleanse you from your sins and the sins that others have done against you. I would make you new. It means that your identity and name could not remain as Bad because you would be choosing to enter into My Kingdom which is Love, and nothing bad is allowed. You would need a new name. And you would have to choose to forgive so that you can be forgiven. It means that you would learn the plans that I have for you. They are plans for good and not for evil, to give you a future and a hope. You are a warrior, and my Kingdom is made up of many mighty warriors such as yourself. I would not only provide you with armor and weapons for protection, but I would teach you to use each weapon with precision and to overcome the evil one; and I would assign warrior angels to accompany you.*"

Bad's eyes grew wider with each word Jesus said. She did want to be a warrior. And when she looked back on her life, it all seemed very empty. Jesus had said that her weapons were false protection. Could she believe that? She had relied on them her whole life. She knew that she wanted to belong to this new Kingdom, the one of Love. But the pain of the past suddenly overcame her and was so powerfully severe that she leaned over and wretched what seemed like black bile, right there on the altar! She was horrified!

Jesus beckoned for Nicole to draw close to Bad. She was overwhelmed with compassion for the girl, and as she knelt down beside her and wrapped her in her arms, that thing Jesus had done before with Little Nicki, happened again. The dividing walls of separation between Nicole and Bad came tumbling down, and Nicole was Bad, and Bad was Nicole. She could now feel everything that Bad was feeling, and it was terrifying!

Jesus quickly led Nicole/Bad into a prayer of repentance from sin and renunciation of former gods, idols of her heart, things she had trusted in, relied on apart from Christ. He led her to ask Him to break all ungodly soul ties with those she had bound herself through sex and ungodly relationships.

Then Bad made a declaration of faith in Jesus Christ. "Lord Jesus, I ask You to be my Lord and Savior. I don't understand everything right now, but I will be faithful to You. I do believe that You love me and that You are Truth and Good and Peace, and I will serve You as Your warrior woman. Please be my defense, my shield and my sword, and I will depend on you." And then she began to lay down every weapon of defense that she had clung to so tightly. It was a longer process than Nicole originally thought. Not only did she need to lay down the weapons in her hands, but then she opened her coat and began pulling out guns and bombs and things Nicole didn't even know existed!

When she was done, Jesus stooped down and picked up every weapon and placed them in a very large, black bundle that carried her burdens and her weapons, and laid them on the altar. He then poured red liquid, His blood over the bundle, lifted His eyes toward heaven and called out for the fire of the Holy Spirit. Bad's eyes grew wide again and she jumped back as fire did indeed strike the altar in such power that the black bundle was incinerated within seconds. Gone. That was the thought that began growing in Bad's mind, and the doubts about what she had just done began to awaken fear and panic.

Jesus quickly touched Bad's shoulder and turned her toward Him. When she looked up into His eyes, her vulnerability touched His heart of compassion so deeply that tears began to fall down His cheeks. He pulled her into His loving arms and said, "*Don't worry My warrior woman, they are gone but I am going to give you better ones! Much better! And you will never need to be vulnerable again as long as you stay close to Me.*"

GOOD

Then Jesus looked up, smiled and exclaimed, "*Oh praise God! It is time. Follow Me!*"

He led her to the other side of the room past the door Nicole had first entered so long ago, to a place where there was a large curtain that she had not noticed before. As she stood there contemplating this new surprise in the tabernacle, she didn't notice that Jesus had disappeared. She was captivated by the beauty of the curtain, then realized that its beauty was enhanced by a glowing light coming from behind it. As it beckoned her, she gently pulled the curtain aside, and Bad was immediately struck with a sense of awe, for there before her was a large golden throne, and sitting on it was the King.

King Jesus rose from His throne and called forth the one named Bad. She reverently stepped forward and knelt at Jesus' feet with her head bowed. In a loud and mighty voice, Jesus drew His Sword, raised it high into the air and proclaimed, "*This is my beloved daughter in whom I am well pleased! I have chosen her and she has chosen Me! Let it be known in all the earth and in the heavenlies that the one previously known as "Bad" has died, and I have raised her in the newness of My life through the power of My blood, the blood of the Lamb.*" Jesus then brought the Sword down and rested it on the top of Nicole's head. "*I, Jesus Christ, the Nazarene, the Son of God, do hereby decree that you will now be known from this day forward as Good, My beloved one.*" As He said this, He gently touched the Sword to each of her shoulders like Nicole had seen kings do in movies in a knighting ceremony.

Then Jesus lifted Good up from her knees and began placing His armor, His life upon her. Good was surprisingly very pleased with her new name, and even more surprised and pleased with the armor. It fit so perfectly and was so light and easy to wear that she was afraid it might not offer much protection. Jesus just laughed in delight, grabbed her hands in His and began dancing around and around in celebration. Good's fears lifted in the exhilaration of the moment, and Nicole felt more peace than she had in many days...that is since Good's entrance.

That night when Jake came home from work, he was relieved when his wife hurried over to him with a smile, a big hug and a lingering kiss. And because Nicole had been learning that the things that happen in the spiritual realm are reflected in the physical (and vise-versa), she should not have been surprised to see that Jake had brought her a gift...an adorable not-so-little puppy. He wasn't black like the puppy in the garden, but he was a guardian. Jake explained that the fawn colored Anatolian Shepherds were bred to be protectors and to watch over their families. He also said that this little puppy would grow to be about 150 pounds, give or take. Good was delighted! A puppy and a protector! A big one! She named him Jo. It was instant love between the two, and Jo quickly became Nicole's shadow. He loved people, but even as a puppy, he took his roll as guardian very seriously. His first display of protection happened as their cat Shall-Be walked into the room. When Jo saw this strange animal, he growled and then went and stood between it and Nicole. Even though they laughed and tried to explain that the cat was not a threat and that he belonged there, this action endeared him to both Jake and Nicole.

THE LIAR

"Today is the day of destruction and you are going to get up, kill your kids and destroy everything in the house when Jake goes to work!" the voice boomed throughout Nicole's mind as she woke up.

"Who are you?" she asked.

"I am a part of you like Bad was, and I am going to take you over and destroy everything!" it said.

Jake was already up and in the shower. She sat up bed and it felt as if the room was swirling with invisible beings all around her, but the voice continued to taunt her. *"You are going to destroy! Kill and destroy! Destroy!"* She could see herself getting the kitchen knives and....Oh this was soooo bad! She was disturbed to the point of panic, and did the only thing she could think to do. She picked up the phone and called Lynn.

When Lynn picked up, Nicole frantically blurted out, "I don't want to do it! I don't want to kill my kids! Help me! Help me please!"

"Nicole!" Lynn shouted. "Calm down and tell me what you are talking about."

She explained, "I heard a voice say that I am going to kill my kids and destroy the house! What am I going to do? I'm really scared! Help me!"

Lynn calmly asked, "Whose voice said that to you?"

"It said that it was a part of me."

"That's a lie. Nicole, do you want to kill and destroy?"

"Of course not!"

"What does John 10:10 say?"

Nicole got her Bible and read, *"The thief does not come except to steal, and to kill, and to destroy. I have come that they may have life, and that they may have it more abundantly."*

"Who is the thief?" Lynn asked.

"Satan," Nicole replied.

"And what does he do?"

As the light of truth dawned upon Nicole's mind and heart, she said, "Steal, kill and destroy."

"So whose voice did you just hear?"

"Satan's. So I don't have to listen to him, do I?"

"No you don't. But you do have to tell him to get out of your mind and your house in Jesus' name."

"OK! In Jesus' Name, Satan, you are not a part of me and I will not listen to you or obey you. Get out of my mind and my house right now!" Nicole commanded.

Instantly there was a shift in the atmosphere of the house. The fear was gone. The voice was gone. The swirling was gone. And there was peace in Nicole's spirit and mind. "Wow! Truth is powerful!" Nicole said as she sank to her knees. She had just realized how close she had come to accepting the lies of the Liar. "Jesus, if I had believed those lies, I most likely would have acted on them. Thank you Jesus for the power of the Truth which set me free and for Lynn who spoke the Truth to me!"

"Did you know that you just spoke a Biblical principle?" Lynn asked.

"No. What principle?"

"Go look it up....John 8:31-32. But Nicole? Don't accept every voice you hear as part of yourself. And don't believe everything you hear. Test it against God's Word. While you're at it, that's another principle you should look up...1 John 4:1."

"Thank you sis," Nicole said. "And I mean it! Thank you for being there for me and for speaking the Truth."

"Don't worry about it. Somebody did it for me, I'm doing it for you, and you'll do it for somebody else someday. That's the way this works because that's another principle...But never mind. I think you have enough to chew on for one day," Lynn laughed.

Nicole laughed too. "Ok Teacher! Thank you for not overwhelming me with homework!" It felt good to laugh!

THE DEMON

Nicole began to think about the room with the boxes where she had found Bad. She was a little disturbed…ok, a lot disturbed by the thought of how many boxes she had seen. She was wondering if there were any more little girls locked inside that room; and she questioned that if one of those had held a piece of her past, did they all hide other pieces of her past? She decided to check it out in hopes that she was wrong. Inside her mind she went right to the room and opened the door. It was still full of boxes, but before she could pull any off the shelves and peek into them, she noticed one on a middle shelf at eye level. It was a clear box and inside was a horrifyingly nasty looking demon that was glaring and growling angrily at her. Nicole screamed out, "You don't belong here!" and would have fainted with fear, but Jesus immediately showed up and pulled her out of the room and shut the door.

Nicole sat down and began sobbing. "Jesus, I'm so afraid of demons! Is there a demon in me? How can that be? I belong to You!"

Jesus came near to Nicole and sat down beside her. Taking her hand in His, He lovingly but firmly said, *"Nicole, you went to a place that I did not take you to. You went on your own, apart from me, and there is danger in that. Always before, I have led you where I wanted you to go, and then you were safe. Stay with me, close, and I will lead you and protect you."*

Nicole was so ready to comply. "Ok Jesus! You can bet that from now on I am only a follower. But Lord, I am very tired of all the memories, the pain. I want all this to be over. I keep remembering all the boxes in the room in my mind, and there were so many of them. I refuse to become discouraged, so I will try not to think of how many there were. But Lord, please show me the room again when all the boxes are gone so I'll know that it's over."

Jesus didn't say anything; He just leaned over and kissed the top of Nicole's head.

Over the course of time, IS had become increasingly uneasy as he watched Nicole's heart growing softer and softer toward the Man of Galilee. He had tried several plans to see what could be done to thwart this growing attraction (he refused to use the L word...Love). IS knew that the holds he had on her were only in place because they had been forced on her. If she chose him, the soul ties that would be formed would strengthen those in existence and would set up new ties that were even stronger. If she wouldn't choose him in her waking moments, perhaps she would in her dreams...

He called forth Mare, the terror spirit of dreams. "I am assigning you a very important case. I command you to pour out a full blown attack upon Nicole in her sleep. Don't bungle this up or there'll be hell to pay!"

"Yes my lord," answered the confident spirit.

WILL HE

It hadn't been more than a few days after Good's transformation that Will He appeared. Nicole woke up one morning and there he was, a boy of about 11 years of age or so, sitting on a little stool, wearing a baseball cap turned sideways on his head, chewing a big wad of gum, and punching the baseball glove on his left hand with his right...like he was ready for the game of his life. When he saw that Nicole was awake, he smiled real big and said, "Oh hey, kid! How are ya?"

Nicole, being a bit disturbed, sat up in bed and asked, "Who are you?"

"I'm Will He, formerly Willie. They named me Willie, but I changed my name to Will He because they wanted me to kill you. I didn't really want to do that, and the more I watched you, the more I wondered if I really should. So I changed my name to Will He, as in Will He kill her?" And then he just smiled again while smacking his gum and punching his glove.

Nicole, barely awake, just yelled out "Jesus!" and ran into the tabernacle in her mind, her safe place.

107

He was sitting near the fire with a Bible in His hands. "Jesus, a boy named Will He is after me! He wants to kill me!"

Jesus put His Bible down and lazily looked up at her. *"Nicole, it's ok, honey. Just calm down. Come here and sit beside Me for a bit."* He beckoned her to Him and she sat down on the floor beside His feet.

After sitting quietly for some minutes, Nicole's heart rate returned to normal, but the implications that she might be part boy were almost more upsetting than Good's rage had been. It was beginning to make sense to her though. Just the day before when Jake reached over to kiss her, she had experienced the oddest sensation of wanting to punch him in the nose, along with thinking a few choice words that certainly did not feel like something she would say or even think. They had been more like what a boy would think and do. With this realization, her heart began to pound again, and she began to cry. "Jesus, I just can't be a boy. I am a wife and a mother! Please help me Jesus. Please help me!"

Jesus put His hand on her head and said, *"Bring him here to me, Nicole."*

Inside Nicole's mind she went back to where he was still sitting on the stool waiting for her and told him to follow her. She brought him into the tabernacle, and when Will He saw Jesus, he immediately swallowed his gum, removed his cap and threw his glove on the floor behind him, then stood at attention like a soldier would in the presence of the General Himself. In acknowledgement, Jesus nodded and said, *"Will He."* Still standing at attention Will He saluted and said, "Sir!"

Jesus stood up and began pacing back in forth in front of Will He and Nicole. Then instead of talking to Nicole, Jesus spoke directly to Will He as He continued to pace. *"Son, you've done a good job. I'm proud of you for using your head and thinking for yourself, because had you obeyed the orders assigned to you by My enemy, you would have killed our Nicole here, and that would have been the wrong thing to do."*

Will He stood a little taller and loudly said, "Glad I could help, Sir!"

Jesus continued. *"There is one thing that concerns me though, Will He. And that is that you did disobey orders."* Jesus stopped pacing and looked directly at him. *"I would like to enlist you in my army, but you see, son, the soldiers in My army must always obey My orders. I believe you would make an exceptional soldier, but I need to know that I can count on you to obey Me on My command. Can you give Me your word that if I enlist you into My service that you will obey Me?"*

Will He responded, "Permission to speak, Sir." To which Jesus nodded in affirmation. "Sir, I know that I failed my assignment, but as I watched Nicole and listened, I became more aware that the assignment I was given was evil. There were several times when I had opportunity to carry out my orders, and in preparation for them, I became aware of some very huge warriors that were on the opposite side, Your side, and I sure didn't want to cross them! In fact I began to hate my orders, and that's when I changed my name. I want to do good, not evil, and so when I saw that Bad got a new name and armor and was going to be in Your army, I thought that maybe You could use me too. I really want to be a soldier. I want to be on the same side as those great big warriors who work for You, Sir!"

Jesus smiled. *"Well said, Will He, My boy. All right then, kneel here before Me, son."* As Will He proudly knelt at Jesus' feet, Jesus continued. *"In the authority and power of the Holy Spirit, I forgive the sins of this young man, Will He, and by the power of My blood, I release him from all previous assignments and reverse any curses placed on him by the enemy. I speak to the evil spirits and command all demons and spirits of discipline assigned to him to release him and to return from whence you came. You will in no way ever come back or inflict any part of Nicole or her loved ones. Will He, I cleanse you from all sins and their affect over you, I seal your spirit with My Spirit, and I anoint you as My own son and welcome you into My service."* Jesus drew His sword, and as He had done

109

with Good, He touched one shoulder and said, "*Will He, as a soldier in My service, I now change your name to William, which means Strong-willed Warrior; Protector.*" As Jesus declared this new name, He touched William's other shoulder with the Sword. "*William, you may now stand before Me as a soldier in My army.*"

William slowly stood to his feet, but did not look up into Jesus face, for he was ashamed of the tears in his eyes. Jesus took hold of his chin and lifted his face up, then wiped the tears from his eyes. William again hung his head, and said, "Sir, I know men are not supposed to cry. It's just that I am so relieved to be done with my old job, and so honored that You would give me another chance. Thank You, Sir. Thank you!"

After William blew his nose very loudly with a Kleenex he had retrieved from his pocket, Jesus laughed and asked, "*Who said that men don't cry? Don't you know that I cried a lot when I was a Man living on earth?*"

William's eyes grew large at this announcement, then he proclaimed, "Well Sir, I'm glad that I'm just like You, Sir!" And he stood even more straight and proud in front of his new General than he had previously.

Jesus turned His attention back to Nicole who had been watching this interaction between the two in some amazement. "*Nicole, with your permission, I will relieve this young man from his duty towards you and will enlist him into My army. Is that ok with you?*"

Nicole shook her head, trying to comprehend the fact that she wasn't going to have to be a boy. Then she cried out, "Yes, by all means, please take him!" Then realizing that William's feelings might be hurt at her rejection of him and anticipation of his departure, she went over to him and took his hand in hers. "William, I want to thank you for not killing me. Thank you even for protecting me. I hope you understand that this isn't personal; and it isn't that I don't like you. I do! It's just that I'm a wife and a mom and I can't be a boy. But I'm so glad that Jesus loves you and has a special job for you in His army. You are going to be an awesome soldier and warrior! God speed William!" Nicole reached over and kissed his cheek.

William blushed and said, "Aww shucks, kid. I understand. I wasn't into being a wife and mom either!" They both laughed, then Jesus commanded, "*Atten-tion!*" William jumped to attention so quickly that it took Nicole by surprise. She stepped back as Jesus then shouted, "*Ab-ouut face!*" William proudly stepped into place behind Jesus and waited for the next order. "*Forwarr-d march!*" William began marching looking straight ahead at his new General, then for just an instant, he turned and looked back at Nicole. He winked at her as he said, "See ya kid."

Nicole watched in amazement as a huge warrior stepped into line behind William. She watched until they had marched out of sight through another door. Along with being grateful that this chapter of her life was over so quickly, a silly thought raced through her mind as she got out of bed and prepared to start her day...One thing was for sure. Her life was anything but boring!

WHAT IS MONIQUE?

The walls of division within Nicole's mind seemed to come down slowly and there was still some sense of separation. It was such an odd sensation. Nicole knew that the girls were her and she was them and that their memories and feelings were really hers, but the process of integration was not fast and easy. There was a lot to process and work through. So in the meantime, each girl had their own tastes in food and clothes, and unfortunately, they were almost always complete opposites. Good loved chocolate, but Little Nicki hated chocolate. She loved strawberries, which Good despised. Good hated pink, Little Nicki's favorite color; Little Nicki hated black, Good's one and only color. With practice, Nicole began not to hear their individual voices so much as just to feel the battle going on within her about what to eat or what to wear. She began to think that maybe this is what it was supposed to be like. Maybe everyone had to ask themselves, "What do I feel like today? Do I feel like wearing black or do I feel like wearing pink? Or do I feel like wearing something completely different?" The problem was that she felt all of it all at once, which made decisions practically impossible when she listened to her feelings. She found that compromise helped. Black pants, pink shirt. Strawberries with chocolate. And she found that sometimes she just had to remind everybody that she was in charge and then take control.

On this particular day, Nicole stood in front of her closet contemplating what to wear, and she began to realize that she was sensing a different presence. She was seeing her clothes through completely different eyes. She had grown used to this feeling, and said, "Hello, I'm Nicole. Who are you?" Immediately she saw a very pretty young woman wearing a stylish dress with bangle bracelets on her arm.

In a French accent the woman smiled and replied, "Hello, Nicole, I am Monique. I will help you to put your wardrobe together so that you will be very pretty!"

Nicole liked her. She never felt very pretty and outgoing, and being Monique gave her confidence. The problem was, it was false confidence, and Jesus brought this up several days later when He asked Nicole why she hadn't brought Monique to the tabernacle to meet Him. Nicole hadn't even thought about it because she was feeling so good about this new girl. She didn't seem to have any painful memories or emotions; she was just fun. But Jesus reminded Nicole that He wanted to be a part of everything in her life and that it was very important for them to come to Him together.

She knew He was right, so she and Monique entered the tabernacle together, hand in hand. Jesus did not address Monique. He spoke right to Nicole. *"Nicole, where did Monique come from?"*

Nicole hadn't thought about that before. She turned and asked her, and Monique said, "When you were young, you asked your father what nationality you were. He said that you were a little bit of everything, and not much of anything; but that your last name was French. You had the impression that French people were beautiful and confident, and because you wanted this, I came to help you."

Jesus looked very serious as He said, "*Nicole, she is not a part of you. She is built on lies and can not stay. You have placed false confidence in her that will not stand. I am to be the source of your confidence. Will you give her to Me?*"

Nicole was upset. She was thinking that Jesus was robbing her of happiness that she surely deserved after going through so much pain. She had rebellion in her heart and when she looked up into Jesus eyes, it was like she could see into His heart, and it was breaking. She couldn't stand to hurt Him! And His pain caused her to see her rebellion and to remember where it would lead if she held onto it. After a moment of soul searching, she chose to release Monique to Jesus. He had always placed the girls back inside of her when she had wanted to give them to Him in the past. Maybe He would give Monique back as well.

Nicole took Monique's hand and led her over to Jesus. She knelt down at Jesus' feet and placed Monique's hand in His. Jesus lovingly touched the top of Nicole's head, then picked Monique up. The floor beside Jesus opened up and He threw Monique into the pit. Nicole watched in horror as the source of her confidence burst into flames and fell down, down, down.

She began to cry and ran out of the tabernacle. She couldn't believe that Jesus would be so cruel! For several days she felt sad and mourned over the loss of her friend. On the third day, her real friend Lynn spoke the truth to her and said, "Nicole. STOP IT! Obviously she was not a part of you, and if she wasn't a part of you, what do you think she was? Why would Jesus destroy her?" This made Nicole begin to evaluate Monique from a new perspective and she saw the truth that she hadn't wanted to see before.

Nicole dashed into the tabernacle and threw herself into Jesus' arms. "Oh Jesus, please forgive me! Please forgive me for wanting and loving something that was not a part of Your Kingdom! I don't know what Monique was, but I can see now how I was relying on her instead of You, and I hate to think of the dangerous place she would have led me to with out Your intervention. I might not have even been aware of it until it was too late!" Nicole shivered at the thought, then continued. "I do need confidence though Jesus, so please help me to be and do whatever You want me to be and do, and I will trust in You to help me!"

Jesus just held onto Nicole and the two cried tears of relief together for some minutes. Then Jesus said, *"Well Nicole, the reason why I was able to save you was because you surrendered her to Me. Surrender is one of the most important keys in My Kingdom and I hope you will never forget this lesson."*

IS was enraged. He had lost several spirits of death assigned to Nicole through Willie, and now he had just lost another of his powerful pawns! It had been so perfect too because Nicole had unknowingly accepted and loved this demon. He called for Mare. "I want a full report on Nicole. You have had ample time to fulfill your function in her life and I am not seeing any results."

Mare bowed low before this master and said, "You know my lord that nothing pleases me more than operating fully within my function and fulfilling your will. Knowing the importance of this case, I have assigned my best minions and have personally been overseeing it myself. We have relentlessly hounded Nicole in her sleep with many of my best nightmares and night terrors upon her. We have called upon your own Succubus spirits as a means of offering comfort in response to the terror in the dreams. Her response is rejection of us as she immediately calls out to You-know-who, and she is even doing this in her sleep now."

IS rolled his eyes at Mare's lack of using even a choice name for their enemy.

Mare continued. "As you know, my lord, we have also worked with your own Incubus spirits, imparting sexual content

114

and desire into her dreams based on what we know of her preferences; then have offered sexual stimulation. It pains me to report that nothing from that angle has worked either.

"Even though these things are downloaded into her mind, there are several problems. I feel that it is important to tell you that it is not our fault that Nicole has not taken the bait. One of the biggest problems is that there is always a huge warrior standing between Nicole and us. You know that because she belongs to You-know-who, we can not go to her, she must come to us."

"Well why don't you talk her into walking past the offensive hindrance, you stupid spirit?" IS demanded. "It can not stop her from following her own will."

"We have tried everything we can think of, my lord," Mare responded, then continued. "Another problem is that Nicole has come to recognize our tactics and actually renounces the dreams and spirits attached to them when she wakes up, so that our sphere of influence even in her vulnerable sleeping state is being weakened."

Mare took a deep breathe and in a very quiet, ashamed tone he said, "And then there's the issue of her smelling us." He flinched ahead of time, already knowing and fearing the wrath of his master.

IS snorted. "You nincompoop! You are supposed to be cloaked!"

Mare bowed lower to the ground and said, "We have been, my lord. It seems as though Cantor has been given permission to remove the veil, and you know how strong our stench can be. We haven't been able to get near her lately because as soon as we do, her fear of fire and sensitivity to the smell of smoke wakes her up immediately and we have to pull back."

It was IS who took a deep breath this time. He was seething in anger and frustration as his plans seemed to be thwarted time and again. Well, there was still the stronghold of pain…

THE PROBLEM OF PAIN

Nicole had been in pain of one kind or another for so long that unbeknownst to her, it had become wrapped up in a familiar spirit. The stress of a life time of trauma had taken a toll on her body, and even though she was experiencing tremendous mental, emotional and spiritual healing and freedom, physically she was beginning to suffer various inflictions and diseases. It seemed like she could do nothing but sleep and was barely able to get out of bed. When she did, she was so sick that she felt useless. One doctor told her that there was nothing he could do for her and that she was just going to have to live with it. Since she was unwilling to accept that diagnosis, she went to another who gave her medicine that made her feel better, but that had other serious side effects which she was also unwilling to accept.

One morning in the middle of this seemingly hopeless dilemma, she asked God what she was supposed to do. Jesus answered quickly with a question, *"What have I told you to do, Nicole?"*

Immediately she knew the answer. Several years before, Jesus had told her that He wanted her to do three things, and she suddenly realized that she had not been able to do them. "I'm so sorry that I haven't been able to do those things for You, Jesus, but I just can't with this sickness. I've asked You to heal me, but You haven't done that yet. I believe and know You can, so I'm waiting."

Jesus asked, *"Nicole, would I tell you to do something that was impossible for you to do?"*

She thought about it a moment. The impact of the truth hit her like a ton of bricks. "That's it isn't it? Of course You wouldn't! So if You are not behind this illness, then I know who is!"

Jesus smiled and said, *"It's about time little one! I have not healed you because I want you to learn to use and apply My authority and power to physical problems as well as spiritual and emotional. Many physical problems are actually attacks of the enemy set out to destroy My people or to render them useless. Satan is like a roaring lion seeking to devour, but he patiently waits in hiding until the opportune moment to strike in such a way that his victim won't know that it's him. He is a master of disguises and hides behind masks of sickness, disease, infirmities, mental disorders and emotional problems, hoping that you won't recognize him. You need discernment to be able to tell when something is just a part of living in a dying world and when it is a spiritual attack. When I show you that it is an attack, I don't want you to sit back and wait for Me to do what I've gifted you to do. I want you to take action and heal the sick, cleanse the lepers, raise the dead, cast out demons. Freely you have received, freely give (Matthew 10:8). So, Nicole, now that you know this is an attack, what do you need to do?"*

"I need to take authority over the Spirit of Infirmity, don't I?" Nicole saw Jesus smile, so she continued. "In Jesus' name and by the authority and power He has given me, I command you spirit of infirmity to release me and leave me."

Jesus said, "That's good Nicole, but unless I tell you specifically to send the demons somewhere, it is important for you to command them to go directly to me when you tell them to leave because I know what to do with them. You see, if you don't tell them where to go, many will wander around, looking for someone else to attach to, usually someone close to their previous host. It is also ok if you ask Me to send angels to come and gather up any that are rebellious and disobedient and who refuse to leave."

That thought horrified Nicole. To think of demons leaving her and attaching to one of her boys was too awful to contemplate, so she hastily added, "You, Spirit of Infirmity will go to Jesus and wait for His judgment of you. And Jesus, please do send me angels to make sure this spirit obeys!" Nicole didn't feel any different in that moment physically, but spiritually, there was joy. And not five minutes later, the fever that had wracked her body for a whole year was suddenly gone. Praise God!

Nicole tried to be obedient and even though she was better, she was still unable to do the things God had told her to do on a regular basis because of the pain that continued to torment her. One night when she was unable to sleep because of the pain, she lay in bed praying. Jesus called out to her from the tabernacle and she found herself cuddled up in His lap as He rocked her in front of a fire.

After some time, Jesus asked a strange question. *"Nicole would you like to be healed? Do you want the pain you are so familiar with to be gone?"*

She understood what He was asking her and she began to evaluate. If there was no pain, it would mean that she would be able to do things that had been impossible before. And that was a good thing, wasn't it? The pain had been something that had hindered her from doing much of anything. Without pain, she would have greater responsibilities. She suddenly found that she was reluctant to let it go. Had she come to rely on the pain as an excuse when she didn't want to do something? Or when she was afraid to do it? She realized that she had been using the pain as a defense mechanism. A sick, false idol that she had depended on for life but in truth, was ushering in Death. She looked up into Jesus' eyes and saw His love for her. His love was so great and powerful! She didn't want to disappoint Him, and in that moment she knew that even though she was afraid of releasing the pain, if she didn't, it would stand in the way of her relationship with Him and His love.

Now with Jesus beside her giving her courage, she turned to Him and committed her life, every part of it to Him...all the good, and all the bad; all the sin, her sin and the sins of others done against her, all the blame, all the guilt and shame, all the pain. She was ready to release it. She deliberately knelt down at the foot of the cross and poured her heart out to her Lord.

Suddenly she became overwhelmed with pain. Emotional pain that Good had still been carrying and was now giving over to her; physical pain that was rooted in past events; pain of a broken heart; and tormenting pain that was being inflicted by demons. She had held onto these things long enough. It was time for Good to give her memories and emotions of pain to Nicole.

IS, however, was unwilling to lose more of his major strongholds, and so, as the walls came down and the transfer of pain was in process, he began a physical assault on Nicole with the intent to kill. He was adamant that if he couldn't have her spirit, he would take her body. The spirit of pain began squeezing and twisting Nicole's physical heart, taking the form of a heart attack, while demons of torment began to stir up emotions with such intensity that within the torture of her soul, she cried out for release, even unto death.

Jesus saw what was happening and jumped into action so fast, that IS had no time act any further. He carried her into the healing room and laid her at the foot of the cross, then leaned over Nicole and whispered, *"What do you want little one? The time has come for you to choose, and choose quickly. Do you want to embrace the pain or do you want to be healed?"*

Nicole threw her arms around Jesus' neck and cried out, "Oh please take the pain if You can! I don't want it any more! Please forgive me Jesus for relying on it instead of You!"

Jesus laughed joyously and said, *"I was hoping you'd say that! I do forgive you. Ok, Nicole, now you must renounce the Spirit of Pain. Do it quickly!"*

"In Jesus' name I renounce the Spirit of Pain. I don't want you any more and command you to leave me body, soul and spirit. In Jesus' name I command you to go directly to Jesus and wait for His judgment of you; and I call upon the angels of God to come and make sure that the demons obey."

As soon as the words were out of Nicole's mouth, two large shining angels appeared and reached into Nicole's heart. When they withdrew their hands, they were each holding two small, ugly pixie-like demons who were dripping with blood, kicking and screaming in anger, pain and torment themselves. Jesus whispered, *"When you renounced them, I covered them with my blood. They hate that!"* Nicole watched as the warriors carried the demons away, right out through the roof, and she suddenly realized that the tormenting pain had stopped. She sat up and took a very deep breath, a breath of life.

After she rested a moment, Jesus said, *"Nicole, I am going to show you a special secret of mine that I hope you will share with the world in time."* He pulled a little golden box covered with many beautiful jewels out of His pocket. *"Did you know that I never waste anything? I will never erase the past, but I love to take all the bad things that our enemy tried to use against you to keep you from My love and to destroy you, and I change it into something that we will use against him and that will bring glory to Me and My Kingdom; and it will make you strong. In this little golden box are the ashes of your life, all that remains after burning your black bundle. Now watch and see what I will do with them!"*

He looked deeply into her eyes and smiled as He reached into her heart and began to heal the broken places. Then He took the box and planted it in her heart. *"My love, I give you beauty instead of ashes, joy to replace your mourning, and the garment of praise for the spirit of heaviness. Through the blood of the Lamb and by the word of your testimony, others will experience hope, healing and freedom and will overcome as you have."*

There was a momentary sharp pain in the girl's heart, and then a miraculous, warm, glowing light began to flow through her body and her soul. She was set free from the pain that had once consumed her! Joy began to well up from the deepest part of her spirit and flow through every fiber of her being. She began to sing and dance with joy, and Jesus danced with her. They danced until she fell to the floor exhausted. It was then that she noticed she was wearing a new gown! A beautiful, sparkling white gown, a garment of praise over her armor; and she realized that the girl who had knelt at the foot of the cross only moments before, had been transformed and had danced in victory as a woman.

THE ARMORY

After the joyous celebration in the healing room, the music became quieter and Jesus said, *"Nicole, come with Me. I have something to show you."* He helped her up and led her out of the healing room back into the main room of the tabernacle.

In Nicole's other reality, she was physically, emotionally, mentally and spiritually drained after experiencing the things that had been going on in the healing room. It was really quite amazing how the things that took place in the spiritual affected her physically. She laid down on her bed to rest and was looking into her newly remodeled walk-in closet, admiring the organization of it and enjoying all the things she had placed on the shelves that represented different aspects of her life. She realized that they were all things that she loved! The thought went through her mind that there were no spooky ghosts in this closet! At that very moment Jesus spoke to her and said, *"Nicole, you know that everything that happens in the physical realm is a mirror of what is happening in the spiritual. I know you are very tired, but come with Me again for what I have to show you will renew your strength."* Jesus held out His hand to her, and she found herself once again, back inside the tabernacle.

Jesus removed a large tapestry that was hanging on the wall behind the altar, and under it was another door. He took out a key from His pocket and opened the door. Beckoning for her to follow Him, they entered the room and stood quietly while Nicole's eyes adjusted to the dimly lit room.

Nicole sensed that there was something familiar about this room, but she was unsure what it was. "Jesus, what is this room? Why does it seem as if I've been here before?"

Jesus just smiled, knowing that she would soon become aware.

As she looked around, she realized that it wasn't the things in the room that were so familiar, although she recognized some of them, but it was the shape of the room, the walls of the room, and the shelves. "The shelves! That's it! This is the room in my mind where I saw all the boxes sitting on shelves that I knew held pieces of my past. This is the room where I saw the demon in the box and got scared out of my heebee jeebees, and then You told me not to go places unless You took me there. And look at it now! I asked you to show me this room when all the boxes were gone and I thought it would be empty. But look at all this cool stuff!"

Jesus laughed at Nicole's excitement. *"It is not a coincidence that your closet was finished just in time for me to reveal this new room and its purpose to you. You have learned the principle of 'putting off the old, renewing your mind, and putting on the new' very well, Nicole. As you chose to deal with the things in the boxes one at a time as I showed them to you, you were 'putting them off' so to speak. As you allowed Me to show you the truth and you chose to believe and act on the truth, you were renewing your mind and putting on the new. All of these things in here are those 'new things' that you will need as you go back out into the world, to live, to love, to fight and to rest outside this safe place."*

Nicole's excitement momentarily vanished as Jesus' words registered in her mind. "Jesus, I don't ever want to leave this place! Please don't make me!" Nicole pleaded.

"Hold on there lady!" Jesus answered. *"Don't be worried. This safe place will always be here for you and you will be able to come and go freely. But you are ready to go into the world, to share my hope, healing and freedom with others. This is My plan for you, and what I have been preparing for you since before you were even conceived. Be strong and of good courage; do not be afraid, nor be dismayed, for the LORD your God is with you wherever you go (Joshua 1:9). I created and formed you Nicole. Fear not, for I have redeemed you; I have called you by your name; You are Mine. When you pass through the waters, I will be with you; and through the rivers, they shall not overflow you. When you walk through the fire, you shall not be burned,*

nor shall the flame scorch you. For I am the LORD *your God, The Holy One of Israel, your Savior;... Since you were precious in My sight, You have been honored, and I have loved you;... Fear not, for I am with you;... Everyone who is called by My name, I have created for My glory; I have formed you, yes, I have made you....You are My witness and My servant whom I have chosen, that you may know and believe Me, and understand that I am He. Before Me there was no God formed nor shall there be after Me. I am the* LORD, *and besides Me there is no savior. I have declared and saved, I have proclaimed, and there [is] no foreign god among you; Therefore you are My witness that I am God... And there is no one who can deliver you out of My hand;... Do not live according to the former things in your life... Behold, I will do a new thing...I will even make a road in the wilderness and rivers in the desert...to give drink to My people, My chosen. I have formed you for Myself; And you shall declare My praise"* (Isaiah 43).

Nicole knelt down in humility, in reverence and awe as this Holy One standing before her spoke. The thoughts of this new life that He had shared began to wield a yearning that was stirring in the depths of her spirit and was flowing freely into her soul as she began to envision His plans and desires for her. Doubts and fears were blocked from her as she willingly chose to embrace His words.

Jesus helped Nicole to her feet. Anticipation and excitement began to awaken questions, but before she could speak, Jesus began explaining about the room they were in and its purpose.

"This is your armory, my woman of victory. You see, in this room are keys of My Kingdom, weapons of warfare, and tools for cultivation. It appears dark in here to you right now, but as you learn to use these things according to My Kingdom purposes, your understanding will increase and the light will become brighter."

Jesus took her hand and led her over to a large glass case, under which were keys of all shapes and sizes. *"I give you access to My keys, My authority to unlock My Kingdom blessings and power, and to lock up My enemies as you take them* captive. *Whatever you bind on earth, will be bound in heaven, and whatever you loose on earth, will be loosed in heaven. I even have the keys of hell and of death, and these will not be able to overcome you (Matthew 16:19, Revelation 1:18). I give you authority over these keys, and I desire for you to learn about each one and how to use them appropriately."*

Nicole was reluctant to move away from the keys because she had a special attraction to them, especially old ones, and many of these looked ancient. But He said, *"Don't worry, you'll have plenty of time to study them later. Right now I just want to acquaint you with all the equipment here."*

He then turned and showed her the next part of the armory. *"You had no idea that when you laid down your defense mechanisms and useless weapons that you would be given a complete set of armor."* Jesus pointed out the naked manikin that had held her coat of armor. *"You are already wearing the armor, for you are Good and she is you. Never take this armor off, even when you are sleeping."* And then He picked up a Shield and a Sword and handed them to her while explaining that they are mighty in warfare, effective in protection against the enemy and in slaying the enemy as well. He also showed her many other weapons that would be useful in pulling down the strongholds of the enemy.

"Nicole, I want you to practice all aspects of the armor you are wearing until it becomes like your own skin. And I expect you to practice using every weapon of warfare. Don't be afraid of making mistakes. I will be right there to teach you, correct you, and to instruct you in every way that is pure, holy, righteous and true, so that you may be complete, thoroughly equipped for every good work I want you to do" (2 Timothy 3:16-17).

Then He moved over to another section of the armory. *"These are tools for cultivation. You see, even though you will always be living in My Kingdom, You will be sharing My love with others around you. You will need these tools to help prepare them to hear the truth, and tools to help plant the gospel of My love, and tools to help remove the weeds the enemy will plant hoping to choke out the good seeds."*

Jesus took a step back and looked at Nicole, the girl who had become a woman and was now a warrior. The excitement in her eyes told Him that she was ready to begin training. In that moment, the roof lifted as it had before, but this time, instead of a violent wind, a warm, soft breeze flowed into the room, encircling the warrior and anointing her with the Holy Spirit to go out into the world and accomplish His purposes in and through her.

CHAPTER 9
TRAINING BEGINS

Nicole was sitting in her bedroom in her favorite chair having her regular morning devotions with Jesus when she felt a shift. It wasn't an earth quake because nothing in the room was moving, and yet it felt like her world had just been shaken into place. She didn't understand it completely, but immediately realized that something was different. It was as if something in the spiritual realm had just become a part of her physical realm; like two flat planes that had existed separately with one above the other, had just been readjusted to the same level, connected, and locked together.

"Jesus, what is happening?" she asked as she gripped the arms of her chair. She wasn't exactly afraid, just disconcerted.

"*It's ok Nicole. I'm giving your life a spiritual and physical chiropractic adjustment. It's time for the things you've been experiencing in your mind to become a reality in your life,*" came the answer. "*I exist outside the Tabernacle just as you do.*"

At that moment, a Whirlwind came in from the window on the east wall. It swirled around the room and came to rest in front of her. A voice spoke to her from the Whirlwind and asked, "*Nicole will you give Me your feet?*"

Nicole recognized that she was speaking with the Holy Spirit. Her reaction surprised even herself, for as soon as she heard this question, she knew her fear. She said, "Lord, if I give you my feet, you might make me go to Africa, and I don't want to go there!"

As the Whirlwind continued to swirl in front of her, the Holy Spirit asked, "*You must never assume that you know where I will take you, for if you do, you may run in front of me, out from under the protection of my wings. But the question is this. Will you love Me enough to give Me your feet even if I send you to a place you don't want to go?*"

"Lord, when You put it that way, of course I love You enough to go anywhere You send me," Nicole responded. "So Yes, I do give You my feet, and if You want me to go to Africa, I'll go."

The Whirlwind gently moved closer until it had enveloped her feet and legs. Then the Holy Spirit asked, *"Nicole will you give me your body, your health, your hopes, dreams and the desires of your heart? Will you give me all of the people you hold dear to your heart?"*

Nicole was beginning to understand the purpose of the Whirlwind. It was testing her to see if she would truly be willing to surrender to Him. She thought for a moment about this question and then replied, "Lord, I know that all my hopes, dreams and desires are nothing if they are not Your desires and plans. So yes, I give You everything that I want in life and ask You to exchange them for You plans and purposes." Nicole thought about the next part of the question. Could she release the care of those she loved to Jesus? She was very honest as she told the Lord how she felt. "Jesus, I am afraid that if I give You my husband and my boys that You will take them from me. I don't know what I would do without them!"

The Lord answered from the Whirlwind, *"Nicole, are you really in control of their lives? Can you stop me from taking them if I desire to do so?"*

And Nicole realized that she truly was helpless to control their destiny. She realized that in holding onto them, she was holding back the work of the Holy Spirit in them and was spending energy worrying about things that she could not control. She also realized that she was allowing them to hold a place in her heart that only Jesus was to occupy, the place of fully trusting and relying on Him. She answered, "Lord, Yes, I will also give you my husband and my boys. I realize now that I was believing a lie. Please forgive me for worrying, for trying to take Your place in their lives and for being prideful."

The Whirlwind slowly moved up Nicole's body until it had covered all but her neck. Much to her relief, she was not feeling strangled or confined. *"Nicole, will you give Me your mouth, the instrument of your speech and your nose, the instrument of your breath?"*

Nicole said, "Yes Lord, I give You my mouth and my voice. I want all that I say to be for Your praise and glory. I also give You my nose. I want every breath I breathe to be Your life going in and coming out."

The Whirlwind moved up over her mouth and nose. *"Nicole, will you give me your eyes and ears?"*

"Yes Lord, I give you my eyes. I want to see the things You want me to see. I give You permission to show me things through Your perspective, to give me discernment and to show me the spiritual realm as You desire. I also give You my ears. I want to hear Your voice more than any other," Nicole responded.

The Whirlwind swirled upwards until it covered her eyes and ears. *"Nicole, will you give Me your mind?"*

"Lord, You know my heart and that my mind is already Yours. In fact all that I am belongs to You. But yes, I recommit my mind to you and commit to knowing all I can about You, Your Word and Your holy ways so that I can walk in them close to You."

As the Whirlwind moved up over the top of Nicole's head and hovered there, the Lord spoke softly to her. *"Well done, Nicole, my beloved. There is one other thing that must be done before we can begin your training. You must be baptized. I know that your baptism as a child was not your choice or desire, and while I have honored the commitment made by your parents, it is now time for you to make this commitment to Me as a part of your own free will."*

The Lord's timing was perfect, for had He asked this of Nicole the day before, she would have been more prone to argue. But through the intensity of this encounter with the Holy Spirit and the freshness of her complete surrender to Him, she sat contemplating what He was asking of her instead of running from the thought of it.

There was another who had become aware of the things that were taking place inside Nicole's sitting room as well. The demons that had been assigned to watch her and to alert him to activity such as this had done their duty, and he had arrived in record time.

While she was still completely engulfed in the protection of the Whirlwind, the Lord opened Nicole's eyes so that she could see lord IS as he seemed to float down from the air and land right outside her sitting room window on the west side. She knew that this was more than just a vision when Jo, who had been sleeping beside her chair, woke up and began growling with the hair on his back raised as he stood between Nicole and the window. What she saw was a beautiful man, probably the most beautiful person she had ever seen. His facial features were so beautiful in fact, that Nicole tried to think of another word to describe him because she didn't think that men were supposed to be beautiful; but no other word seemed to fit. He had striking black hair and was dressed in black, but he was wearing a purple cape. She saw that he was speaking to someone or something, but could not see who, or what.

She heard him say, "And why was I summoned at this time?"

To which she heard the panicked reply, "They're talking about baptism!"

At that moment, IS turned his head and looked in the window straight into Nicole's eyes. She suddenly knew that this was a prince in Satan's kingdom, and the very disconcerting revelation that pierced her soul as she looked back into his eyes was that she knew he was familiar to her.

Before Nicole could panic, the voice of the Lord in the Whirlwind that was still swirling around her began to speak bringing comfort and direction to her. *"Nicole, this is an arch enemy of yours. I am protecting you and he can not come near you. You see, he can not even enter the room."*

Nicole heard what the Lord said, but she had not taken her eyes off of the beautiful being. She was repelled and attracted to it at the same time as he continued to hold her gaze.

The Whirlwind jealously shook Nicole to break her gaze, and spoke in a very commanding tone. *"You gave your eyes to Me and I am telling you that you are not to gaze into the things of Satan! He will surely turn your heart and your mind away from Me if you do, and it is My commandment that you shall have no other god before Me!"*

As soon as Nicole's eyes broke away from the beautiful man's, she immediately felt ashamed, and something that went even deeper that that. She felt defiled. She fell to the floor in sorrow and cried out to Jesus. "Lord, I am so sorry! It is true that I gave my eyes to You and it breaks my heart that I so quickly and easily allowed them to be taken off of You. I was attracted to him, and yet I feel so dirty! Oh Jesus, help me!"

Through the Whirlwind, the Lord now spoke to Nicole gently. *"Nicole, My beloved, I know your heart. You are forgiven and cleansed. Keep your eyes only on Me. Stay under the shadow of My wings and I will protect you. You have just been re-introduced to one of the most powerful princes in the kingdom of darkness, and it requires strength to stand against him. It is good that you have seen that your strength lies only in Me. In time you will learn much about this enemy and his army so that you can defeat him in your life personally; and as you overcome him yourself, you will be able to lead your family, your church, your community and beyond into freedom from his reign as well. Just remember that you must never engage in any form of relationship with him at all. As long as you keep your eyes on Me and your ears attentive to My voice, I will lead you into victory."*

Nicole was feeling much better in one sense, but was becoming fearful as the Lord was making it sound like this thing was going to be something she would have to encounter again! "Lord, why don't You just get rid of him for me? You saw how easy it was for me to fall, and You know that is not what I want. I know You are much more powerful than he is, so please just get rid of it for me!"

Jesus said, *"Nicole, remember that you are now a warrior! You have all the weapons, keys and tools that you need to conquer this enemy. At this time, the only way that I will defeat him for you is as you engage in battle with him yourself at My command. You see, he and all of Satan's rulers of darkness were given permission to rule over this earth through Adam's sin. Very soon, at the end of this world, I will overcome them once and for all and take back the authority that was given away, but for now, I rule through My people. I will teach you how to use the weapons effectively; to destroy the strongholds of Satan over My people and the land; and to move the principalities in the air out of the way so that the portal between heaven and earth is cleared of enemy interference."*

Nicole did understand this plan, she was just reluctant to accept it after this encounter. "Lord," she said, "I surrender to You. I want nothing to do with this enemy, but I will trust You."

"Good job, Nicole," Jesus replied. *"You will not need to deal with him again right away because you have a lot to learn before your next meeting with him. He has come at this time because he knows that if you choose to be baptized into My Kingdom, he will loose more strongholds on your life. You see, baptism is like a legally binding document in the spiritual realm. Churches teach that baptism is an important institution for several reasons, but most have not understood this critical aspect of it and thus have failed to teach it in its entirety.*

"As you know, Nicole, you totally belonged to Me the minute you first called out to Me as Lord, confessed your sins and repented of walking in darkness. You were immediately clothed in righteousness by My blood and transferred from Satan's kingdom into Mine. Positionally I saw you seated in the heavenlies with Me in your first minute as a baby Christian. But Satan, being the usurper that he is, continues to claim lordship until he is legally served notice. Baptism is that legal document that Satan cannot refute. The document notifies all of the spiritual realm as well as the physical realm of a change in kingdom loyalty. In the spiritual realm, baptism informs Satan and his demons that you are no longer a part of his kingdom or under his authority, but that you have been transferred into My Kingdom and are now under My authority. This is why I want

131

new Christians baptized immediately when they enter into my Kingdom.

"I know that you are terrified of putting your head under water, Nicole, but it is vitally important that you do this if you are serious about continuing to obey Me. Will you do this for Me Nicole?" Jesus asked.

Nicole understood the importance of this after Jesus explained it, and was ready to call the pastor and ask him to come over right then. Joy and laughter rang out from the depths of the Whirlwind at Nicole's eagerness, and then the Lord said that she would be protected until it could be arranged. While joy continued to embrace her, the Whirlwind began to move away from her. It swirled slowly through the room and exited out the west window where the deceitfully beautiful man had stood a moment before.

As Nicole got up to find the phone and call the pastor, she marveled at the things she had just experienced. She knew it was real, but wondered if anyone else would believe it. She realized that this was a turning point in her life. This experience was something that had been common inside her mind and spirit, but now it was happening outside her mind…The spiritual was meshing with the physical! What a trip!

Nicole was baptized the next Sunday right after church. The angels were singing and the demons were cursing. IS was seething in quiet rage that erupted as Nicole came up out of the water, baptized in the power of the Holy Spirit. The angels were dancing and the demons were running for their lives, for IS was on the warpath, looking for someone upon whom he could inflict his murderous fury.

CHAPTER 10
JIHAD

It was within the church that Nicole's first real battle as a warrior began. Christian women who were stuck in bondage as she had been, began coming to Nicole for help. She hadn't advertised at all. In fact, it had been just the opposite. She had been silent about her journey because she knew that most people wouldn't understand what she had experienced. And yet they had found her.

She was beginning to be deeply disturbed in her spirit by the darkness she saw that was invading her church, and she was powerless to stop it. Spiritual gifts became something that was invalid for this day and age, and bondage, deliverance and emotional healing seemed to become bad words. It was unacceptable to think that Satan could affect Christians who worshipped God; and yet Nicole knew differently.

An unseen but very real dividing wall was being erected and it seemed like those in leadership had begun speaking a different language. The words they used were the same, but she felt that the meaning was completely different. Even the way they interpreted scripture was foreign to Nicole. And it wasn't just their church. Nicole was hearing it preached in sermons on the radio, yet most Christians were unaware of the differences. Christians were just Christians weren't they? And the Bible was God's truth wasn't it?

A struggle began inside Nicole as the enemy relentlessly tried to shut down the ministry she believed God had called her to. The teachers were becoming more vocal and she was beginning to sense opposition even though it hadn't directly come against her yet. She began to question and then to doubt herself. She believed that the church leaders were godly men that she respected and loved. She began to wonder if she was wrong; if the things that she had experienced were all lies. Maybe she had imagined them or maybe she was crazy! Something that felt like a blanket of fog began to settle over her mind and everything seemed confusing. She believed that Satan was real and that he was her enemy, but he was becoming like some illusive thought that caused her to feel like she had done something wrong if she so much as spoke his name. She felt like she was becoming a spiritual zombie and she didn't like it.

There was one person she believed she could talk to that might be able to help her understand the questions she was wresting with. She asked Jake to go with her and they went to visit Andrew.

After Nicole shared her dilemma, Andrew didn't say much, he just got out the Bible and begin to read. "Matthew 4:24, '*Then His fame went throughout all Syria; and they brought to Him all sick people who were afflicted with various diseases and torments, and those who were demon-possessed, epileptics, and paralytics; and He healed them.*' Matthew 8:16: '*When evening had come, they brought to Him many who were demon-possessed. And He cast out the spirits with a word, and healed all who were sick.*' Mark 1:39: '*And He was preaching in their synagogues throughout all Galilee, and casting out demons.*' John 14:12-14: '*Most assuredly, I say to you, he who believes in Me, the works that I do he will do also; and greater works than these he will do, because I go to My Father. And whatever you ask in My name, that I will do, that the Father may be glorified in the Son. If you ask anything in My name, I will do it.*'"

Andrew explained that one-third of Jesus' ministry was preaching, one-third was healing, and one-third was casting out demons. He challenged her to study this out and to decide if she believed that His work was still relevant for today.

The power of God's Word broke through the darkness, and by the time they left Andrew's house, the fog in Nicole's mind was gone. She should have recognized the clouding of her mind as the work of the enemy. She repented and renounced Doubt as she realized that doubting God's work had allowed it in.

The elders had told her that she couldn't trust experience and so Andrew's challenge to study God's Word for herself in this matter was just what she needed to do. She didn't want to continue with something that was not of God, but she also didn't want to blindly follow anyone. Nicole made a commitment to stop discipling and to seek God for a whole year, and then see where she stood.

Nicole cried out to Jesus, "Lord, I know You are real! I believe in You. I've been confused and I know that's not of You. So Jesus, I am laying down everything I believe except for my belief in You. I'm laying down all my experiences, all my memories, everything I think I've learned, the way that I have interpreted Your Word...everything! I don't want anything that is not of You. I am empty and I want You, Jesus, to fill me with the truth. I will be diligent to study Your Word and I will read nothing else for a year. I am desperate for You and the Truth! Help me Jesus!"

And so every day for one year, Nicole spent hours reading and studying the Bible. She could see herself holding out empty hands, asking Jesus to fill them. And He did. He put the very things that she had laid down at His feet back into her hands, into her mind, and into her heart. At the end of that year, Nicole had grown in confidence and boldness. She was equipped and prepared to stand firm in the battle that was to come. God's timing was perfect for at the end of that year, several ladies were asking her for help. Even though Nicole knew that God wanted her to disciple, she also knew that she needed to do it under the spiritual covering of the church, in submission to them, and if they didn't approve, then it would not be right for her to continue.

She approached Don, the elder over the counseling department, and explained again what she believed. In the past he had always had accepted their differences. This time he gave her one of their biblical counseling manuals to study. "Nicole, it's time to bring unity through our doctrine as we counsel. Look through this manual and then I'm sure you'll want to join our team."

As Nicole began to read the manual, anger and rage began to boil in her blood. Soon, she was unable to even see the page in front of her. All she could see was blackness. "Lord, what is this? I am so angry at the people who are quenching Your Spirit and who are condemning people to lifelong bondage." Through the darkness, the Lord made it clear that a time of testing was coming upon her, and He began to burn two things into her heart. *She was to present, but was not to defend. He was her Defender. The second was that she was to say and do everything in love.*

She made an appointment with Don so that she could return the manual. She explained, "I believe that the Holy Spirit speaks through His rhema Word as well as His written Word and I believe that the gifts of the Spirit are valid and necessary for us today. I feel that this material puts God in a box and tells Him what He can and can't do. To me, it quenches the leading of the Holy Spirit and I can't operate in that box. The Holy Spirit is my Guide. I feel as if your material wants to take His place and I will not allow it to dictate my life."

"Well, Nicole, that's a dangerous place to be," Don sighed. "You are opening yourself up to hearing the voice of deceiving spirits. We should only listen to the written Word of God and then we won't be deceived. It's common for most believers to begin their Christian walk with beliefs such as yours, but as they mature, they come to understand the truth of God's Word. It's time for you to put aside your immature belief structure that can lead people astray."

She couldn't believe her ears! "So you're saying that out of the fear of being deceived, I should ex out the Holy Spirit's voice; and that your material is the only means of accurately explaining what the Bible says as interpreted through your doctrine?"

"It is our job as shepherds to keep the flock safe, Nicole. To protect them from false teaching."

"It's your job to know the Shepherd's voice, Don, and to teach other's how to hear Him. It sounds to me like you are leading the people into a shadow of Catholicism where only those who have studied this doctrine are able to accurately interpret God's Word rather than teaching people that the Holy Spirit will guide them into understanding the truth of His Word."

Don could tell that she was not following his lead and he didn't want to lose her. In a consoling tone he said, "I'm sure that if you'll come to the training classes, you'll understand what I'm saying. How about it Nicole? Will you give it a try?"

She was quiet for a moment and then sadly said, "I'm sorry. I can not sit under your teaching. You think that I'm unbiblical in my beliefs if they don't line up with yours, and I'm telling you that they don't and can't. I think that you are quenching the Holy Spirit and I won't align myself with any doctrine that would do that."

Don shook his head. "Then there's only one thing I can think of to do. We'll evaluate your ministry and beliefs and see if we can work this out. I've seen the fruit of your ministry and I'm sure we're saying the same thing, just using different terms."

Nicole didn't believe that would do any good, but she agreed. She soon realized why the Lord had told her to present and not to defend, for the process of examination turned into a six month long test. No matter how clearly she tried to present biblical answers to their questions, they didn't seem to understand; or maybe they did, but just were not satisfied with her answers. If she had taken a defensive stand, she would have been a basket case! At the end of that time, it was clear to Don, the elders and to Nicole and Jake that Nicole's beliefs did not line up with theirs and that she would be turning in her resignation from all leadership positions in the church.

No one felt good about this, and in a last ditch effort, another elder asked, "Nicole, why can't you just submit to us?"

"I am," she replied sadly. "Resigning is the only way that I believe I can submit to you."

As she left that meeting, her heart was broken for the church. She was broken hearted over the relationships that had been changed forever. Broken hearted for the precious women who were bound by the enemy and now had less of a chance at finding the hope of being set free. The only consolation she held was that she had remained faithful and that she had presented without defense, and had spoken truth in love. And in that moment, Nicole knew that there was nothing left for her to do. "Jesus, this is Your church. These are Your people. I leave it completely in Your hands."

That night Nicole had an especially disturbing dream. She dreamed that *she heard beautiful singing and went into a store-front building where it was coming from. People were singing a beautiful song about freedom. She wondered if this was a church and she stood at the back listening. Most, if not all of the people were Caucasian men. The song ended and after a brief silent pause, all who had been singing, loudly shouted out, JIHAD! And then the nature of the room changed and the people became aggressively violent. Several of the men came charging at her and she turned and tried to run out of the room. She didn't know what JIHAD meant other than hearing that word in connection with the Muslims, but she did know that she was in obvious danger and that they would most likely kill her if they caught her. She made it out the door and around the corner. The man who continued to pursue her was white and middle aged. She found herself stuck up against a wall and he was only about a foot away. She was afraid, but not terrified. She prayed, "Jesus, please blind him so that he can't see me." Then she started to walk away. The man looked a bit puzzled and said, "I know you are near. You won't get away." But she just walked past him and all the others who were raving about in a violent frenzy, like they were looking for someone or something to kill.*

In the morning when Nicole shared the dream with Jake, chills went down her spine when he told her that *Jihad* meant *holy war* to the Muslims.

"Lord, what does this mean, if anything?" Nicole asked. The dream had been so graphic, she didn't feel that it was just one of those "pizza dreams." In the name of protection, had this new wave of theology invited Jihad, holy war, to step inside the church? It was not Jihad of the Muslim faith, yet she saw that in the spiritual realm it could be just as deadly and destructive. Down through history, the church had been at war with itself. Christian against Christian. Mark 3:24-25 came to mind. Jesus had said that if a kingdom or a house were divided against itself, it could not stand. Had Satan placed a curse of division against the church? It sure felt like that. And if so, what could she do about it?

Jake and Nicole knew that they could no longer continue in that church. With hurting hearts, yet unwilling to cause division, they left quietly and decided to try a little church closer to the ranch in Samaria.

The first Sunday they attended, they both knew that this was where God wanted them. As Nicole sat listening to the worship songs she realized how spiritually dry she had become. The Spirit gently flowed over her and into her, and tears rose up from somewhere deep inside and spilled down her cheeks like welcome rain after a drought. The Holy Spirit was welcome there, along with the gifts of the Spirit; however Jake and Nicole realized that there was a lot of healing work inside their hearts that God needed to do before they were ready to step into their places of service within that body. Nicole knew that emotional pain could easily open the door for Satan, and she prayed for protection. She chose to forgive the leadership at the previous church and to walk through that process daily as painful thoughts and feelings rose up inside her mind and heart.

As time went by, the pain became less dominating. She was discovering that there were many other people who had the same convictions and basic beliefs about the work the Holy Spirit was doing and wanted to do in His people today, just as He had two thousand years ago. God led her to Peter Horrobin's books, "Healing Through Deliverance," and she went through his online discipleship course, "Ellel 365." It confirmed the things the Lord had done in her and the things He had taught her. It built her faith and confidence in Jesus and caused her to love Him more. In time, God began opening the door of ministry for her in this new place of worship where the Holy Spirit's gifts were welcomed and she was free to speak and do the things He placed on her heart.

One afternoon while Nicole was in town shopping, she ran into some friends from Community Bible, the old church. Feelings of resentment began to rise inside her, but she shoved them down. She had forgiven them, hadn't she?

Nicole could hardly ignore the true state of her heart any longer when several weeks later, she once again found herself in the company of several friends from C.B. They were genuinely glad to see her and invited her to attend a class with them. Not wanting to offend them, she hoped she had sounded nice as she declined. In reality, the thought of stepping into that church again made her feel sick to her stomach and she was surprised at the intense feelings of anger and even hatred for it that had risen inside her.

Over the next several months as Nicole thought about these things, the battle inside her mind was fierce. She felt that she was righteous in her anger as she built up a case against them. They were so wrong in their exclusion of the Holy Spirit which caused multiple consequences for the people in that body and those caught in the ripple effect. And then there was the still small voice warning her that she was on dangerous ground, but she pushed it aside and felt justified in how she had been faithful to God and had done everything right through their examination of her ministry. She didn't recognize that she was embracing a critical spirit and clothing herself with pride that had begun to harden her heart, or that her heart was encasing a root of bitterness that had slipped in unaware through the open door of pride and was buried so deeply inside like a murderous weapon, hoping to be undiscovered.

Yet, so great was God's love for His church and for her, and knowing that time was of the essence in reaching her before the hardness of her heart began to shut Him out, the Lord Jesus came to her in a dream one night as she slept and began revealing the things she had refused to see in her waking moments. The words that were ringing in her ears as she awoke from the dream were, "*Nicole, your heart is full of defilement and bitterness; and it has become hard, encased in pride. This is not My heart for C.B. Do you want to know My heart?*"

Nicole got up, poured a cup of coffee. Did she want to know God's heart for C.B., namely the leaders? What she could answer honestly was that she didn't want defilement, bitterness or pride in her heart. She opened her Bible to begin reading where she had left off. She had just taken her first sip of coffee and just about choked when she read the first line of Psalm 133. "*Behold, how good and how pleasant it is for brethren to dwell together in unity.*"

"Ok, Lord. Thank you for making your point so completely!" Nicole smiled. "But seriously Jesus, You know that I was willing to work with them as a harmony part to their melody, but they were unwilling to work with me. They saw the harmony as a bad note. So how can there be unity between us?"

"*Pursue peace with all people, and holiness, without which no one will see the Lord: looking carefully lest anyone fall short of the grace of God; lest any root of bitterness springing up cause trouble, and by this many become defiled.*" Hebrews 12:14-15 rang through her spirit and she knew that unity had to begin within herself. She had not recognized her pride or how she had become defiled with the root of bitterness until now.

A picture of the Iris in her flower garden came to mind. Someone had given her what looked like a piece of dead root. Several weeks after planting it, it began to grow. Several years later, the plant was so large that it was overtaking her other flowers and so she started to dig some of it out. What she found was that the root had produced many other roots! Of course she knew now that those were bulbs and that was their nature. It was also the nature of bitterness. Hide underground, grow, multiply and take over.

The Father said, *"Nicole, I see your heart as beautiful, a thing to be treasured and cherished; something I value so much that I sent My Son to redeem it, to buy it back from the evil one. I see your heart as perfect because it is covered in and under the blood of Jesus, and it is Mine. I have chosen to make My home in your heart because you have chosen to love Me. And yet, your heart is harboring sin and ungodliness."*

"Yes it is, and I'm so sorry to have defiled Your home, Jesus," Nicole responded.

The Holy Spirit answered, *"There will be things throughout your life that I will continue to bring to your attention, and you will continue to confess, repent and renounce. That's the process of sanctification, of you becoming like Me. But my point is this, Nicole. Just as your heart is not perfect, neither is My church, My body. The body of believers you gather with in Samaria is not perfect, yet it is My church. The body of believers at Community Bible is not perfect, but it is My church. The elders and leaders are My people, just as you are. Their hearts are not perfect, and yet, they love Me. I have made My home in their hearts and they are covered in and under the blood of the Lamb. I am working in them even as I am working in you. They are My responsibility, not yours. Release them to Me. Let Me do My work in My church. And release the pain and anger and bitterness you have harbored toward them to Me. Then just watch what I will do in you."*

Nicole was sure she could hear the joyful laugh of her Redeemer, and she bowed her head in shame as she cried. "Lord God, I am so sorry for allowing bitterness in. I don't want it, and I don't want to carry responsibility that isn't mine. Please forgive me and wash me clean of it! I do release C.B. and the elders to You."

"You are forgiven, My daughter." Knowing that the root was buried deeper than she was aware of, the Holy Spirit asked, *"Nicole, are you willing to humble yourself and confess your part in the direction this church has taken?"*

"My part? What do you mean Lord?"

Her thoughts suddenly turned to a period of time several years past while she had been in attendance at C.B. She had recognized a spirit of Destruction that had begun attacking the church and its people in various ways. No one else saw it, but she did. It was moving through the congregation and took three lives and one marriage, was wreaking havoc in relationships, was causing car accidents and financial crisis. She decided to take control and had begun to come against it and bound it and commanded it to go; and for a time, it seemed that it had. The crisis had stopped. And now she saw that it hadn't gone at all, it had just taken on a different form of attack.

"Jesus, what would You have had me do?" Nicole prayed. And the Holy Spirit answered her.

"Nicole, I gave you the spiritual eyes to see. I set you as a watchman over that church, and it was not your job or your position to deal with the spirit of Destruction. You had power to deal with it, but you didn't have the authority. It was your job to warn the elders of the things I showed you. They held the authority and responsibility."

Nicole was suddenly broken. "Oh Lord, please forgive me! I do remember thinking that I should warn them, but I believed that they wouldn't listen or do anything about it and I took matters into my own hands. I can see how prideful that was and how I stepped outside of my area of responsibility. I'm so sorry!"

The Holy Spirit led her to Ezekiel 33:1-9 and began to teach her what it meant to be a watchman, an intercessor. *"There are times when a watchman is called to be a warrior, but it*

143

must always be done under the authority of the leaders. As a watchman, your first duty is to warn them of the danger. If they give permission, then because of your vantage point, as you see the enemy approaching, you attack. But if you warn the leaders and they don't give you that authority, then you have done your job and are released. The results or consequences are their complete responsibility."

"What do You want me to do about it now, Jesus?" And Nicole knew that the first thing was to deal with her own heart. She bowed her head and she began confessing her part, her pride, her sin.

In her repentance, her heart was broken as the Holy Spirit cracked open the hard casing of pride. He told her, *"Now I want you to put action to your choice and walk in humility and love."*

Nicole wondered what He meant, and suddenly she knew. She needed to call every elder at C.B. and ask for their forgiveness in not reporting the spirit of Destruction to them all those years ago. Wow, that would be hard, but she would do it as soon as possible.

Jake came into the living room yawning. He gave Nicole a quick kiss, then headed for the coffee pot. As he got settled in his chair with his Bible in his lap, he looked over at his wife and saw the tears he hadn't noticed before in his sleepy state. "What's wrong hon?" he asked.

Nicole explained what God was showing her and that she needed to not only ask for the elder's forgiveness, but that she needed to first choose to forgive them so that she could be free from bitterness.

Jake listened thoughtfully then said, "This does brings back a lot of feelings and unanswered questions. I remember talking to different people about specific situations and each person would describe the same thing so differently that it seemed like a completely different circumstance." He sipped his coffee then began putting his thoughts into words. "I guess what it comes down to is that when we disagree with other Christians, we have to distinguish between their actions and their motives. It is possible to do the wrong things for the right reason. But that doesn't mean that what they are doing is not damaging. It's seems that when the focus is on actions, it is easy for things to escalate and become a holy war, and no one is more motivated than a soldier thinking they're serving the Lord."

He paused as he considered his next words. "Human nature quickly takes us from making sacrifices for God to wanting to sacrifice others for God, thinking that we need to defend Him and His Word. We want to destroy the enemy of God, but we mistakenly define that enemy as other believers that have a different theology than us or who are on a different level of understanding than we are. And that's when we become a destructive tool of Satan instead of a true warrior for God." He paused, and then said, "But even when we address those issues, we have to look for the heart. Is their heart for serving God? And it may be; but it just may be a deceived heart."

Nicole sat quietly thinking about the elder's motives. What Jake said made a lot of sense to her. She did believe that their motives were to love and serve God with their whole hearts. She remembered that forgiveness was a process and made a choice to forgive them and to continue to forgive them for their actions every time she felt pain or anger; she would thank God that their motives were for Him; and she would continue to release their hearts to the Holy Spirit so that she wouldn't interfere in His work. Nicole clearly saw that if God had not called her attention to the state of her own heart, she would have risen up in the spirit of Jihad and started a holy war of her own!

"You know," Jake said. "Maybe God's Kingdom is like an elephant."

Nicole laughed. "What's this? A new parable about the Kingdom of God?"

"I don't know about that," he replied. "But I'm thinking of the story about the blind men who touched different parts of an elephant, and each one described it differently because they couldn't see the whole animal.

Maybe each church or denomination is touching or holding onto a different part or function of God's Kingdom."

"I think I see what you mean," Nicole said thoughtfully. "C.B. has a strong emphasis on God's Word, and even though they may have come to interpret it differently than I do, they are teaching Truth and making a difference in many people's lives through the Truth. I do believe that God is bigger than our misunderstanding of His Word, and He will reveal the Truth to those who want to know it." She thought for a moment then added, "And in all honesty, I'm sure that our denomination doesn't have all its doctrine exactly right either. We just don't know what that is or we'd change it."

Jake added, "Exactly. God has placed our hands on the spiritual gifts part of His Kingdom. It would be awesome if we could all work together in one church, but maybe God doesn't see it the way we do. Maybe He's not looking at just the leg or just the trunk. Maybe He's looking at the whole elephant saying, 'Look how well the legs are working as My people go out into the world spreading the gospel. And see how well the trunk is functioning in doing the heavy work in My Kingdom like feeding the hungry. And how well the tail swishes the flies or demons off through spiritual warfare.'"

Nicole was reminded how thankful she was for her husband. She reached across the side table between them and squeezed his hand. "I love you, Jake. You are the most humble, the most wonderful man in the whole world! I am so thankful that God has given you the gift of mediation, of being able to see all sides of issues; the ministry of reconciliation like 2 Corinthians 5:18 talks about. You know, that was Jesus' ministry as well."

Not being comfortable with Nicole's praise, he joked, "Yes I do, and I'm quite proud of it!"

They laughed then sat contemplating all these things for a moment. Nicole said, "I think you've discovered the key I was looking for to help me understand how to '*dwell together in unity*' and to '*pursue peace with all people.*' I don't have to expect us all to share the same doctrine; however, I must make sure that my heart is free of bitterness and full of God's love so that no matter how others view or treat me, my heart, mind and body can respond in His love."

Jake joined her in prayer, and as they prayed, she could see the Holy Spirit reaching into her heart and removing the defiling, bitter root.

"What would you like me plant inside your heart, Nicole?" Jesus asked.

Much Afraid in "Hind's Feet on High Places," the book by Hannah Hurnard, came to mind. "Jesus, I want the seed of Love to be planted in my heart in place of bitterness."

He smiled and said, *"Done!"*

Later that day, Nicole made the phone calls to the elders. She didn't expect them to understand and they didn't. But they all seemed to appreciate her confession. Don was the last person she talked to and he had asked, "What would you have wanted me to do about it anyways, Nicole?" And she had replied, "I don't know, Don. But it would have become your responsibility to get direction from the Lord. I robbed you of that responsibility, and I believe that the consequences have been devastating." He had replied, "I don't know about that, but what I do know is that I'm proud of you for being faithful to your convictions, Nicole."

There was a release in her heart after those calls. It felt like Love.

Nicole had been watching a spot on her cheek for some time. She had been a little concerned that it might be skin cancer and considered going to the Doctor, but she kept asking God how she could pray for others to be healed if she hadn't experienced His healing first hand. She didn't want her prayers to come from just head belief, but heart belief, and so she had done everything she knew to do in the spiritual and physical realms. She had plead the blood of Jesus on it daily, bound the Spirit of Skin Cancer, cursed cancerous cells in Jesus' name, asked for healing, claimed healing, renounced Doubt and Fear when they raised their ugly heads. She was treating it faithfully with aloe vera. And nothing had changed until the following morning after the root of bitterness had been removed from her heart. As she washed her face, she noticed it was not nearly as large!

Immediately she realized that the bitterness in her heart had been a spiritual disease that gave Satan a stronghold or place from which he was able to inflict this physical disease on her. She had often compared bitterness to cancer because their properties seemed to hold the same components. It was just that one was of the spiritual realm and the other was of the physical, and she realized that the Lord had just opened her eyes to another one of the keys of His Kingdom. She now understood that in praying for physical healing, the root may be spiritual and need to be addressed and taken care of before the physical problem could be resolved.

"Thank You Jesus for healing my heart and my body!" Nicole rejoiced.

And every day after, as she prayed for Community Bible with God's heart instead of her old, critical one, the spot continued to shrink until it was gone.

~~~~~~

Miles away in Washington D.C., Sam Adams boxed up the last of the files he had kept hidden since he had begun to suspect foul play, and he was secretly sending them to his new address. Under the guise of retirement, he would be continuing his research in hopes of stopping some very bad people in high places and positions of government from fulfilling their very bad plans.

"Lord, I plead the blood of Jesus over this box and these files. Please blind them from the eyes of the enemy and help them reach their destination unseen and unharmed." He picked up the box, looked one more time around his old work place, then hit the light switch as he walked out the door for the last time.

148

PART 3
WINGS

CHAPTER 11
GOING DEEPER

Eternal life is not some far off destiny.
Rather it begins now, at the moment of salvation in Jesus Christ.
In His own words, Jesus explains it this way:
"And this is eternal life, that they may know You, the only true God, and Jesus Christ whom You have sent."
John 17:3

When Jake and Nicole had moved to their 15 acre ranch on the outskirts of Samaria, it had been a secluded, quiet place away from the constant oppression of the world. It was close enough to the city for Jake to commute to work, and the perfect place for their three boys to enjoy their teenage years. It was also a perfect place for Jesus to continue to use the keys to open Nicole's memories and emotions that she had given to Him, and for her to put into practice using those keys, tools and weapons that He had given to her. The ranch was the perfect place for healing.

One morning several years later, Nicole woke up with two words in her mind and heart. GO DEEPER. "Lord, what are you trying to tell me?" It was earlier than usual, but the words were ringing in her spirit and she wanted to understand. She got up and turned the coffee pot on.

Nicole opened her Bible and was directed to Proverbs 24:10-11. *"If you faint in the day of adversity, your strength is small. Rescue those who are being taken away to death; hold back those who are stumbling to the slaughter,"* (RSV). Her desire had been to help others find hope, healing and freedom, and she had helped some. But as she read these specific words, it was like they had taken on life and they sank deep into her heart.

She could feel Jesus' heart of love and pain for those who were stuck in bondage as she had been. *"Rescue...hold back....*" The words of this verse were becoming a visual picture in her mind's eye and a more intense longing within her heart.

"Jesus, what can I do?" She began examining her life. The boys were grown and had lives of their own now. She was keeping up things at the ranch and discipling several women a week. "Lord, there are so many!" she cried out. "What can I do to reach more of them? I want to help. Show me!"

She didn't hear a voice at first, but her eyes were directed to the first part of the verse. *"If you faint in the day of adversity, your strength is small."* And then she knew that before she could really rescue others in large proportions, she needed to find her strength in her relationship with Jesus and surrender to Him. "Lord, this is how I try to live now. What more can I do to love you?"

"Go Deeper," were the words that again filled her heart and mind. And so Nicole set her spirit, soul and body on discovering daily what that looked like, and with every day that passed, the desire for helping others was growing into a passion. She began to recognize the need for a place of healing and training away from the world, just as the ranch had been for her.

She began to call their home Ramoth Ranch, representing a place of refuge and healing. Ramoth was one of the seven cities of refuge in the Old Testament, and it was located in the province of Gilead that was famous for its special healing balm or ointment. She began to envision little bungalows on the ranch where women could come and experience God's hope, healing and freedom just as she had, equipping them to go back out into the world and be effective women of warfare in God's Kingdom. Nicole had been a little reluctant to share her thoughts with Jake. He had always been supportive of her and what God was doing in her life, but he saw things from a much different perspective than she did. Not a wrong perspective, just different. Nicole had learned that by God's design, Jake helped to balance her life out as he saw things more from the logical perspective and she from the spiritual. She also knew that God listened to her husband, and when he prayed, God always seemed to answer. And she knew that Jake would not ask God for something if he didn't think it was right.

So one evening after dinner when Jake was sitting in his chair reading with Jo curled up at his feet, Nicole believed it was the perfect time to share this growing vision. It was all she seemed to be able to think about, and she couldn't wait any longer to enlist his support. She believed with all her heart that this vision and burning desire was God's heart and desire, so with hopeful expectations that Jake would understand and begin to embrace it as well, she approached the subject with him.

Nicole brought two cups of steaming hot tea into the living room. She set one down next to Jake, then she sat down on the sofa near his chair. After taking several sips, she asked, "Hon, would this be a good time to talk about something that's been on my heart?"

He looked up at her questioningly. "Sure. What's on your mind?"

"You know my heart for working with women," she began. "You know that I am passionate about sharing the hope, healing and freedom that I've found with others who are bound up without hope. I've been thinking about our ranch here. We've never really named it, but I've been thinking that I'd like to call it Ramoth Ranch, after Ramoth Gilead."

Jake nodded his head but didn't say anything. Nicole knew that he was familiar with her passion and with the connotations of the name in the Bible.

She continued. "I've been thinking about how this place has been a refuge and a place of healing for me, and that maybe God gave us this place to share with others who need to find healing and deliverance as well. I was thinking that maybe we could build a few bungalows and this could become a place of ministry to women who are hurting like I was."

Nicole noticed that Jake's expression was not brightening up with acceptance and anticipation like she'd hoped for. She leaned forward and continued. "Oh Jake, just think! We could have worship and discipleship every day, and even teach life skills like managing money, work ethics and job training as well as healthy living so that they would be prepared for life spiritually, emotionally, mentally and physically. Doesn't that sound awesome?"

The look on his face told her what he thought before he even said anything, and awesome was not going to be the word he would use. "Nicole, I'll have to think about naming the ranch. I may be ok with that. But you are talking about having people live here with us 24/7. You never do things half way, and you would be consumed with this venture. You would wear yourself out and your health would go down the tubes, not to mention our lives. No Nicole. Our home will not become a home for women."

Nicole's heart seemed to drop. Rarely did Jake say no to something she desired, and when he did, it meant no. But she was so sure that this burning desire that had grown so large within her was from God. Why would He put this vision and desire in her and not in her husband? Before hope died within her, she asked, "Jake, will you at least pray about this? I know it would change our lives, but if this is from God, wouldn't you want to know and to obey?"

Jake patiently answered, "I'll pray about it Nicole. But I can honestly tell you that I do not share this vision with you right now, and if this is of God, He will have to change my heart big time. There is no way we could do this unless that happens."

In spite of the disappointing pain that was beginning to form in her heart, she knew that what he said was true. And if she was honest with herself, she would have to admit that she had not told him sooner because she had been afraid all along that he would feel this way.

"I'm sorry to disappoint you, hon," Jake said. He got up out of his chair and pulled Nicole up and into his arms. "You know I love you."

She returned his embrace and replied, "Yes, I know you do. I love you too." But because the vision had become so large within her, his rejection of it began to cause her heart to break, and with the breach came the threat of isolation.

IS was in heaven...figuratively speaking of course. Here was a little rift in the tightly bound relationship of husband and wife. If he could cause enough disunity to break up this marriage, he would win. He would work on stirring up feelings of rejection, pain, isolation and strife...And then there was the broken heart. Hmmm, he could do a lot with that!

Over the next several weeks, Nicole found herself suddenly overcome with sorrow and tears for what she thought was God's plan, but that could never come to pass. Jake had told her that he just didn't believe that it was God's plan for them, and that was that as far as he was concerned. But Nicole couldn't let it go and it was quickly becoming a dividing wall between them. She knew that something needed to be done.

There was a prayer meeting that Jake and Nicole would occasionally attend, and one evening when Jake was working late she decided to go. She felt led to share that her heart was burdened for something that Jake was not burdened with, and that it was causing division; then asked them to pray for her.

True to their way, they had her sit in the "mush pot," the middle of their circle as they began to pray over her. They didn't just tell God what their concerns were. They also expected Him to answer and were ready to listen. Karen stood nearby with pen and paper ready to write down whatever word of wisdom or knowledge God spoke to them. So they began to pray, and God began to give words and even a picture to several of the others. By the end, when Karen read back what she had recorded, God had begun to humble Nicole's spirit, tear down the walls and to mend the breach in her heart.

God clearly let Nicole know that what had begun as His heart for women had grown to such an obsession within her that it had taken on the stink of the enemy and had grown from there to something that He was not involved in. Pride had crept in and caused a rift or breach between herself and Jake. The word of the Lord for her was that if Nicole would repent and entrust her burden and vision to Him, that He would bring her back to the place where she would meet His true heart in the matter, and that He would bring Jake from the other end of the spectrum to the same point; that they would meet in the place that God had for them, together in unity.

It was the picture that fascinated Nicole and that she would never forget. Jesus gave her brand new, red running shoes. The significance of running shoes brought comfort to her soul because she realized that with Jake's rejection of her idea for the ranch, she had felt as if she had been taken out of action. Jesus was letting her know that that was a lie and that she would be running again! Jesus was the Prince of Peace and so as she ran in His shoes, there would be peace and not discord with her husband; there would be trust, confidence and reliance on God…peace and not obsession. The color was also very significant. When she heard that the shoes were red, her first thought was that she didn't like red. Why red? Then she realized that red was of the utmost importance, for it symbolized the blood of Jesus, victory. Everything she did needed to be done under the covering of the blood of the Lamb or it would be nothing except and open door for the enemy.

When Nicole got home, she hit the floor in her praying spot beside her bed. "Oh Lord Jesus, I am so very sorry for allowing pride and obsession to overtake me! Please forgive me Jesus! I choose to submit to Your plans; I accept them and Your red running shoes. Please heal my heart and help me know how to follow You." Peace and contentment filled her heart as she was once again in the right place with her Lord, but she knew there was another that she needed to speak with.

A vision of fleas and other small parasites came to her mind. She realized that these represented small things that wanted to stay hidden but that would continue to torment and destroy. Her ideas and pride had opened the door for Satan to come against their marriage. Even though she confessed her sin to God, if she didn't make it right with Jake, there would be things that would still attach to her bad feelings and steal the life out of their marriage, just as parasites would on a body.

Jesus said, "*Nicole, don't assume that you know where I'm taking you when you begin to follow Me. Remember that your strength is small, but Mine is powerful. Make sure that you stay behind Me because the evil one is out there ready and waiting for you to take one step outside of my shadow. If you turn your eyes in the wrong direction, he will lead you astray. Because of your small mind, the dreams and visions I give you may look like one thing to you and something completely different to Me. If you are not careful, I will turn a corner and you will keep going straight and you will miss the blessings I have in store for you.*"

As soon as Jake got home, Nicole ambushed him. "Jake, honey, please forgive me for allowing myself to become obsessed with a desire that was not of God and that caused division between us. I will submit myself to God's plans and to you."

As he hugged her he said, "Of course I forgive you. I want you to know that I don't think your idea is a bad one. I know it's important. It just can't happen here, and you just can't be available 24/7. We'll wait and see what God does with this."

It felt so good to be in unity with her husband again. As Nicole climbed in bed and closed her eyes she heard Jesus say, "*Well done my woman of warfare. You have learned that obsessions and disunity with your husband lead you away from Me, and that trust and unity lead you into…Well, just wait and see where they lead you in this matter.*"

And Nicole fell asleep to the sound of the joyful laughter of her Master.

CHAPTER 12
JUMPING IN

Nicole had laid down for a quick afternoon nap, and woke from the dream in a cold sweat. What did it mean? She had learned that God often spoke to her in dreams, and occasionally they were an attack from Satan. This one was so heavy, she either needed to understand it's meaning or needed to have it wiped from her emotions. As she was preparing a cup of hot tea trying to shake off the disturbing affects of the dream, a car drove up her driveway. Because of its isolation, it was unusual to have people come to the ranch without calling first.

Nicole opened the door to see her friend Brenda stepping out of the car. Immediately Nicole understood the dream. God had been preparing her for this moment. Brenda was still in her pajamas, her hair was a tangled mess, and her swollen red eyes caused her to look like she'd been in a fight; but because of the dream, Nicole knew this was a spiritual attack, not physical. She took her friend into her arms and led her into the house.

They sat down together on the couch and Nicole began to pray. After a moment Brenda said, "I don't know what's wrong with me. I've been pacing the floor since yesterday after church. Words and sounds keep coming out of my mouth that I don't understand, and it's not good. They're not tongues from God. I'm going crazy. I can't think straight. I feel like my body is being controlled by something and I don't know what it is or what to do. The only thing I could think of was to come here, so I did."

Nicole hugged her friend and with all the hope, comfort and confidence that Christ had given her, she replied, "You came to the right place, sweetheart. Jesus brought you here and He will help us work through this together, ok?"

Brenda smiled faintly, then a tortured look came over her face as a snake like demon began strangling her.

Nicole didn't see it with her natural eyes, but the Holy Spirit opened her spiritual eyes to see it and she immediately bound it, took it captive in the name of Jesus, and commanded it in Jesus' name to release its hold so that Brenda was able to breathe and talk. For several hours, the Lord revealed the open doors in Brenda's life that had allowed this demon access to her body. Brenda had been growing in the Lord, and it was now time for all the darkness to be exposed and eradicated. And it didn't want to leave without a fight.

When Jake came home from work, he walked into the front door, saw what was happening and went into the bedroom and closed the door. Nicole had been wondering how he would react to all of this, but about that time, another demon raised its ugly head and she knew that she needed prayer support. She found Jake and briefly explained what was happening. He willingly came and prayed with them. The battle went on all night as demon after demon was exposed, its rights to Brenda were terminated, the curses were broken, and the demons were sent to the feet of Jesus. By morning, the Holy Spirit occupied the places in Brenda's soul and body where the demons had previously been. Even though she hadn't slept in two days, she looked one hundred percent better than when she came.

The Lord had been true to His Word. This experience was foundational in beginning the process of knitting Jake and Nicole's hearts together for the future that He had for them. Jake began to realize the importance of this type of ministry, and Nicole realized that Jake had been right about her inability to have people needing ministry in their home 24/7. She also realized that this was the first time that she had dealt so openly with demons in other people. She had helped others recognize, renounce and destroy strongholds Satan had had in their lives, but they had never manifested like these had. In a funny sort of way, it felt as though she was being given wings.

CHAPTER 13
BELIAL AND THE BROKEN HEART

Nicole was already in bed when the phone rang at 10:15. She sat up and waited as Jake answered and was relieved when she realized that it wasn't one of the boys. Phone calls that late usually weren't good. Jake handed the phone to her and shrugged to say that he didn't know who it was.

"Hello," Nicole answered.

"Hi Nicole, my name is Brandy. You may not remember me, but I met you once when you were in L.A. for Susan's wedding."

Nicole recognized the European accent and remembered meeting the woman with very sad eyes. "Hi Brandy! Yes I do remember you. What can I do for you?"

"Well, I've been having some trouble and I tried talking to a couple of pastors, but they didn't know what to do with me. A friend told me to go talk to a priest. I was desperate enough to do that, and he was nice but he couldn't help me. He told me that I needed to talk to someone who understood spiritual warfare and deliverance. I remember Susan telling me that you might do that. Would you be able to help me?"

Wow. How should she answer that? "Jesus help me here, please," she silently prayed. "Brandy, can you tell me what has happened? Why do you feel that you need deliverance?"

"It's a long story, but basically, I am in so much pain, and it's so bad now that if I don't get help, I know I'm going to die."

Nicole asked, "Where are you now?"

"I'm at home. I can talk with you on the phone, but I don't have the money to get up there."

"That's ok; we can talk on the phone tomorrow. But can you tell me what kind of pain you're talking about?"

Brandy took a deep breath, "I'm hopeless. I'm depressed. I don't want to go on living like this," she answered. "I've been in hell and I can't seem to get out of it. My life is hell. This world is hell! I go to bed in fear and sleep with nightmares. I wake up in terror, and I can't identify the source of my fear, it's just there! It's a part of me and I just can't go on living like this."

Nicole asked, "Brandy, do you know Jesus? Have you asked Him to forgive your sins? Have you surrendered your life to Him and asked Him to be your Lord, to live in you and help you?"

"Yes," she answered. "I did that four years ago, and my life got worse after than it was before. And I never would have thought that was possible!"

"Ok, Brandy. Let's pray right now, and then we can talk tomorrow." Nicole prayed a short prayer and went back to bed, but not to sleep. "Lord Jesus, I don't know how to help this lady. If I think about it, I get scared. She's so desperate and her life is on the line. What if I don't help her enough and she ends up in worse trouble?"

She heard what she was saying and recognized fear. Interesting. Brandy talked about fear and terror. Nicole had been learning about "the strongman," and how important it is to identify it and bind it as Matthew 12:29 teaches. "*Or how can one enter a strong man's house and plunder his goods, unless he first binds the strong man? And then he will plunder his house.*" "Lord is fear a strongman here? Please forgive me for fearing or doubting. I know that I don't have to worry because this is not my work, it's Yours. I trust that You have brought her to me and I will trust that You will give me the wisdom I need to help her. Thank you Jesus."

Peace settled over her like a warm blanket and before she knew it, her morning alarm was going off.

In the morning as Nicole prayed for Brandy, the story of the Moses and the children of Israel came to her mind. God had called Moses to set the people free from the bondage they were under in Egypt. When he went to Pharaoh, instead of initially setting the people free, they were abused more than they had been before; but through obedience and perseverance, freedom had come. She realized that was a physical picture of a spiritual reality, and prayed that would be the case for Brandy as well.

Later that day, Brandy began to share her story over the phone. Her life was riddled with rejection and abandonment from the moment of her conception, throughout her childhood and continued into her adulthood. Nicole's heart was bursting with compassion for this woman as she continued to share her story of being tricked into the slavery of the sex trade and was trafficked to the US. She had managed to escape, but had ended up homeless in LA, living on skid row and then found a women's center who gave her a place to live until she was able to get her own place. The center was where she had met Susan, their mutual friend.

This young lady had seen more trauma in her 30 something years than anyone Nicole had ever known, and by the end of the phone conversation, Nicole realized that God wanted her to meet with this lady face to face. The problem was that she lived four hours away. She said, "Lord, if you want me to go, I'll go, but you will have to prepare the way."

As Nicole prayed about this, Jesus gave her scripture confirmation that He wanted her to go. *"For while your obedience is known to all,... I would have you wise as to what is good and guileless [innocent] as to what is evil; then the God of peace will soon crush Satan under your feet" (Rom. 16:19-20, RSV); "I have given you authority to tread upon serpents and scorpions, and over all the power of the enemy; and nothing shall hurt you (Luke 10:19); and "You will tread on the lion and the adder, the young lion and the serpent you will trample under foot (Ps. 91:13, RSV).* So she took this literally and began to bind the demons and evil spirits over the Hotel where Brandy lived, and proclaimed that they would be trampled on the

161

moment she set foot in that place! She began calling upon God to release His mighty warrior angels upon the hotel to bring the demons into subjection of the Most High God.

That night after dinner when Jake was out raking leaves in the yard, Nicole went out and began telling him about Brandy. When she told him she thought that Jesus might be asking her to go and meet personally with her, he said that he wasn't against the idea and that he would pray about it. Then Nicole told him the other part she had been hesitant to mention.

She began, "Hon, I hope you'll also pray about your own reaction and don't try to judge one way or another about me going until you really pray about it. The thing is, Brandy lives in a crack hotel in the middle of skid row." The rake quit raking and Jake's head jerked up as he looked at her with a frown on his face. Before he could say anything, Nicole hurried on explaining. "She is not on drugs; she only lives there because that's all she can afford. She feels safe there because God is protecting her, and if God wants me to go, I'll be safe too. I'll willingly agree to whichever decision you make. So will you pray about this with an open mind?"

Jake looked at her a moment and shook his head as if he was wondering how he had ended up with such a crazy woman. But he just said, "Isn't there some place you could meet?"

They both tried to think of somewhere, but didn't come up with any options. Finally Jake said, "Well, I'll pray about it." And he went back to raking the yard.

After thinking and praying, Jake agreed that if Brandy said she could come, then he would allow her to go. Nicole called her that very day.

Two weeks later, Nicole stepped off the bus in downtown L.A. After greeting one another with a hug, both women felt as if they had known each other forever. Because of Brandy's work schedule, Nicole had arrived at 5:00 pm, and it was already dark. They would need to work all night so that Brandy could get to work the following morning by 7:00 am.

They left the depot and went to a coffee shop for a quick bite to eat, then headed to the hotel. Nicole felt as though she had entered another planet as they left the car in the garage and began their walk through the streets. Lights and litter and cars and people of all sorts were everywhere. The streets were alive and horns were honking. But there was no fear. As they walked, Nicole sensed that there was a shield around them and she mentioned this to Brandy.

"You are exactly right!" Brandy commented. "I have never been in danger here or hurt by any of these people. I actually trust them more than I trust people sitting in a church! I haven't had much luck with them, the church people I mean. But I do know that God is always protecting me."

As they arrived at the front doors of the hotel, Nicole said out loud, "In Jesus' name I take authority here, and in the power of the Holy Spirit, I bind all demons and evil spirits. You will be trampled on as I walk into this place and you will be silent and ineffective. I call upon holy angels of God to come and discipline any who try to interfere in the work of the Lord God Almighty!"

It wasn't nearly as dirty as Nicole had imagined it might be. They walked through halls and up an elevator to Brandy's room. They met several people who were very nice, and other than that, all was quiet. In fact, it was quiet all night long as Nicole began leading Brandy through the Steps to Freedom in Christ by Neil Anderson, a tool she liked to use.

As they began the forgiveness step and Nicole prayed that Brandy's heart would be filled with incomprehensible love toward her abusers, the Lord told her, *"Brandy's heart can not hold My love. Look and see."* Then He gave Nicole a vision. She saw Jesus' hands cupped together with Brandy's heart sitting in them. The heart was not only broken, it was shattered and crushed.

163

The fragments were being held together with thin red strings of Jesus' blood. Then she saw a demon, a large reptile looking beast casting a shadow over her heart, and many smaller demons cutting the strings with their sharp claws as they whispered, "Worthless. Unlovable. Stupid. Ignorant. Idiot. Whore. Ashamed. Hopeless...." Then there was a tormenting Spirit of Fear that was marching across the pieces of her heart, causing pain and terror with each step it took, continuing to break each piece into smaller fragments.

Nicole was breathless as she realized how few strings were left that were holding Brandy's heart together and she shuddered inwardly to think what would happen to her if every string was broken. She cried out, "Jesus help us! We need You NOW!"

"*Belial.*" As soon as she heard the name in her mind she understood the shadow above Brandy's heart and who the strongman was. In reading 2 Corinthians 6:15 one day not that long ago, the name Belial had stood out to her, so she had researched it.

"Brandy, I think that it's time to do some spiritual warfare."

Brandy said, "Cool! I'll get my anointing oil! I keep it close because there is so much evil all around me that I anoint myself and my apartment all the time."

"Awesome," Nicole said. She was pleased that the idea didn't frighten her. "Brandy, have you ever heard of the name Belial?"

"No. What does it mean?"

"It's the name of a principality whose goal is to destroy or cause destruction, and it means *worthlessness, good for nothing, wicked, ruin, destruction, ungodly, evil* and *naughty.* Other words that describe it are *corrupt, scoundrels and troublemakers,* and it has come to signify a name of Satan. I don't think it is Satan, but because Satan can't be everywhere at once, he has set up an army of various ranking officers under him, just like in a physical army. I believe that Satan has generals under his command, and that each one has been assigned a specific function or job that reflects his own nature and character, and every general has an army of demons working under them. I believe that Belial is one of these generals or principalities, a powerful and influential spirit that represents his master Satan and his function of destruction."

Brandy said, "The worthlessness and good for nothing part sounds like I feel; and the wicked, corrupt, evil, scoundrels and troublemakers sound like everybody else in my life. Well not everybody…present company excluded…but you know what I mean," she smiled.

"Yep. There are two sides to this coin, and both serve the same master. On the one hand, there is the abuser, and on the other, the victim. The abuser takes on an identity of pride or self importance, and the victim takes on an identity of worthlessness. We see Belial's captivity everywhere in society, in abusive relationships, in prostitution, in slavery of all kinds.

"To some," Nicole continued, "Belial promotes pride, the love of self and the deceptive belief that as their own master they can and should do anything they want to or that feels good, brings them pleasure or fulfills their selfish goals and ambitions. They often operate under anger and rage, manipulation and control. Under heavy deception, they think that they are so important that they can get away with anything. They have no idea that in this place of pride they have given themselves up and placed themselves under the rule of Belial, the god of worthlessness."

"That would be my ex-husband," Brandy said.

Nicole nodded. "On the one hand, this self worship devalues others and the spirit of worthlessness makes it ok to harm others. Without a sense of worth or value, there is no hesitancy to do the wicked, vile things that the master of the flesh commands. On the other hand, the victim falls prey to the lies that they are valueless, worthless and unlovable. They tend to live under a blanket of insecurity and fear of rejection and abandonment which opens them up to the controllers and manipulators."

"And that would be me," Brandy commented.

"Belial or worthlessness will take down and destroy both if there is no intervention. I want to make it plain that God's love and forgiveness extends to everyone, no matter how evil they may have been, if they repent," Nicole explained. "In the end, Satan will claim the spirit, soul and body of abuser and victim if they do not belong to Christ. However, while Satan can destroy a Christian's soul (which is the mind, will and emotions) and their body, he can not claim or destroy their spirit. They will spend eternity in heaven where there is no more suffering, sorrow or pain."

"I just want to go there right now. I'm so tired of the pain. I wish it weren't a sin to kill myself," Brandy mused.

"Brandy," Nicole said, "First let me say that there is hope for you and for those whose souls have been captured and abused. I believe that you have a badly broken heart and Jesus wants to fix it and heal it. Just for the record, we're talking about your spiritual heart here, although the pain can manifest in the physical heart. I think that Belial has been a strongman in your life since you were conceived. When a child is unwanted by its parents, Satan is always right there ready and willing to claim it. I think that Belial claimed you when nobody else did. He instilled his identity and sense of worthlessness in you since the beginning and has manipulated and controlled you throughout your life. When you became a Christian, your identity was changed, so Belial has had to work very hard at keeping you away from Jesus and from learning who you really are. He knows that Jesus can fix and heal your heart, and if that happens, then he looses you.

"Your heart was already broken when you became a Christian, and Jesus began stitching your heart back together with stitches of His blood. Belial, as a strongman, is hovering over your heart, casting a shadow that hinders God's light and truth from penetrating into your heart, so even though you know a lot about Jesus with your mind, it isn't sinking in. He also has all these other demons that are working for him that are continually tormenting you and inflicting more damage and pain to your heart. Every time one of them whispers 'stupid' and you believe it, they are tearing out a stitch that is holding your heart together. If you don't stop believing their lies, Jesus will not be allowed to fix and heal it."

"How do I do that?"

"We need to break off the rights that allow Satan or his army to claim and torment you. Belial and his lies attack the very core of God's love and the work of Jesus Christ on the cross who willingly sacrificed His own life because of His love and belief in the value and worth of every human being, and that means you too Brandy. You must recognize the lies that you have been believing and choose to renounce them, stop believing them no matter how you feel, and choose to believe the truth about who God says you are."

"But you don't understand. I am stupid! Because of the genetic code that was given to me through my parents, I am unable to learn the way other people do. I can't remember things right. I can't learn the truth like you can, and if I learn it, I forget it. When I need it, it won't be there in my brain for me to use."

"Brandy, I have to tell you that you are believing a major lie of Belial! You may have a learning disability, but that doesn't mean that you are stupid. Many people have problems exactly like yours. You have been told this your whole life, but in the short time that we have been interacting, I can tell you that you are not stupid. Let me try to explain something to you.

"There is a difference between your brain and your mind. Your brain is physical, and your mind is spiritual. As a child of God, your spirit is what connects you to God and His Spirit so that you can experience relationship with Jesus and His love. One of the Holy Spirit's jobs is to be your rememberer, to communicate with your mind so that you will know what He tells you even if your brain has trouble processing it."

"More than anything I want to be close to Jesus and to obey Him. But I never feel God's love. I never hear His voice speaking to me like you do."

"That's because your heart, which is the connection between your spirit and your soul, is badly broken. Your spirit that is connected with God's Spirit is working fine, but Your soul or personality and sense of self is still under Belial's captivity because your mind has been infected with lies which affect how you feel, the choices you make and the things you do. Your heart represents the place where Jesus lives inside of you. When your heart house is broken, Jesus can be pouring His love in, but it just flows right back out without giving you time to experience it. When He pours His cleansing, healing blood in, it flows right back out without having time for you to notice its affect. Belial knows that a broken heart will isolate your soul from your spirit and stop your relationship and communication with God. The lies you believe cause you to continue to live and operate under hopelessness, depression, anxiety, fear, anger, and on and on. The belief that God has abandoned you, that He doesn't really love you, and that you truly are worthless grows until you want to die. I think this is why suicide is on the rise. Belial is breaking hearts and destroying hope all over the place."

They were both silent for a minute, lost in thought. Nicole was realizing that there were several things that needed to happen in order for Brandy to be set free. They needed to renounce Satan's claim on her and dedicate her to the Lord; her soul which housed her beliefs needed adjusting; and her heart needed healing.

Nicole finally said, "Brandy, your identity has been hidden inside your broken heart. Are you afraid that if Jesus heals it that you won't know who you are any more?"

Tears began running down Brandy's cheeks. "Maybe I am. I am afraid of everything! What if He heals my heart and I'm still stupid and don't know what to do? What if I still can't hear Him or feel His love? Then I'll know for sure that it's me, that I really am worthless! I can't handle another rejection!" Brandy's tears became sobs.

Because of the vision God had given her of Brandy's heart, she knew that this was the tormenting Spirit of Fear that was marching across the pieces of her heart, causing brokenness, pain and terror with each step it took. "In Jesus' name I bind the tormenting Spirit of Fear along with those of Pain and Terror that are working with you. I bind your feet with cords of Jesus' blood so that you are unable to continue trampling through Brandy's body, soul or spirit, causing her pain or terror through fear. In Jesus' name I separate you and your cohorts from your functions in Brandy's life and strip you of all authority. You will no longer be able to break her heart and keep her from God's love. In Jesus' name, I claim Brandy as God's beloved daughter, and I claim the truth of 1 John 4:18. *There is no fear in Love, but perfect Love casts out fear, because fear has to do with torment.* In Jesus' name, I command you tormenting Spirits of Fear, Pain and Terror to leave Brandy's body, soul and spirit, and go to Jesus' feet to wait for His judgment of you! Lord Jesus, please send Your angels to escort this spirit into Your presence. I know that You hear us Jesus, and that it is Your will to free her from fear and torment so that she can be perfected in Your love. Thank you, Jesus. Amen."

Nicole picked up her Bible and began reading. "*Psalm 34:18, The Lord is near to those who have a broken heart, and saves such as have a contrite [repentant] spirit. Psalm 51:17, The sacrifices of God are a broken spirit, A broken and a repentant heart — These, O God, You will not despise. Isaiah 61:1-3,... He has sent Me to heal the brokenhearted, To proclaim liberty to the captives, And the opening of the prison to those who are bound;... To comfort all who mourn, To console those who mourn in Zion, To give them beauty for ashes, The oil of joy for mourning, The garment of praise for the spirit of heaviness; Psalm 147:3, He heals the brokenhearted And binds up their wounds. Isaiah 42:3-4, A bruised reed He will not break, And a smoking wick He will not quench; Isaiah 53:3-5, He is despised and rejected by men, A Man of sorrows and acquainted with grief.... Surely He has borne our griefs and carried our sorrows; Yet we esteemed Him stricken, Smitten by God, and afflicted. But He was wounded for our transgressions, He was bruised for our iniquities. The punishment for our peace was upon Him, And by His stripes we are healed."*

Nicole gently asked, "Brandy, do you believe that Jesus can fix your heart?"

"I don't know," she sniffled. "I guess I believe that He could, but I don't believe that He will. It's no wonder that everybody in my life has rejected and abandoned me. Even God doesn't want me!"

"Let's say that the tables were turned and I am you, the one with the broken heart, and you are me, would you believe that Jesus would heal my broken heart?"

"Yes, of course. He loves *you*."

"In Jesus' name, I command that all the mouths of Belial and the enemy will be quiet and closed so that Brandy can hear God's truth. Brandy, Jesus loves you too. I think that this is a matter of faith. In order for you to overcome the lies, you are going to have to choose to know the truth, believe the truth and act on the truth no matter how you feel. Your feelings will change over time. Would you look up John 3:16?"

"I know that one. *'For God so loved the world that He gave His only begotten Son that whosoever believes in Him, shall not perish but have eternal life.'*"

"Good. Now put your name in place of 'world and whosoever.'"

"*'For God so loved Brandy that He gave His only begotten Son that if Brandy believes in Him, she shall not perish but have eternal life.'*"

"Now look up Hebrews 11:6."

"*'But without faith it is impossible to please Him, for he who comes to God must believe that He is, and that He is a rewarder of those who diligently seek Him.'*"

Nicole said, "Good, now look up Proverbs 3:5-8.""*'Trust in the* LORD *with all your heart, And lean not on your*

170

own understanding; *In all your ways acknowledge Him, And He shall direct your paths. Do not be wise in your own eyes; Fear the* LORD *and depart from evil. It will be health to your flesh, and strength to your bones.'"*

"Great! One more. Look up Jeremiah 29:11-14."

"*'For I know the thoughts that I think toward you, says the* LORD, *thoughts of peace and not of evil, to give you a future and a hope. Then you will call upon Me and go and pray to Me, and I will listen to you. And you will seek Me and find Me, when you search for Me with all your heart. I will be found by you, says the* LORD, *and I will bring you back from your captivity.'"*

"What is God telling you through these verses?" Nicole asked.

Brandy was quiet for a moment then said, "God wants me to know that He does love me. He wants me to trust the truth that He loves me and that He thinks of me. He wants me to live and to have peace and hope for the future. He wants me to trust in His truth and not in the lies I've been listening to and believing; and that if I will seek Him and trust Him He will reward me. He'll set me free and heal me."

With a huge smile on her face, Nicole clapped her hands in joy and hugged Brandy. "Yes! See Jesus does speak to you!"

Brandy smiled faintly, "Yeah, I guess He does. Maybe I just haven't been able to hear Him. It seemed like something changed when fear left and then you told the enemies to be quiet."

"If you will let Jesus heal your broken heart, and will do your part, it will get easier to hear Him and for His truth and love to stay inside your heart so you can experience Him. Do you want that Brandy?"

"Yes. Yes I do. But what do you mean when you say if I do my part? What is my part?"

"We can get rid of the demons, but the hardest part of deliverance is what comes after. It means that you will have to put off the old way of thinking and constantly be evaluating every thought that comes into your mind. The

171

enemy will no longer have rights to you, but you can be sure that he'll be right there with his same old tricks, throwing those old lies right back at you, hoping that you'll take the bait. So you need to take every thought captive, and if you see that they are Belial's lies you renounce them, tell him to get lost, and immediately replace those thoughts with God's truth. If you see that they are God's thoughts, you hold onto them. That's called renewing your mind in the truth, and that's what Ephesians 4:22-24 is about. You aren't going to feel like believing the truth because the lies are all so familiar, and they are habits of thinking. It takes a lot of work to change habits."

"I understand what you are saying," Brandy replied, "but it seems overwhelming."

Nicole squeezed Brandy's hand and said, "We just need to take this a step at a time and keep our eyes on Jesus and then we won't sink. The first step is for us to renounce Satan and Belial's claim on you from the moment of your conception."

"Ok, I agree with you on that. What do we do?"

"Tell Satan and Belial that you are taking back the person that God created you to be. Renounce them and their rights to you, and then give your body, soul and spirit to Jesus."

Brandy bowed her head. "Jesus, I can see that Satan and Belial claimed me because nobody else wanted me. I can't say that I'm sure that you even want me, but I will believe it because Your Word says it's true; I just can't feel it yet. But I know that I don't want to be claimed by the devil! I want to be free of him! So in Jesus' name, I renounce the claim that Satan and Belial made on me from the moment of my conception clear through today. I choose to give my spirit, soul and body to Jesus. Please accept me Jesus. Amen."

"Good, Brandy. That is the first step, and now you have some choices to make. Will you choose to believe that Jesus loves you and to accept His love, even if you don't feel it? Because this is truth and truth is what sets you free. Are you willing to do this Brandy?"

"I do want to be free. Yes. Jesus, I am sorry that I have doubted the truth of Your love for me. Please forgive me. I choose to believe that You do love me and have plans for my life even though I don't feel Your love right now. Please let me feel You sometime soon, please! And help me to have faith when I don't. In Jesus' name, Amen."

"That's beautiful, Brandy," Nicole said. "The reason you can't feel God's love is because of your broken heart. Remember, I told you that He's pouring His love in all the time, but it just flows right back out. So if you want to, we will get rid of Belial and his demons and then Jesus can heal your heart. Is that what you want?"

"Yes! Of course. I don't want to be no demon's puppet!" Brandy replied.

Nicole smiled at Brandy's analogy. "Ok then, there is just one more question I have to ask you. It has to do with freedom and forgiveness. We want you to be free from the bondage of the enemy, to be loosed from him. To loose means to unbind, untie, set free or forgive."

"Are you telling me that I have to forgive Satan?"

"No, absolutely not! But you do have to forgive the people who hurt you. They are not the true enemy. Satan is. Jesus tells us that if we want to be forgiven, set free or loosed from the enemy's captivity, then we have to choose to forgive, set free or loose the people we have hanging from our hook of unforgiveness. We cut them free from our hook and hand them over to God. Holding onto unforgiveness will only hurt us, not them."

"So you're saying that if I want to be set free I have to forgive the people who have hurt me my whole life?" Brandy asked.

"I'm not saying that, Jesus is. Let's read Matthew 18:21-35."

After they read this, Brandy said, "Ok, Jesus does make it very clear that if I want to be forgiven and free then I need to forgive. I'm not sure I can change my feelings."

Nicole took hold of her hands and said, "That's the beautiful thing about God, Brandy. You don't have to change them. He doesn't expect you to. All He's asking you to do is to trust Him enough to obey by making the choice to forgive, and He'll take care of the rest. It's a step of faith."

"Ok. I'm ready. So should I pray?"

"Yep. Do you want help?"

"I think I know what to do," Brandy said. "Lord Jesus I thank You that You are willing to forgive me. I know I don't deserve it. And I choose to forgive the people who hurt me that I've been angry with and have had unforgiveness in my heart for. I will trust You to change my feelings. I hope You will forgive me now and set me free from the evil spirits. In Jesus' name, Amen."

"Yeah!" Nicole shouted. "Now we are going to renounce Belial, his demons and his lies. Would you like me to help you or do you want to do this on your own?"

Brandy took Nicole's hands in hers. "I would like you to help me because I don't really know what I'm supposed to do now. I just know that I want them gone."

"You can repeat after me, but if you don't understand something or you disagree with it, stop and tell me. Or if you hear interfering thoughts and can't focus, tell me that too, ok?"

"Ok."

Nicole started and Brandy repeated, "In Jesus' name, I bind the strongman Belial and take him captive under the power and authority of the Lord Jesus Christ and His blood. We also take all the demons working for him captive. We tie them up with cords of Jesus' blood.

"Lord Jesus, we ask You to send warrior angels to come and discipline any demons or principalities that refuse to obey. Jesus, I confess giving a place in my mind, will, emotions, spirit and body to Belial and his demons. I know that I have listened to their lies my whole life, and I see them now for what they are. I choose to renounce those lies and I choose to believe the truth. I won't listen to or believe in the lies any more. I choose to believe the truth that God loves me and has chosen me to be His daughter; that He accepts and loves me so much and that I am so valuable to Him that He sacrificed His own life so that I could live with Him forever! I choose to believe that He has plans for good in my life and that He won't ever abandon or reject me. I choose to believe that God understands my physical limitations and that His Holy Spirit is my helper and will help me to remember and know the things I need to understand. I choose to believe that Jesus is my healer, emotionally, mentally, physically and spiritually.

"I confess that I have given in to a Spirit of Fear because I have not trusted in God to take care of me and to help me. Please forgive me Jesus for not trusting You. I choose to put my faith and trust in You, and when I am afraid, I will trust in You. In Jesus' name I renounce and reject all Spirits of Fear, Torment, Pain and Terror. I do not want you and you are not welcome in my life anymore.

"And now in Jesus' name, I command that the demons be separated from their functions and stripped of their ability to communicate with each other or any spirits outside of what we are doing. In Jesus' name I break all curses spoken against me or placed upon me, and I claim the freedom from curses that Jesus gave to me when He reversed all curses at His death. I send all curses back upon their originator, Satan.

"I confess to You Lord Jesus that I have been involved in many ungodly relationships, and I ask You to forgive me, cleanse me and heal me of those; some I was an unwilling participant in, and others I was willing. I choose to forgive my abusers.

Please break all the ungodly soul ties between those people and myself. I only want to be connected to You Lord Jesus, and to the people that You bring into my life that You want me to be connected with.

"And now, in Jesus' name, I command the Spirit of Fear, Belial, and all other demons with him, to leave my spirit, soul and body without hurting me, and go to the feet of Jesus to wait for His judgment and direction for where you are to go."

In her spirit, Nicole saw a very large angel come and tie Belial's hands behind his back. He was kicking and swearing up a demonic storm, but all the other little demons were standing in shock and confusion. The angel blew what appeared to be a warm wind over the devil's storm winds. Belial and the others were swept away, carried on the wings of angels. And then there was peace. Brandy was at peace for the second time in her life.

Tears of joy and relief flowed down both ladies faces, and they thanked Jesus for His redemption.

Nicole saw the vision of Brandy's heart again. It was still in Jesus' hands, still broken, shattered and crushed, but there were no demons tormenting it, and no shadow blocking the light. And what Light! Nicole had heard of God's Glory light. She knew that it was His presence showing up in a tangible way. And when Glory light shone, amazing things happened.

"Brandy, I see that Jesus is ready to do something in your heart. Do you feel, see or hear anything?" Nicole asked.

"I hear Jesus calling my name. But he's calling me Ana, not Brandy."

"Do you know why He is calling you Ana?"

"Ana is my real name. When I was trafficked, they changed it to Brandy."

"Ana. That's amazing!" Nicole said. "Do you know what the name Ana means?"

"No. Do you?"

"I do. I happen to believe that names are very important and I often look them up to see what they mean. I remember that Ana means 'favor or grace!'

Brandy looked those words up in the dictionary, and then looked at Nicole in wonder. "Do you know what this means? God wants me! He has always wanted me! The favor part means that God approves of me, supports me, and chooses me. The grace part means that God has given me the gifts of His love, mercy and favor. And He's made me into something lovely and beautiful! I remember my grandmother cursing my name and telling me that it was a stupid name and that she didn't know why my mother picked it out for me. But now I know why! God chose that name for me and for some reason she listened to Him!

Nicole saw the vision of Brandy's heart again. The Glory light was still shining on it and she noticed that it had been reshaped, and instead of being held together by thin red strings of Jesus' blood, it was stitched with strong red stitches and was also held together with a solid covering or casing of Jesus' blood. Even though it was not completely healed, it had been made much stronger in such a short time!

"Ana," Nicole said. "I would like to anoint you with your real name if that's ok with you?"

"Please!"

They stood to their feet and Nicole anointed Ana's head. "Lord Jesus, thank You for naming Ana as a baby, for revealing Your love for her now, for beginning the healing process of her heart. Brandy, in Jesus' name, we strip you of your identity that was rooted in a broken heart, and we anoint you Ana, whose identity is found in the favor of God, in love, joy, peace and hope of Jesus Christ. I dedicate you as Ana, God's beloved daughter."

The presence of God was so beautiful, that neither woman wanted to look to see what time it was. But finally, Nicole saw that they would soon need to head back to the car.

Nicole had something she wanted to encourage Ana with before they left. "Ana, in Isaiah 61 it says that Jesus came to bind up the broken hearted. I think that it's important to think about what that means. If my finger were to be almost cut off and I go to the hospital, they will sew it back on and wrap it up or bind it. Does that mean that it is completely healed?"

"No. I think I see what you are getting at," Ana said. "God has stitched and bound up my broken heart, but it is not healed yet. Right?"

"You are a quick study!"

"Huh?"

Nicole giggled, "That means you learn fast. So you are right that it is fixed but not healed. If I use my finger wrongly, I could break it open again. It's the same with your heart. If you listen to the lies or the fear, you could cause the binding to split open. If this happens, you just confess it to God and ask Him to re-stitch and re-bind it.

"The prescription I'm going to give you in taking care of this healing heart is to spend time with Jesus every day by reading your Bible. Jesus will talk to you through it, and you need to hear what He has to say to you. Practice listening to His voice. There are two kinds of listening. Listen and wait for Him to speak, then listen and obey what He says. Every time you do this, your heart will be growing stronger and healthier. Stay close to Jesus, and His Spirit and His love will be able to fill your heart up and will overflow into every part of your body, soul and your spirit. And remember, if you don't take your thoughts captive, they will take you captive."

It was still dark when they left the hotel and started back towards the parking garage. The streets appeared empty at first glance, then Nicole noticed a movement on the other side of the road and realized that it was a person lying on the bus stop bench covered with a newspaper. Then she noticed another person under a blanket on the sidewalk against a building, then another and another. Such a different way of life. Such pain and suffering all around, and yet she felt as if Jesus were even shielding her heart from all the overwhelming feelings associated with these precious people because even though she would love to be able to help them, it was not her mission at the moment.

Brandy broke into her reflective thoughts by saying, "He did it."

"What?"

"Jesus trampled Satan under your feet just like you prayed," replied Brandy. "It has never been that quiet and uneventful in the hotel, especially at night." She began to tell Nicole stories of screaming neighbors, of death and destruction that took place regularly, and yet they had worked all night long without any noise or interference at all.

Ana and Nicole hugged each other and said goodbye knowing that they would see each other again.

On the bus ride home, before she fell asleep, Nicole was thinking about Belial. She realized that everything apart from Christ is worthlessness, and as people enter into Satan's territory of worthlessness, they become trapped in bondages of worthless things. It didn't even have to be huge things like drugs and sex. She could see how Belial enticed everybody with little things that seemed harmless, but were worthless distractions; and all led to the same trap. She remembered something she had told Ana. "Belial and his snares attack the very core of God's love and the work of Jesus Christ on the cross who willingly sacrificed His own life because of His love and belief in the value and worth of every human being."

She suddenly realized the role of Belial in her own life. The Lord showed Nicole how she herself had fallen under the influence of this principality. He revealed how she was driven to please others because she felt that she would be worth something if she could make others happy. She had never realized that she believed this lie before! And she saw other lies Belial had thrown her way, worthless lies that stole her time and ruled her life. Nicole confessed her sin to God. She repented of believing Belial's lies, renounced them, and purposed in her heart to ask Jesus what He wanted her to do everyday.

Her thoughts returned to Ana and their time together. The whole thing had gone so quickly and smoothly that she began questioning God. There had not

179

been a physical manifestation of demons or principalities. Had she imagined all this? Was the strongman's power over Ana really broken? Had Belial really gone? God didn't answer in the way that Nicole expected.

She must have drifted off to sleep because she was suddenly awakened to a very evil, angry presence hovering directly in front of her. In a deep, guttural voice it growled, *"You can't have her. She's mine!!!"* Without considering where she was, she shot right back at him, "Ana belongs to God, not me, and you can't have her back!" The presence left and Nicole became very aware of the stares of the other people sitting near by. Oops, she had answered out loud and could feel the disapproving stare of the woman in the seat next to her, so she turned and gave her a very sweet smile. The lady drew her magazine a little closer to her face and as she turned her body as far away from Nicole as she could, she heard her say something about the world and nuts. Nicole couldn't help but smile. She knew God's answer to her question was that their work had been effective. She had learned that prayers prayed according to God's heart are tangible things to Him, and that when He answers, He answers in tangible ways! Her faith in God's authority and power had grown by leaps and bounds.

Nicole arrived home exhausted but very fulfilled! That night, at 3:00 am all the smoke detectors in the house went off. Nicole jumped out of bed and yelled for Jake to get up. As soon as they went into the living room, the alarms stopped. When Nicole realized that there was no smoke or fire, the thought went through her head that somebody was mad. They got back in bed and immediately they went off again and quit as soon as Nicole entered the living room. The third time the smoke detectors went off, she had no doubts that Belial was trying to come against her and that he was so stinking full of hell fire that he was setting off her smoke alarms!

She said, "Jake, we need to pray. The devil's mad and is trying to get in here." Jake was so sleepy he would have slept through the alarms if Nicole would have let him, and he certainly didn't feel like praying. But because he knew he wouldn't be allowed to sleep until they prayed, he groggily got out of bed and followed her again into the living room. They asked God to set heavenly boundaries of protection around Ana, their home, family, pets, property and finances to cover them in Jesus blood, and then they went back to bed and slept soundly the rest of the night.

This encounter with Ana and the events of the night increased Nicole's desire and burden for a worship and ministry house. She knew that it was going to take a lot of work for Ana to keep her freedom because this enemy was ragingly angry and a relentless stalker. She wished that she knew of a place that Ana could visit for a short period of time to help her in the adjustment period of learning to renew her mind and that would give her heart time to heal in a safe place. For now, she would claim the truth found in 1 John 4:4. *"You are of God, little Ana, and have overcome them, because He who is in Ana is greater than he who is in the world."*

Nicole began to pray more fervently that God would open something up. She was also beginning to realize that a home like that would need many strong, healed and delivered people of God to minister to the 24/7 needs and to maintain it. As hard as it was to admit, Nicole didn't know of anybody who even had the understanding of healing and deliverance that this would require.

She felt so isolated in this area of ministry, and she needed an army! So she began praying that God would raise up His people, an army of intercessors. Yes, that was exactly what was needed... intercessors! Nicole was beginning to understand that no one could go to battle unless they were connected in the deepest way with Jesus. That realization changed the way Nicole prayed, for what good would a home do if there was no one to run it?

CHAPTER 14
PYTHON

Nicole was learning to fly with her new wings, and IS was very unhappy! This was not supposed to be happening! She was fasting and praying and obeying the wrong God. She was learning that she had power and authority over evil spirits and was not only casting them out, but was teaching others about their power and authority as well. She was giving away his secrets about broken hearts, and people were forgiving all over the place and getting their hearts healed, which was shutting the door on his workers! Something had to be done. He considered trying to drive a wedge between Jake and Nicole, but that had backfired too many times and had brought about the opposite effect. He couldn't even use Jake's lack in the understanding of Nicole's calling against them because Jake had been watching the fruit in the lives of the women who were coming to her for help and had come to believe that even though he didn't completely understand it, this ministry was valid and important.

No, he needed something new, and decided to enlist ideas from some of his cohorts, so he called a meeting of the high counsel.

The stench in the court room was foul and became fouler with the arrival of each demonic entity. Even though this was not a formal hearing, IS sat behind the judge's bench to remind all the others who was in charge. There was a tendency for them to all think that they were the highest and mightiest which would often result in conflict requiring intervention from one higher and mightier, which would be him. When they were all in attendance he called the meeting to order.

"I assume you all got the memo concerning the reason for this meeting. I hope you have come prepared with thoughts and ideas that will help me find a way to shut down Nicole's ministry. I now open the floor to comments...." The room erupted into chaos as they all began talking at once, believing that they had the best and only answer. IS stood from his high bench, casting a fierce shadow over the room, and banged his gavel down so hard that the room reverberated as if a great earthquake was taking place. The affect was immediate and when it was quiet he said, "One at a time as I acknowledge you, you peons!"

IS listened to each suggestion ranging from burning their house down at night while they were in it, to killing Nicole in a car accident. Nothing pleased him, and as he looked around the room, he noticed Python sitting coiled and still. "Divination, you are very quiet. Have you nothing to offer?"

Python coiled himself up a little tighter and then lazily began to stretch himself out while he hissed, "Ah contraire your highness! I have been lissstening to these imbeciles with their brainlessssss ideas and have been thinking of something a little more subtle, but deadly."

IS quieted the room down as murmurs were beginning to sound against Python's insults, and then said, "Please do share. I am intrigued."

Python raised his head a little higher and began. "There issss a woman named Trisha who is in our service, your highness. We are very sssstrong in her and she is an acquaintance of the one we recently lost known as Brandy." Loud hissing and cursing exploded at the mention of their loss, and IS banged his gavel, giving the floor back to Python. "She has also become a Christian..." IS banged the gavel before more noise erupted in response to the repulsive name. Python continued, "I proposssse that we introduce Trisha to Nicole through Brandy. Get her to 'help deliver' this poor bound woman from the clutchessss of the enemy. I have foresssseen a union of friendship through which we may be able to take an advantage..."

The insolent smile that was beginning to form on the face of his highness told Python that he had done well. "I am pleased. Make it so!" IS banged the gavel as a sign of dismissal and sat contemplating the delicious taste of victory.

Nicole had begun sensing an urgency rising up within her that she didn't understand. "Lord, what are You trying to tell me?" He seemed to remain quiet, but the thing that kept coming to her mind was the idea of fasting. She had come to realize the importance of fasting and prayer, but since she had battled anorexia in the past, the Lord had always led her to fast things other than food.

Sometimes it was TV and movies, sometimes it was electronics all together, and sometimes it was fasting all books except the Bible, and even once, it had been her morning coffee.

The Holy Spirit had taught her that fasting was a powerful key in His Kingdom. It opened the door of her heart to the presence of God in a more concrete way and she was better able to hear what Jesus was telling her. It was not magic, but it seemed to strengthen her relationship with God. The attitude of self sacrifice and of love for Him kicked that monster of pride right out her heart's door so that when she saw what God was doing, she was able to join Him without getting in the way. It helped her to remember that life was not about physical comfort, but about her relationship and reliance on God. She saw how self-discipline through fasting helped to produce the spiritual fruit of self-control which was also an important key in setting others free, for it seemed that most often, captivity occurred when there was an imbalance of either a lack of self control or an over abundance of false control.

Nicole was now thinking that it was time for her to begin to fast food. She believed that God had healed her and that to never fast food was like continuing to take medicine long after it was needed. When she took this to the Lord, she sensed that He was pleased that she was ready to go to a deeper level of discipline and trust in Him. He assured her that she would need to be obedient to Him in this, but that it was going to be vitally important for the work He was preparing her for.

The verses that seemed to be on her mind were Isaiah 58:6-9. *"Is this not the fast that I have chosen: To loose the bonds of wickedness, To undo the heavy burdens, To let the oppressed go free, And that you break every yoke? Is it not to share your bread with the hungry, And that you bring to your house the poor who are cast out; When you see the naked, that you cover him, And not hide yourself from your own flesh? Then your light shall break forth like the morning, Your healing shall spring forth speedily, And your righteousness shall go before you;*

The glory of the LORD shall be your rear guard. Then you shall call, and the LORD will answer; You shall cry, and He will say, 'Here I am.'"

Nicole was staying in contact with Ana, and one morning when they were talking on the phone, Ana told her about a friend of hers. "Nicki, I wish you could talk to Trisha. She is having a lot of issues because her father sold her into prostitution when she was a little girl, and she and her family were also involved in the occult. She is a Christian now and has been trying to change, but she struggles so much! Do you think there is any way you could help her?"

"Why don't you give her my phone number and we'll go from there," Nicole suggested.

Several days later, Trisha called. They talked for awhile, and Nicole was convinced that it was a divine appointment. She and Jake talked and prayed about it and decided that they would invite her to come for a weekend visit.

Nicole called Trisha and explained her proposal. "I don't know what the strongholds of the enemy are on your life, Trisha, but I do know that Jesus came to set the captive free. Are you ready to be set free?"

"Absolutely! I've been trying to do all the right Christian things, but I'm not getting anywhere. I feel like there are things that are holding me back and I don't know what they are or how to overcome them."

"Well," Nicole said, "Jake and I would like to invite you to come up to the ranch for a few days if you are ready to search God's heart for the answers. I don't know what it would look like exactly. I can tell you that it wouldn't be a vacation because searching God's heart is a lot of work; but I would like to offer to help you with that process."

Trisha was silent for a moment and then answered, "Wow, that sounds like an offer I can't refuse! Let me pray about it and I'll get back to you. Hey, you aren't going to do weird deliverance stuff on me are you? I was just thinking about how I've gone to a few churches that wanted to deliver me and they just abused me. I don't mean to be rude; it's just that I don't really know you and I don't want to go through that stuff again. It doesn't do any good."

"No offense taken," Nicole responded. "I'm glad if you'll tell me how you feel, and I'm sorry God's people have hurt you. Before you come, I can promise you that I will do everything I can to seek God's heart through prayer and fasting for His spiritual discernment, wisdom and knowledge so that we can walk in obedience to His direction when you are here. And I will not do anything without your approval and consent.

"That makes sense, and I appreciate what you are saying. It means a lot to me that you would offer to spend time with me."

Nicole said, "That reminds me to ask you to be honest with me as well. I am very willing to give my time to help you. I love watching Jesus set the captives free. But if you aren't really serious about being set free, then I would expect you to tell me. Neither one of us wants to waste our time."

"I hear you," Trisha replied. "And I respect that. I'll think and pray about this and let you know."

Trisha came two weeks later on a Saturday morning. Nicole and Jake liked her right off the bat. She had an easy sense of humor that they enjoyed, and after lunch, Nicole asked, "Well, are you ready to begin our search?"

"Let's roll," was her answer.

"We are going to begin with communion, and worship Trisha. If there is anything that is blocking or hindering your relationship with Jesus, I am going to ask Jesus to reveal it to you, ok?"

"That's a good idea. I know that we need to be close to Jesus in order to combat the enemy," she answered.

Nicole hadn't planned on Jake joining them, but as they prepared for communion, she felt the Holy Spirit nudge her to ask him to be part of that as their spiritual covering. Jake was happy to be included and he served them the Lord's Supper, and then dismissed himself.

As the two ladies sat quietly worshipping God following communion, the Holy Spirit allowed Nicole to see what was happening spiritually inside Trisha's body. This giant snake-like demon had wound itself around the insides of her body and had rooted itself deep inside her heart. Its body continued through the heart and up through her throat to her head where it's mouth was embedded in her brain. Without saying anything to Trisha about what she had seen, Nicole began to pray.

Trisha suddenly grabbed her heart and doubled over in pain. "I think I'm having a heart attack! It hurts so bad and it's hard to breathe!"

Because of what she had seen, Nicole knew that this was not a heart attack, but a spiritual attack. She took authority over the spirit and said, "In Jesus' name I cover you snake demon with the blood of Jesus and command you to release your death grip on Trisha right now!" The pain stopped in that very moment and Nicole told her what she had seen.

"That makes sense to me," she said. "Hey, I think I know what this is. I've heard of something like this before, and I think it is the spirit of Python but I don't remember anything about it." They looked it up on the internet. "This is very interesting!" Nicole said. "Python is a Spirit of Divination. According to Strong's G4436, it's the same Spirit of Divination that the slave girl in Acts 16:16-19 had been operating under as she followed Paul around, annoying him until he cast it out of her."

"Wow, this spirit is ancient," Trisha declared. "I never thought about it like this before, but the things I just happen to know about people are a result of a Spirit of Divination, of Python, the same spirit that Paul kicked out!"

"Spirits never die," Nicole explained. "They just transfer from person to person down through history. They also identify themselves according to the job and function that is assigned to them, and take on the characteristics and nature of that assignment. So whether or not it is the exact same Spirit of Divination, we don't know. But it has taken the same function and assignment as that of the slave girl. It may have been assigned to you through your involvement with the occult, or it could be a generational spirit that has been passed down through your family bloodlines."

"Hum," Trisha thought. "I know my grandmother was into witchcraft and in looking back, I'll bet she did use divination. My mom is a Christian and she hasn't been gifted with anything like that. Can it skip a generation?"

Nicole answered, "I'm sure it can. Your mom might have been a carrier for the seed and not functioned in the fruit. Usually though, carriers have some visible traits if you know what to look for."

"Yeah, but my mom is a Christian and has been for a long time, so Satan wouldn't be able to influence her, would he?"

"If things were passed down generationally and she never recognized or renounced the curse, it is most likely affecting her in some way. Often it can be physical infirmity and disease, or emotional turmoil like anxiety and depression, constant financial problems, continual relationship problems, being accident prone, things just always going wrong, or any number of ongoing problems or torments. Without breaking the generational curse, no amount of prayer seems to make a difference. Does your mom have any of these symptoms?"

Trisha sighed. "You hit the nail on the head with almost everything you just mentioned."

"The hope is that Jesus can break this off of you Trisha, and stop it from being passed down your family line any further."

Nicole jumped and grabbed her leg as a searing pain reverberated through it. Trisha jumped when Nicole did, and then asked, "What's wrong?"

Nicole started to tell her that it was just a momentary pain when she saw four very large rats. One was sitting next to her leg and she knew that it had been the source of the pain, and the other three were surrounding her legs as if they were planning on sinking their teeth in at any moment like the first one had. As she looked back at the first rat, it turned and looked at her, and when it realized that she could see it, Nicole saw fear wash over its face. It turned around and ran with the others following close behind it.

"You're not going to believe what I just saw," Nicole said. "There were rats. One bit my leg and the others looked like they were getting ready to."

"I've experienced rats before," Trisha explained. "They are spirits that are assigned to discipline people. I don't think that Satan is very happy with you right now for helping me. I'm sorry about that."

"Well, it's not your fault. In fact I'd say that this is confirmation that we're on the right track and the devil is trying to stop us. I'm thankful that the Lord opened my eyes to see what was happening. This isn't the first time I've had pain like this. The Doctor had told me that I had the beginnings of fibromyalgia. Now I know what it really is, and if I have any other pain like this again, I'll know what to do. Right now in Jesus' name I speak to the rats and any other disciplinary spirits. I will not accept discipline from any spirit other than God. You have no authority to discipline me, and in Jesus' name I rebuke you and command you to leave this house and property right now. Jesus, please send your angels to guard us."

Trisha smiled. "There are angels all around your house and the ranch. I saw them when I first drove up." She was quiet for a moment, then said, "I'm thinking about the implications of Python's rule in my life. I've been able to go into churches around the nation and operate under counterfeit spiritual gifts of prophecy and words of knowledge, and have been welcomed and encouraged to use these gifts. I knew they weren't of God, but I just thought I had this special ability. I don't mean to offend you, but the church people I know are fools. They go to church on Sunday and Wednesday nights and live like the devil the rest of the week. I would enter a church service, and I can see now that it was Python that would show me things about people. All I would have to do was to tell someone sitting next to me something about a person on the other side of the room, and before I knew it, they would have me up front speaking words of prophecy and knowledge. It was all a show! I could look around and tell you who was engaged in pornography; who was having an affair and who the other party was. Python must have been especially happy when we encountered ministers and church leaders who were struggling in those areas. I would lay the bait, and sure enough, you'd be surprised at how many would sell their souls to the devil and hire my services. I'm ashamed of it now, but back in the day, I was proud of how many Christians I could take down. Not once in all those years did one person discern that I was operating through witchcraft and demonic wisdom...at least nobody ever confronted me on it or stropped me. That's a sad commentary on the state of the church!"

"Yes it is," Nicole agreed. "The church has become proud, fat and lazy. I think that God is teaching us about the enemy so that we can come to understand who we are up against and how to overcome. You have identified one aspect or function of Python, which is to seduce or draw God's people away from Him, often through sexual sin. I'm wondering if he works with the Jezebel spirit."

Trisha thought about it and said, "I think you're right. She is a very strong religious spirit that does operate under witchcraft and seduction to destroy God's work and His people."

"I'm not sure the seduction is always sexual though," Nicole said. "I think it can include any thing that would entice or pull people away from God. I'm reminded of a woman I knew who operated under what I later came to understand was a Jezebel spirit. Everyone thought she was this awesome Christian...and just for the record, I do believe that she really thought she was too....She would

190

give people scripture verses that she said God had given to her just for them. She would give encouraging words to people that would seem just right for their situation. But she would never pray for them. She was operating in divination and even though she was using scripture, it wasn't from God. When I got to know her more, I saw that she was a controller and she would use God's Word like a whip to manipulate people into her sphere of influence. Those who were close to her had come to avoid her because of her judgmental, critical and controlling attitudes. She had become so overtaken by the spirit that her body was hunched over and she was in severe physical pain. She would call and ask me to pray *for* her but she never wanted me to pray *with* her. Several times I just started to pray right then, but she would become very fidgety and cut my prayer short and come up with some reason why she had to hang up. I fasted and prayed and asked the Lord to show me what this was that was controlling her, and I believe He told me that this was a Jezebel spirit. But what He showed me was a large snake, actually a lot like the one I see in you. In her it had wound itself up and around her whole body, constricting her physically and pulling her body down so that she was unable to stand up straight, and its head was protruding through her face. I wondered what the snake had to do with Jezebel, but now I am thinking that this is a picture of Python and Jezebel functioning together. When I talked to her about this, she got angry and told me never to bring it up again. I wasn't able to pray for her after that. She became a very isolated, sick, lonely woman, and she actually died a few months after that."

Both were quiet and lost in their own thoughts for a moment and then Trisha said, "You said something earlier about relationship problems. That's something that I've always had a problem with. It seems like when I talk with friends, they hear me saying one thing when I mean something completely opposite, like our lines of communication are twisted. I'm always arguing with people and feelings are always getting hurt."

Nicole said, "I think that is one of the things we read about Python.... Yep, it says that one of his goals is to interfere or stop communication with God and with other people. I can see how Python interferes with communication on several levels besides divination. He knows that if there is communication, then there is relationship, and he wants to block relationships. Python causes communication between people to be misconstrued or misunderstood which causes division and strife instead of unity and peace within those relationships. God is all about relationships and unity, and Python is all about isolation and division."

Nicole continued thinking this through. "This must be why he hates prayer and the Word of God so much; they lead us to relationship with Jesus. He twists or perverts the Word of God within a person's mind so that they can not understand it and so that they believe the lie that they are incapable of reading it on their own. I've seen this same thing happen when truth was spoken through sermons or Godly counsel."

Trisha said, "Well that describes me. I haven't been able to read the Bible and understand it or listen to sermons and get anything out of them. I thought it was just me. And then there's all the drama in my relationships! I'm sitting here thinking about all the ways this Python has had a hold on me. Nicole, I want to be free from this. I'm tired of all the relationship misunderstandings and fights that I seem to always be involved in; all the drama. I want to be able to have a close relationship with Jesus and to read the Bible and understand it. I've always thought that it was only understandable to certain people and I wasn't one of those, but I see now that that's a lie and that my mind has been blinded by Python. Can you cast it out?"

Nicole answered, "We can totally do this together with Jesus." Then she added, "But you have loved the perks of Python, Trisha. You must decide where your heart truly lies. Are you willing to renounce the false gifts it gives and the attention and sense of importance that come from those gifts? Are you willing to study the Bible and learn to obey God's voice and none other?"

Trisha thought for a moment and then she smiled. "It's true. I have enjoyed Python's perks. I like how you put that. But I am very serious about being free and following God. So yes, I will renounce everything that has to do with this demon and probably the Jezebel spirit you mentioned earlier too. And I am willing to do whatever it takes to learn to listen to Jesus and to only obey Him."

So they began to pray. God led them to first deal with Trisha's heart.

"Trisha, we know that the things that are physical are reflections of spiritual truth. I was just thinking about how that applies to Python. In the physical realm, pythons love to hide in the dark, in cool, moist places. They like to live close to their food source, and they kill their prey by constriction. I've seen pictures of little children cuddled up with pythons that are larger than they are. They think that their pet is loving them, when in reality it is just absorbing the warmth of their body in a self centered embrace that could quickly become deadly when the snake got hungry. How do you think this applies to Python in the spiritual realm?"

"Well," Trisha pondered, "the place where Python is rooted is in my heart. It was a dark, moist place. It's been dark because Satan's kingdom is darkness and it was moist with sin. It's all cuddled up there but hasn't needed to constrict and eat me because I've been feeding it other food for a long time. Every time I would engage its gifts, abilities, or communication issues that led to broken relationships, I was feeding it with the spiritual blood of others, just like I would feed a mouse or rat to a pet python. As long as it was full, it didn't need to hurt me. Blood flows through my heart, and life is in the blood. Python has been basking and hiding in the blood of my sinful heart and it's been a place of refreshment for him. He's been stroking me with his perks like you said because I've been giving him everything he wants. He's been very happy until now."

"Wow. That is a powerful analogy. What do you think the sin of your heart has been?"

"Pride. I know it's been pride. Can I pray about this right now?"

Nicole smiled and nodded. "Of course!"

"Lord Jesus," Trisha confessed. "Please forgive me for being prideful, for listening to and engaging in Python's purposes and functions. I know that I have caused many people to stumble, and I am so sorry for that. Please forgive me for using divination to destroy Your people and Your church. I don't want the false gifts that Python has given me any more. I only want the true gifts of the Holy Spirit. I choose to renounce those false gifts and abilities and will continue to renounce them instead of engaging them if they show up again. I know they've been familiar to me for so long, so Jesus, please help me to recognize them for what they are. If you want me to make right what I've done, then please show me what to do and I'll do it. Amen."

"Trisha, do you understand soul ties?" Nicole asked.

"Yeah, a little bit. I know that they are invisible spiritual ties between people and that they are bad."

"Not all are bad. God actually created them to be good; to unite or connect people together like in marriage, in parent/child relationships and in godly friendships. It is a joining of the mind, will and emotions that makes husbands and wives 'one flesh,' and that gives parents the connection with their children that allows them to influence or train them until they are of an age where they are responsible for themselves. In godly soul ties, the Holy Spirit is able to be a partner in that relationship as He moves back and forth between the two parties. Satan takes advantage of this spiritual ability in a perverted form. If he can get people to engage in ungodly relationships where soul ties are formed, then demons are able to transfer back and forth between these ties, and gain influence to oppress an unsuspecting target. Sex between unmarried couples is one of the major ways that they are formed and established, along with relationships where there has been abuse, trauma, excessive control and manipulation...."

"Oh great. So like I must have millions of ungodly soul ties. What do we do about that?"

"You confess and renounce them, and then we ask the Lord to break them off of you."

"Let's, do it! Will you help me?"

"Yes. But first, I think you need to renounce the Jezebel spirit since that has been a major influencing factor in seducing Christians sexually, which creates soul ties."

"Yeah. Ok." Trisha began, "Lord Jesus, please forgive me for allowing the Jezebel spirit to use me. I don't want to control and manipulate and seduce Your people anymore. Please forgive me for this. I renounce the Jezebel and Python spirits. I don't want them or their gifts anymore. In Jesus' name, Amen."

Nicole said, "Good Trish. Now you can repeat after me and we'll ask God to break the ungodly soul ties." Trisha nodded, and they began. "Lord Jesus, I am so sorry that I allowed myself to become defiled through sex with so many people, and that through those relationships, I opened myself up to all these ungodly soul ties. I have already confessed my sins and believe that You have forgiven me, but now I am renouncing prostitution and ungodly relationships and I'm asking you to break off the ungodly soul ties between me and all those people I've had sex with. There are too many for me to name or even remember, but You know who they are Jesus. In Jesus' name I take captive every evil spirit that has attached itself to me through all my ungodly relationships and I command every one of you to release me and to go to Jesus' feet to wait for His judgment of you. In Jesus' name I cancel the assignment of every evil spirit in my life, and I release the power of the Holy Spirit to create new Godly assignments for my life. I also command all parts of other people's souls that have joined with mine to go back to their owner, and I call back all the parts of my soul that have been scattered all over the place to return to me so that I can be whole and can become the woman God created me to be. Now Lord Jesus, I ask You to please break off all these ungodly soul ties. I believe You are doing this, and I thank You. I also pray that You will cleanse me from my sin and from theirs by Your precious blood, and that You heal my soul and restore it in Jesus' name. Holy Spirit, please close off all spiritual openings where these soul ties were, and set Your seal upon each one. Amen."

After a moment of silence, Trisha said, "You know what I saw? It was like this ugly spirit with long hair that came up from my stomach and on out of my body through my head and then rode away on a broomstick. Do you think that was Jezebel?"

"Ask Jesus."

Trisha was quiet for a moment, then laughed. "Jesus said that, yep, that witch flew the coupe! I feel so peaceful. I had no idea that I was connected with so many other people and their demons."

"Awesome!" Nicole said. "Thank you Jesus, for releasing Trisha from the Jezebel spirit, but Lord I pray that You will send out an angel after her to capture her and take her to You so that spirit won't be allowed to affect others. Thank you, Jesus. Now we need to take care of the generational curses and soul ties. Are you ready?"

"Yeah. Help me out again, ok?"

"Sure. Lord Jesus, I confess that my family ancestors have participated in witchcraft and sin against You of all kinds. I know that their sin has affected me, and I choose to forgive them. In Jesus' name I renounce their sins. I do not want them to be a part of my life in any way. I ask You Jesus to cancel all curses that have been passed down, and in Jesus' name I command all evil spirits that have attached themselves to me through the soul ties of my ancestors to release me and go to the feet of Jesus to wait for His judgment. Lord Jesus, please break off all ungodly soul ties between my ancestors and me. Please cleanse and heal me with the blood of the Lamb, restore my soul and set your seal upon my heart, mind, will, emotions, spirit and body. In Jesus' name, Amen."

"Trisha, I believe that Python's rights to you have been destroyed! Lord Jesus, is there anything else we need to know or do before we cast out this constrictor?" Nicole prayed.

Trisha cried out, "I see it! It's trying to constrict, but a really big angel with a sword in his hand is stopping it!"

"Is there anything else that comes to your mind that would give Python rights to you and to your heart?"

"Not that I can think of."

"Then it's time to take authority over it and demand that it go."

"Great. Will you do it? I feel like I'm having a hard time focusing."

"In Jesus' name, I bind you Python and I call upon angels of God to punish you if you try to inflict constriction or pain upon Trisha. I release clarity in Trisha's brain and mind.... Is that better?"

"Yes! Thank you Jesus."

"I think Jesus wants to begin by freeing up your heart. I will help you, but you need to take part in this. So repeat after me and add anything else you want to."

"Ok."

"Python, you no longer have rights to Trisha, and we have rights and authority to remove you from her life." Trisha was repeating but making it personal. "So in Jesus' name, we command you to release Trisha's heart and come out of it."

Trisha said, "It's coiling up tighter and squeezing so hard! Ohhh!" She screamed in pain, and before Nicole could even ask for help, she saw an angel take its sword and jab it hard. Python yelled and Trisha screamed in pain again as the demon quickly withdrew itself from her heart. The pain stopped, but the battle was not over. It was easy to trace Python's moves as he left Trisha's heart and wrapped himself around her throat and brain, choking her so that she could barely breathe or talk. She grabbed her throat in an attempt to loosen the invisible constriction, and her eyes began to bulge.

Nicole addressed Python again. "In Jesus' name, I command you to release your hold on Trisha's throat!" He did. Then in one last attempt to keep a hold onto his victim or to damage her, he attacked her head by giving her a terrible headache. Trisha's hands went from her throat to her head, and she groaned in pain.

"In Jesus' name, I command you Python, to release Trisha's brain, head and mind!" He did.

When Trisha was able to speak, Nicole said, "Trish, you need to take authority and command it to leave your body, soul and spirit."

"Gladly!" she responded. "In Jesus' name I command Python to leave my body, soul and spirit and to go to Jesus' feet and wait for His judgment."

Nicole asked, "Do you see, hear, feel or sense anything?"

"The pain is gone and everything is just quiet. I don't know. I'm not sure that it's gone. What do you think? Can it stay if we tell it to leave?"

"It can only stay if it still has some right that it's hanging onto. I don't sense anything one way or another either. Nicole prayed, "Well, Lord Jesus, we would like confirmation that this spirit is gone, and if not, we need You to tell us what to do."

Trisha said, "I feel like we need to take a break."

Nicole agreed. Jake came in and they had a bite to eat. As they were eating, Jesus reminded Nicole of a disagreement that she and Jake had had earlier that week. It hadn't seemed like a big deal at the time and they both had just decided to ignore it with out resolution, but now Nicole knew that she had to ask Jake's forgiveness because it was an open door for Python to cause division within their marriage. God was showing her that before she could effectively minister deliverance to someone else, she needed to have all the holes in her life closed up and sealed.

So after lunch, she asked if she could talk with Jake in the bedroom. She asked his forgiveness for her part and told him that she would willingly and joyfully accept and submit to his decision in the matter.

Jake was a little surprised and said, "Thank you for your trust honey, but why are you bringing this up now?"

"I'm repairing the breaches so that Python can't get into our marriage." She hugged him and said, "I love you!"

"Who's Python?....Oh never mind. I love you too." As Nicole walked out of the bedroom, Jake just shook his head, smiling. Nicole was evidently on the warpath again.

Jo and the ladies went for a brief walk and when they came back, they turned on the worship music. Immediately Trisha began experiencing pain at the base of her neck. As it intensified, Nicole prayed and asked Jesus to show them what was going on.

"I see what looks like a silver cord rooted in the back of your neck and it is stretched out behind you for miles and miles. Do you know what this might mean?" Nicole asked.

Trisha knew immediately what it was. "It's the connection I have with the occult. It connects me with the others and demons go back and forth through it. It's like a phone line where I can hear what they are telling me and vise versa without a phone. It even works kind of like a device that helps me astral project so that I can leave my body and be with them in my spirit."

Nicole was stunned. "Wow! That cord needs to get cut! It is a soul tie with the enemy and you won't be free as long as it's connected to you. Are you willing to renounce and cut off all your involvement with the occult and all your connections and relationships with these ungodly people?"

"I hadn't thought of it like that until now. But yes! I don't want to be in bondage to Satan or to them. I haven't been in contact with them since I became a Christian. I figured that was cutting my ties with them. But now that you mention it, I'm sure they have been using this tie to keep tabs on me. There have been times when I knew one of them was in the room with me and I just ignored them. But every time that's happened, I've had some problems immediately after. I had forgotten about this cord. It's one of the ways they've been able to control me. So please, get if off of me!"

They prayed and asked Jesus what to do. He had Nicole get the anointing oil and anoint the base of Trisha's neck as she confessed her participation and renounced her involvement in Satanism and the occult. Nicole felt silly, but in obedience to the leading of the Holy Spirit, as Trisha was praying, she began a chopping motion with the edge of her open hand against the invisible cord. When Trisha was done, she prayed, "Lord Jesus please sever this silver cord, this ungodly soul tie between Trisha and anyone at the other end of it." Trisha prayed the same. Then all of a sudden, Nicole jumped about a foot in the air as Trisha let out a long and loud scream.

"Are you ok?" Nicole asked as she grabbed Trisha by the shoulders and looked her in the face.

Trisha smiled. "It's gone now! Python's gone and so is the pain in my neck. I saw a huge angel with a huge red sword come and sever that silver cord. And then Jesus told me to scream. When I did, I saw two more large angels come and pick Python up by the head and the tail. They carried it off to a place that looked very barren and isolated. There was a hole in the ground that was covered by a large metal looking grate, and another angel that was there waiting, opened the lid. The other two angels threw Python inside and then they closed the lid. I can still hear him banging around and yelling to be let out, but the angels flew away. There's nobody there for him to talk to! And I hope he never gets out!"

Nicole breathed a sigh of relief. "I thought you were in worse pain. I guess that even though Python didn't have power over you any more, he wouldn't leave until you renounced your association with the occult and that silver cord was broken. How could I have not remembered the importance of renouncing the occult?"

"Python was clouding our minds to that fact, but Jesus didn't let that stop Him!" Trisha said.

Trisha and Nicole spent some time just thanking Jesus for His miraculous deliverance. He told them that they needed to anoint the place on Trisha's neck where the cord had been and to ask for healing and sealing. Healing from the damage done by the enemy, and the sealing of the Holy Spirit.

They both knew that there was more work to be done, but as Trisha tasted freedom, she suddenly realized just how controlled and manipulated she had been. Even though she had known that her gifts and power had been demonic in origin, she had deceptively thought they were her own and now realized that they were also a manipulation of her to get her to do what Python wanted. She loved the choices that were set before her. She opened up the Bible and read with understanding the whole chapter of Psalm 18!

IS was once again raging mad and on the war path! He had been so sure that Python's plan was going to work, and so hopeful the day that Trisha and Nicole had first spoken. Two of his girls were teaming up, and he had been sure that Python would be able to orchestrate a lovely partnership between the two. He was very strong in Trisha, and she was very experienced. He believed that surely he would be able to use her to gain more power over Nicole. At the time, he had been afraid that it was all just too good to be true. And he had been right The Spirit of God and Nicole's love and obedience to her other Master was getting scary, thanks to that bumbling idiot Python! If he didn't come up with something soon, he knew he'd be in danger of loosing both of these women.

He knew that a meeting had been set up between Nicole and Trisha for another deliverance session. Both were fasting and praying, asking God to reveal the things hidden in the darkness. IS hated those two keys with a passion, for prayer and fasting seemed to open the floodgates of heavenly Light! And he hated to admit it, but he was powerless against the Light. As he contemplated his options, he decided that he would expose some of the lesser gods that were attached to Trisha in hopes of distracting them and getting them off his trail. Then if he had to, he would sacrifice another of his underlings, albeit a very powerful one. Leviathan, with his seven heads, would keep them busy while he tried to think of a way to avoid detection himself; and hopefully he'd be able to plot a plan to destroy Nicole. That detestable girl was fast becoming a very big threat to his kingdom. Such a disappointment! Such a waste!

CHAPTER 15
BITTERNESS, FORGIVENESS AND HARLOTRY

True to his word, as the "day of deliverance" (that's what Nicole and Trisha were calling it) grew closer, IS began to slowly reveal the lesser gods that held a place of influence in Trisha's life. He had Nicole chasing Marduk, a Babylonian god; Mot, the god of death; Asherah, an underling of Baal and companion of Jezebel; Molech, god of the Ammonites along with Chemosh, the Moabite god who both required human sacrifice; Orion, who in cases where salvation occurs, would promote deliverance to a certain extent, then rise up with overwhelming bondage causing hopelessness and despair, rendering the Christian useless; Osirus, Isis, Horus…

So many demons had been revealed as Nicole prepared to go through the process of deliverance with Trisha. When Trisha arrived, she was amazed as Nicole exposed them and they readily came out. Well, not all responded without a fight. At one point, Trisha's mind and body were taken over by a spirit that caused her to enter a trance like state. She sat unresponsive to anything Nicole said or did. It didn't even respond to the blood of Jesus or commands of authority in Jesus' name that had always worked in the past. After several hours of this, in frustration Nicole finally asked the Lord how to break the spell. The only thought that came to her sounded crazy, but she was desperate. So she picked up a Bible and in the physical realm she lightly bashed it down on top of Trisha's head; but in the spiritual realm it was a very heavy bashing. Immediately the demon released her and she came to.

The weekend was almost over and yet Nicole knew that something wasn't right. Trisha didn't really feel any better than she did when she came. So they fasted and prayed, and by the next morning, she knew they had been duped.

She woke Trisha up and told her what had happened. "You mean to tell me that we went through all that for nothing?" Trish groaned.

"Well, not for nothing. It was very important for you to repent of the sins that opened the door for these demons, but even though they have gone, until we bind and eliminate the strongman, he'll be trying to wear you down through constant onslaughts of temptation until you open the door for them again through sin. Then he'll let them back in or invite new ones to take up their function."

"I thought that the Holy Spirit had sealed my body, soul and spirit against them, and that Jesus would keep them away from me." Trisha said.

"He has," Nicole answered. "But because this strongman is relentless and the demons and their ways are so familiar to you, they will do all in their power to cause you to stumble. You have your work cut out for you Trisha. I've often found that deliverance is the easy part compared to the work that comes after."

Trisha snorted, "You call that easy?"

"No, but the real battle is just beginning. You will need to be just as relentless in pursuing your relationship with Jesus. The first step is to position yourself in His presence, as close to Jesus' heart as you can get every day and every night, just like Samuel did in 1 Samuel 3:1. He slept next to the ark of God which housed God's presence. You do this by making time to worship, reading the Bible, praying and including Jesus in every aspect of your day. You need a renewed mind, Trish. That means that you begin to think about things the way Jesus does. It will probably mean that you will have choices to make...to give in to old habits or to change the way you do things. You may have to do some radical amputation such as cutting off certain ungodly relationships, or refusing to go to certain places that you used to go to. You can know what you need to cut out of your life by asking yourself if that person or thing helps you move closer to Jesus or distracts and moves you away from Him. To renew your mind means to find out what God thinks, then do it instead of what you used to do. That's the process of putting off the old, renewing your mind, and putting on the new like Ephesians 4:22-24 says."

"Well it's a good thing that I can read and understand the Bible then. I just wish this was over," she sighed.

Nicole responded, "Yes it is. But don't be discouraged. For some reason, God allowed us to see these underlings. Maybe God is teaching us that there is a process here where I thought we could just go at it and be done with it. Maybe there are layers that need to be uncovered and dealt with. I do feel that the enemy has been having fun sending me on a wild goose chase of uncovering insignificant demons in the hopes that because they are so infamous that we will think we've got the big guy, then you could just go right back into bondage after today. But God has shown us the enemy's schemes and He will be faithful complete the work He has begun in you; it just might be a longer process than we first thought. I'm not sure what or who the strongman is yet, but I know that the Lord will reveal him in His time. Trisha, I'm sorry that I led you to believe that it would be over with after today. I'm in school here, and I am learning too."

"I understand process," Trish said. "Even though I wish it could just be over and I could wake up tomorrow morning a perfect Christian, I didn't get into all this mess in one night and it won't all be gone in one night."

Nicole smiled. "Thanks for understanding. Let's talk to Jesus."

So they put on some worship music and cried out to Jesus. Trisha realized that they needed to bind seeker, scanner and eavesdropping spirits who were basically spies for Satan. Nicole had never heard of this before, but God revealed that these were part of Satan's ranks and needed to be banned.

This seemed to be key because the resistance she had felt before disappeared and the presence of God became so real it was almost tangible. In the spiritual realm, Nicole and Trisha both began seeing a dragon looking creature with more than one head that was thrashing about.

"Lord Jesus, what is this?" Nicole asked.

Trisha spoke the name as Nicole heard the name in her mind. "It's Leviathan," Trisha declared.

"*Nicole,*" the Lord said. "*Leviathan is not the highest strongman, but it is a layer that will uncover the most supreme principality and strongman in Trisha's life. There is one that is hiding in the depths even more so than this serpent. He is hoping that because Leviathan is so big, you will think you are done when he is gone and that he will go undetected. But while Leviathan is a major principality that must be removed, he is also a decoy and removing him will not be the end. You will recognize this strongman and I will show you things that you must know. However, now is not the time to engage in this battle. Go and prepare yourselves. Wait for my direction concerning this matter.*"

Nicole didn't know why they couldn't just bind the strongest strongman and all the others under him and kick them all out at once. But what she did know was that if this was the way God wanted it done, then this was how they would do it.

Trisha went home and for the next several weeks, Nicole fasted and prayed over her and this principality called Leviathan. She searched the scriptures and the Lord revealed its nature, character and function. He told her that she was not to deal with this at the ranch as she had before. This time she was to go to Trisha's, and she was to take help.

"Lord Jesus," Nicole prayed, "I'm fine with going to Trisha's as long as Jake is ok with it, but who do you want to go with me? I'm clueless as to who could do this!"

Nicole spoke to Jake, and he is the one who suggested Karen. Karen was the friend who had been at the prayer group the night God gave her the red running shoes. Nicole called her right away, explained the situation and asked her to pray about it.

Karen didn't even hesitate. "I've never done anything like that before, but yes I'll pray about it. I'd be glad to go with you if that's the Lord's plan."

The following week, after being prayed over and sent out by Karen's prayer group, they arrived at Trisha's apartment. As planned, they had not told her the specific time or day that they would be arriving so that the demons would be unable to hinder them.

Trisha was surprised, and yet eager to get rid of this monster in her life. She and Karen hit it off right away which was a confirmation that they were on the right path. They turned on worship music and spent time worshipping God. When Nicole felt the time was right, they took communion. Trisha didn't have a problem with the bread, the body of Christ; but when it came time to drink the juice, the blood of Jesus, she, or rather something within her, refused.

Nicole spoke to the principality. "I know who you are. You are Leviathan and you are history! But for now, in the name of Jesus, you will go down. I want to speak with Trisha."

Nothing changed. Leviathan sat there inside Trisha's body refusing to move or to speak. Nicole said, "In the name of Jesus, I command you to look at me." Trisha's eyes turned to Nicole's with such defiance in them that she knew this was the enemy. She continued, "Trisha is going to take communion. She is going to drink Jesus' blood, and you can either let her come back and drink it, or I will call upon a large holy angel to come and pour it down your throat...seven times in fact, for your seven heads! It's up to you."

Immediately Leviathan growled and then Trisha was back. Nicole handed her the cup. "Trisha, drink this blood of Jesus quickly." She did, and then Nicole revealed the first plan of attack that was a complete surprise to Leviathan. Jesus had shown her that the first layer that had to be removed was the Spirit of Harlotry, because it had opened the door for Leviathan. If it was not removed, once

Leviathan was gone, Harlotry would open the door for it again and it would come right back.

Trisha asked, "Isn't Harlotry the same thing as Jezebel? I thought we got rid of her."

"Good question," Karen answered. "I believe that Jezebel may have been a part of this spirit because I'm beginning to see how interconnected all of Satan's kingdom is. But I think that Jezebel was a power behind Harlotry, like a soldier is the enforcing power behind the prince. Ephesians 6:12 talks about principalities and powers. Harlotry is like a prince with Jezebel as the power or enforcer of his power. Leviathan is like a prince with Harlotry as the power or enforcer of his power...and so on, right up the ladder of power to the top prince, Satan."

"That makes sense."

Nicole said, "I believe that the key to dealing with this spirit is in Hosea." As they began digging into the Word, they recognized a list of things that described the spirit of Harlotry: *adultery, guilt, shame, idolatry/joined to idols, lack of knowledge, sin against God, forsaking the Lord, stubborn, drunkard, love shame more than glory, defiled, don't know the Lord, pride (self loving, self focused, following God for what He can do for them without thought of love for Him), faithless to the Lord, runs from God to a place expecting life but is a place of death, born alien children, a desolation, oppressed, crushed in judgment, determined to go after vanity/pride, sick, wounded, unable to be cured or healed, evildoers, wicked, destruction, rebellion, lies/deceit, devise evil, a useless vessel, religious spirit/sacrifice, forgets Maker/distractions and materialism, loves money, place of death (Memphis) while running from God, iniquity, hatred, caught in a snare (enslaved), corrupt, yoked to demons (Baal) and became detestable, false heart (can't serve two masters), loves to oppress, to sin and continue to sin, trust in self rather than God, violence, bloodguilt, fallow ground, doesn't recognize God's love, compassion and help.*

The list seemed endless, but as they looked at each thing, Trisha could identify with many. Then God gave them hope. In Hosea 2:15, the Lord said, *"I will ... make the Valley of Achor [Trouble] a **door of hope.**"* YES!

Other places throughout the book they found keys for freedom. *Acknowledge guilt and sin; seek the Lord and his face; return to the Lord; press on to know the Lord; understand and discern these ways of the Lord, live under His shadow (in His presence) and walk in them.* Basically if she would confess, repent, return, renounce, seek God, love God and live with Him and for Him, then in His grace, He would *bind up and heal her, even though she had been unfaithful; He would be faithful and sure to come and bring refreshment to her; she would be able to receive His love and would flourish as a garden; He would answer her call and look after her.*

Trisha was quiet for a moment, and then said, "I want to make sure I understand specifically what all these words mean. I've heard the words 'confess, repent and renounce' before, but I guess I've never really thought about them."

"I'm glad you want to think this through," Nicole said, "because having a clear understanding will help you to make Godly choices in the future. Let's start with a few other foundational words, like salvation."

"I know that salvation means to ask Jesus to come into my heart and forgive my sins. I did that three years ago."

"Trisha, why did you want to be saved?" Nicole asked.

"Because I was into so many bad things I knew that if I kept on, I would die and I knew I wouldn't go to heaven. I guess I was scared," Trisha said.

"I think a lot of people want salvation so that they can go to heaven when they die like you did. While that's a true motivation, there's so much more to God's plan of salvation than that. It's all about love. God loves every single person on this earth so much that even though we all deserve death because of sin, He wants to forgive us so that He can have a relationship with us. Us! Sinners! And He doesn't want to wait till we get to heaven; He wants that relationship with us now, before we die. That's why He sent His Son Jesus, who willingly came to earth as a man so that He could pay the price for our sins through dying on the cross and shedding His blood. Through the power of His blood, He can forgive our sins, and we can have a pure, holy love relationship with the Father."

Trisha contemplated, "So salvation is about God loving me and wanting a relationship with me, but my sin gets in the way of that. When I choose to ask Jesus to forgive me, then I am saved from my sin, washed clean and get a whole new start. Like all my debts are paid in full. Isn't there a verse that says He removes my sins as far away from me as the east is from the west?"

"Yes, that's Psalm 103:12. This experience of salvation from sin is the beginning of a whole new life! And that's because God transfers you from Satan's kingdom to God's Kingdom. My friend Lynn says that salvation is the best and greatest gift ever!"

Karen said, "I agree. Before I was saved, I was just dissatisfied with life. I wasn't a bad person and hadn't done a lot of really bad things, I just felt as if I were wandering around in life with no purpose, no satisfaction, no real love, joy or peace. I was looking for it, but it wasn't in relationships with guys, it wasn't in the hippie movement, it wasn't in the bar scene, it wasn't even in most churches I had been to. When I had finally exhausted all my own resources and was ready to give up hope of ever finding what ever it was I was looking for, one day I just cried out, 'If there's a God out there, then I want to know!' The next day I was walking my dog in the park and a fellow dog walker asked if I knew Jesus. I said, 'Not really,' and she handed me a little booklet called the Romans Road of Salvation.[2] I went home and looked up the verses and it was like Jesus came to me and just held out His arms. I remembered John 3:16 and 17, verses I had memorized as a child. *"For God so loved the world that He gave His only begotten Son, that whoever believes in Him shall not perish but have everlasting life. For God did not send His Son into the world to condemn the world, but that the world through Him might be saved."* I suddenly knew that God had answered my cry and was showing me that He was real and that He cared about me."

"Did you have a hard time giving up all the things that were a part of your old life?" Trisha asked.

"It was a process," Karen said. "I didn't just change overnight, but I was different on the inside. I still went to the bar with my friends, but after a while I just didn't like going and I began to look for a church where I could make new friends that could help me understand more about Jesus."

Nicole said, "That reminds me of the fairy tale of the 'Princess and the Pea.'"

"I don't think I remember that one," Trisha said.

Karen laughed. "A King and Queen were looking for a suitable wife, a princess, for their son, and so they set up a 'pea test.' The idea was that they would invite young women that they thought might be acceptable to come and spend the night at the palace, one at a time. Unbeknownst to each woman, there was a pea that was placed under the mattress of their bed because only a true princess would have the sensitivity to identify such an offensive obstruction. In the morning, they would ask each young lady how they had slept, and if they said, 'Wonderful,' they were dismissed. One morning a young lady finally answered, 'I slept terrible! I couldn't get comfortable and tossed and turned all night long. It felt like there was a rock under my mattress.' She had passed the pea test and it was determined that she was a real princess, qualified to marry the prince."

"That's right," Nicole said. "This is a perfect illustration of what sin in our lives does when we are living in the presence of God. The things we used to be ok with but are offensive to God become uncomfortable and even distressing to us as we become more like Jesus, and the things that offend Him will begin to offend us as well."

"I hadn't thought if it like that before," Karen said, "but that is kind of how the process went for me."

Trisha said, "That's a great story and I can see how that applies to some areas of my life, but there are other areas that I just can't seem to change, even when I know they are wrong and want them to change. Even God hasn't changed them when I've asked Him to."

"Well salvation is the first step in an ongoing process of being changed into the people God created us to be. We must also be saved from our own sin nature and the power of the devil if we are going to live in freedom and relationship with God," Nicole said. "I guess that in order to really understand salvation, we have to understand sin."

"Oh, I understand sin too well!" Trisha said. "It's all the bad things I've done."

"Again, that's part of it," Nicole confirmed. "Sin usually begins with our thoughts. When Adam and Eve listened to the lies of the serpent, deception closed in upon their minds. When they chose to believe the devil instead of God in their thoughts, that's when sin or darkness entered and truth became unclear, foggy. You see it wasn't' just the action of disobedience, it was the turning of their minds away from the truth to the lies of the enemy that opened the door for sin because 'sin hinders the perception of truth'.[3] Once their minds were deceived, they acted on the lies and disobeyed God."

Trisha said, "So you're saying that my perception of truth has been all messed up because I've believed Satan's lies which led me into sin."

"Basically, yes. But Trish, Jesus redeemed you, bought you back again and now you are twice His! You have His mind to think His thoughts, to know His truth, to choose His ways; and you have His heart so that you can love Him in return."

"This doesn't mean that we'll be perfect," Karen said, "We will still sin, but we won't want to practice it. We'll want to walk in the Light so that we stay in fellowship or relationship with God. The book of 1 John chapters 1 & 2 in the New Testament explain this concept better than I can. I think it's important to understand that living rightly with Jesus isn't possible on our own, no matter how hard we try. It's only possible with the help of the Holy Spirit."

"That's so right!" Nicole said. "One of the Holy Spirit's jobs is to let us know when we have stepped outside of God's Light, and then our job is to repent or turn around from the way you were going. That's what 'repent' means. To change one's mind; to be sorrowful over the sins of the past; to hate or to be repulsed by them so much that there is a turning from them;[4] a change of the mind, will, emotions and the actions from one direction to another. From the darkness back to the Light."

"Oh great!" Trisha exclaimed. "I've been in that cycle forever. I get transferred into the Light and then I mess up and go back to the darkness, then I tell God I'm sorry and He transfers me to the Light and then I go back to the darkness...."

"Well first of all," Nicole said, "Once you have been transferred into God's Kingdom, you belong there, just like a child belongs to the family he was born or adopted into; and just because you step out into the darkness like a rebellious child doesn't necessarily mean that you have left God's family. God understands why you've been flip flopping, and has been waiting for the time when He will help you to understand so that you can make different choices and get out of that cycle. When there is a sin-confess, sin-confess pattern, it usually means that there is either a lack of surrender to God or there is demonic bondage. Or both."

"Earlier you said, confess, repent, and...I can't remember the other word?" Trisha asked.

"Renounce." Nicole explained, "Renouncing is a part of confession and repentance at a deeper level. It goes to the root which is usually a belief problem in the mind or heart, and often there is a demon that has attached itself to the lie or the sin. Our thoughts are like houses and will either allow God or Satan to live in them. If we believe a

213

lie, we are allowing Satan to have a place or stronghold in our minds. Since we usually act on what we believe, those lies will influence our choices and behavior. Even when we identify sinful behavior and confess it, if we don't recognize and renounce the lie, we'll continue to sin because Satan still has a home in those thoughts; and those houses or lies are usually buried pretty deeply and heavily guarded by demons who want to keep us from knowing the truth. This can cause the cycle you were talking about."

"Thank God for the Holy Spirit who reveals the things hidden in the darkness!" Karen said. "So basically, renouncing is the process of taking back ground gained by the enemy through identifying those areas we have turned over to him so that we can break his bondage."

"Yes," Nicole replied. "And once we have identified and renounced the lies, then we need to identify and renounce the things we have loved that are part of our old sin nature or habits and that are not part of God's Kingdom. As long as we love the sin, even if we renounce the lie and get rid of the demon, it will come right back and bondage will continue. We have to be willing to relinquish (give up, surrender) and refuse to continue acting out the sin any longer; to loosen ourselves from its grasp, cut it off, give it up, reject it. These are often idols of our hearts and if we want to be free, we must be willing to put them to death in our lives, to tell them to 'Be gone!' Galatians 2:20 and Colossians 3 talk about this. Proverbs 28:13 says, *"He who covers his sins will not prosper, but whoever **confesses and forsakes** them will have mercy."* Once we renounce the lie and the sin, then we can renounce the demons that were holding onto the sin and they will have to go and we will be free to follow Jesus. When we do our part, then the Holy Spirit will do His part. He'll help us and empower us to walk in truth and freedom from sin."

"I do want to be free. I know I'm saved and I am willing to confess, repent and renounce. I just hope I do this right," Trisha said.

214

Nicole and Karen stood up and laid hands on Trisha. "None of us get it right all the time. God looks at our hearts and covers our mistakes and sin with His righteousness. Remember this isn't about following laws or rules, it's about Love. It's about God's Love reaching every part of our spirit, soul and body. We can't change ourselves, but as we surrender to Him, His love affects our old nature and we begin to change to become more like Him."

Trisha laughed. "I want to be able to pass the 'pea test!"

"Amen!" both ladies joined her laughter. Then they began to intercede for Trisha.

The Holy Spirit brought conviction to Trisha and her heart was broken in a good way, just as a broken leg that had healed wrong would need to be re-broken so that it could be set right. She began to realize how she had rejected God and rebelled against Him so completely in her life. She began confessing and repenting which was totally not in Leviathans plans! Suddenly Trisha began screaming in pain and holding onto her legs.

"What is that?" Nicole looked to see what Karen was pointing at. There was something moving through Trisha's legs with an up and down movement like a sea serpent would move. It was causing sever pain, and Karen got the anointing oil and began to rub them. Immediately, the Holy Spirit showed Nicole that Leviathan was trying to cause a distraction to avoid the removal of Harlotry, and that she was to bind it.

"In the name of Jesus of Nazareth, I plead the blood of Jesus over Trisha's body and her legs. I command you serpent Leviathan to be still! You will not inflict any more pain in Trisha, and if you do, I declare that the holy angels of God will turn the pain you pour out back upon your own self and will increase it 10 times." As Nicole declared this last statement, all movement and pain in Trisha's legs stopped.

"Leviathan is trying to distract you away from the deliverance of Harlotry, Trish. We must do this now."

Knowing that the Spirit of Harlotry had to be uprooted through forgiveness as well as repentance, Nicole asked, "Will you accept God's mercy and forgiveness for your sins?"

Trisha looked at Nicole with sorrow in her eyes. "I want to, but I don't deserve His love. You don't know all the things I've done. Maybe this is all a hopeless dream and I'm just wasting your time. I'm not worth your time."

"Trisha, look at me," Nicole commanded. "You are listening to the spirits of Condemnation, Guilt, Shame and Self Pity. Why did Jesus die on the cross?"

Trisha looked away and didn't answer.

"Look at me Trisha and answer my question now!"

Trisha looked back at Nicole, then dropped her eyes in shame. "Because He wanted to forgive sins."

"Ok, yes. Whose sins?"

"The worlds."

"Specifically Trisha. Whose sins?"

"Yours."

"Yes, and who else's?"

In a very small voice Trisha said, "Mine."

"YES! And why would Jesus want to forgive your sins?"

"I don't know."

Nicole knew that she needed to proclaim truth in order to be set free. "Yes you do. Look at me and tell me."

"I can't."

Nicole said in a quiet but authoritative voice, "By the power of the blood of the Lamb and the authority of the Holy Spirit, in the name of Jesus, the Son of God, I bind Belial and all of your cohorts of Worthlessness, Guilt and Shame, and command you to be silent! And in Jesus' name I call upon and release the Spirit of Truth." Then she said, "Now Trisha, answer my question."

Trisha looked a bit confused and asked, "What question?"

"Why would Jesus want to forgive your sins?"

Nicole and Karen were amazed at the transformation as she began to smile and in a child-like voice she said, "Because He loves me!"

They all began laughing with joy at the revelation of God's love for Trisha.

After they took a short break, Trisha renounced the Spirit of Belial as she realized how much he had been influencing her concept of self and how it had kept her from knowing God's love for her. And then Nicole came back to the question that had led them to the recognition of Belial. "Trisha, will you accept God's love, grace, mercy and forgiveness for your sins?"

She smiled, closed her eyes and said, "Jesus, I don't know why You love me, but I accept the truth that You do. I want to thank You for dying on the cross so that you could forgive my sins. Thank You for Your grace and mercy. I know that I don't deserve it, but You gave it anyways and I accept them. I accept Your love and forgiveness."

"That is beautiful Trish," Nicole said as she squeezed her hand. "There is one other question that has to be answered in order to destroy the rights of Harlotry and remove him from your life."

Trisha made a silly face and Nicole asked, "Will you choose to forgive yourself?"

The expression on Trisha's face transformed again from one of silliness to one of seriousness. She was quiet for a moment, then said, "I know I should, but truthfully, I'm not sure that I can."

Nicole knew that she needed a true understanding of forgiveness if she was going to be free and stay free from these evil spirits, because Bitterness was rooted in Defilement, and Defilement would reopen the door for Harlotry at some point.

"Ok then, let's think about forgiving others," Nicole suggested. "Jesus, I ask that you would bring to mind the people that Trisha has anger, hatred or bitterness towards."

Trisha's face twisted in a look of disgust. "You mean that I have to forgive all the people who abused me my whole life? That would take a million years!"

"Well, we'll trust Jesus to help us get it done quickly, but yes you do. Trisha, I want to share what I've learned about forgiveness, and maybe it will help you with this process, ok?"

Trisha nodded her head and propped pillows up behind her on the sofa, trying to get comfortable.

"First, we need to understand why Jesus told us to forgive, and then we'll talk about what forgiveness is and isn't.

"There are several reasons we need to forgive others. Jesus made it very clear that we are to forgive people for the wrong that they've done against us, and that if we don't forgive, we will not be forgiven. Our forgiveness is conditional upon us forgiving others."

"Oh great!" was Trisha's response. "I don't really have a choice then, do I?"

Nicole just smiled and said, "Forgiveness is a process. It takes time to work through everything involved and at first it may seem overwhelming or like it's impossible. It's true that if we want God to forgive us that we need to forgive others, but there are a lot of misunderstandings about what forgiveness is and isn't. That's why I want to help you understand what God is requiring of us."

Nicole had Trisha look up Matthew 6:14 and Matthew 18:21-35, scriptures that taught this principle.

"Another reason to forgive is that healing and forgiveness are connected. Most often, the reason we need to forgive is because someone has done something against us that caused us pain of some kind, physical, emotional or mental. Pain is one of Satan's biggest doors of opportunity that he uses to ensnare us. Anger is often a response to pain, so he waits for our natural God-given emotion of anger to rise, and then demons of Offense, Pride, Resentment and Unforgiveness begin their job of twisting

218

our minds to believe their lies. If we take their bait, then Bitterness takes root in our soul which is like poison that affects every area of our lives. Our spirit, mind, will, emotions and body are all connected, and if our spirit is out of line with God's Spirit through bitterness, we may experience mental torment or illness, emotional turmoil, things like fear, anxiety and depression, or maybe even physical sickness or disease. Not all of these are tied to spiritual issues, but many times they are, and when we pray for healing without dealing with the spiritual root, we wonder why God doesn't answer our prayer. When we forgive, we are pulling out the spiritual root of Bitterness and then we can pray for healing. Those prayers that were hindered by Bitterness can then be answered and the Holy Spirit is free to work in our spirit, soul and body, bringing healing and restoration."

"You mean like maybe some of my physical problems are because I have bitterness, anger and hatred in my heart; and that if I forgive, then God will heal me?" Trisha asked hopefully.

"Yep. I can't tell you that God will heal you of everything, but I can tell you that if your problems are rooted in bitterness, when you truly forgive, those infirmities and torments will no longer have a right to inflict you with their poison. Then you can cast out the demons causing the problems and pray for healing," Nicole answered. "I heard someone once say that 'bitterness is like swallowing poison and expecting it to kill the other person.' Bitterness doesn't destroy the one we are angry with, it destroys us."

She continued, "Also, when we forgive, our relationship with Jesus is unhindered and He is then able to release joy and the power of His Holy Spirit into our lives. This transforms everything! It changes the way we perceive others because then we can see them through God's eyes and with His heart, and then we are able to love instead of hate. That's the power of the renewed mind."

Nicole could tell that Trisha was engaging in what she was saying. "Satan really hates forgiveness because it totally breaks his strongholds over us. You see, bitterness is more than just an emotion. It is also a spiritual principality or strongman that is bent on devouring any one who welcomes it, just like cancer devours the body, or like poison that spreads through the body and then kills it.

"In fact, the Bible uses another word to describe bitterness. **Wormwood** (Strong's Concordance, H3939). The Hebrew root of that word means to curse. There are often parallels between physical truths and spiritual truths, and in the physical world, wormwood is a plant that has a bitter smell as well as taste. It is poisonous and can be deadly. It grows well in poor, dry soil, and once established, it will take over. In the spiritual world, I believe that the representative of wormwood is the Spirit of Bitterness. Four times in the New Testament the word 'bitterness' is used to mean, *'Extreme wickedness; bitter root producing bitter fruit'* (Strong's G 4088), which implies that it is passed on or transferred.

"In the spiritual realm, Wormwood's properties are similar to the plant's properties in the physical. Allowing bitterness in our lives is like planting or giving a place to the Spirit of Bitterness who then bears its bitter, deadly fruit and claims more and more control until it rules us and tries to spread its curse to those around us.

"Bitterness may begin as feelings of unforgiveness, anger or resentment, but if we allow those feelings to remain and nourish them instead of rejecting and renouncing them, they open the door to the Spirit of Bitterness or Wormwood, a powerful ruling evil spirit whose function is to spread destruction through bitterness and hatred. It invites thoughts of criticism, judgment, revenge, and maybe even violence and murder or death into our minds, hoping that we will listen and act on those thoughts. It nurses grudges and feeds pride so that restitution is not an option.

"Bitterness can also be passed down through family bloodlines, and when that is the case, generational curses need to be broken as well. This involves forgiving our ancestors for the sins they committed that opened the door to this principality, for passing it on to us, and then renouncing that Spirit of Bitterness and asking Jesus to reverse the curse."

"Wow!" Trisha responded. "That's scary. It describes my life and my family. It probably has been passed down, but I know I am also bitter toward a lot of people because of what they've done to me. So does that mean that I also have the Spirit of Bitterness? I'm more of a mess than I thought!"

"We all are," Nicole laughed. "But thank God that by Jesus' blood, we can be free immediately of the strongholds of the devil. The first thing is to recognize the problem, so thank You Jesus for helping Trisha to identify a root of unforgiveness in her life."

She continued, "Trish, forgiveness is a Kingdom Key and has great power and authority behind it. To forgive basically means to pardon, release, send away, let go, cancel, cut loose or to be set free from a bond or connection with those who have knowingly or unknowingly caused you pain, offended you, mistreated or abused you or something or someone you care about. Hanging onto bitterness can be compared to being hung up on someone else's hook. When we forgive, it's like we are cutting ourselves loose from a hook that's been binding us. We will still carry the wounds they've inflicted, but we won't be under their control. And once we forgive them, then we can pray for healing of those wounded places, and God will heal from the inside out. There may always be scars, but they will no longer cause us pain."

Trisha interjected, "But those people are so bad! You have no idea what they did to me. They don't deserve to be forgiven!"

"I understand how bad they are more than you think," Nicole answered. "But that's not the issue.

Forgiving doesn't mean that they are 'getting away with something.' When you choose to forgive them, it releases them from your hook, which is really hurting you, not them, and turns them over to God's hook. You can't change them, but God can. They will have to be accountable to God for their actions, and He's the faithful One who has the power and ability to change hearts and to judge."

Trisha was thinking about this and Nicole continued. "Forgiveness is choosing not to hold someone's sin against them anymore by making a choice of the will, not the emotions. Trish, you will never feel like forgiving. No one ever does. It has to be a decision you make with your will out of obedience to God no matter you feel. Here's the thing. Neil Anderson says you are going to live with the consequences of these other people's sins regardless whether you forgive or not. The choice you have to make is how you are going to live with those consequences. You'll either live in the 'bondage of bitterness or in the freedom of forgiveness', as Neil Anderson points out in his Steps to Freedom in Christ.[5] I heard someone else say that 'forgiveness doesn't change history or undo what has actually happened, but it changes the present so that our future is undamaged by what has happened in the past.'"

Trisha smiled. "I like that." Then with an expression of anticipation she asked, "So can we just tell the Spirit of Bitterness to go now? Because I just realized that I'm tired of it and I don't want it anymore. It feels like a heavy weight that I've been carrying around and I didn't even know it!"

Nicole smiled as she asked, "Are you ready to choose to forgive those you have been bitter towards? Because as long as you harbor bitterness and unforgiveness in your heart, the Spirit of Bitterness has rights to stay and it won't do any good to tell it to go. I think we just need to take a minute and pray."

The three ladies got down on their knees while the worship music was playing softly in the background. No one prayed out loud, but silent cries were heard in the spiritual realm.

After a few minutes, Trisha looked up and said, "Oh Wow!"

"What is it?" Karen asked. "What do you see?"

"I see myself sitting on a chair and there's a demon standing behind me. I know this is Wormwood. His skin is white like someone who's been dead a long time and has no color in their flesh, and it's wrinkled like a dried up old raison. He has his right hand on my head and his left hand has gone through my back and grabbed hold of my heart. And I smell him! He stinks like a filthy outhouse or dirty diapers! Oh gross!"

Nicole and Karen laughed. "That's a perfect picture of bitterness," Karen said.

"Quick!" Trisha begged. "Let's get rid of this thing."

"Lord Jesus," Nicole prayed. "I ask in Jesus' name that you will show Trisha who she needs to forgive."

Trisha immediately said, "I see a very long cord stretching out from the demon that's holding onto me. It goes so far that I can't see the end of it. I think it is the generational soul tie of Bitterness."

"Then in Jesus' name confess those sins of your ancestors and renounce them."

After she had done this, Trisha said, "Hey, I see a really big angel with a sword in his hand and he's cutting that cord.....Oh my goodness! I feel like the demon lost some of his power. He looked surprised and turned his head around to see what was happening and now he's raging mad!"

Nicole prayed, "Lord Jesus we ask You to protect Trisha from the rage of Wormwood. I ask You to send angels to restrain him while we work through this process of forgiving."

Trisha smiled, and with relief in her voice she said, "I see them. There's four angels surrounding it and they are restraining it."

"Ok," Nicole said. "You need to allow Jesus to help you know who you need to forgive."

Immediately Trisha started praying. "Lord Jesus please forgive me for being angry and bitter. I don't want this demon, so please help me to forgive..."

Nicole interrupted, "Say I choose to forgive, not help me to forgive..."

"I choose to forgive..." and she began to name people and the specific things they had done against her. After about ten minutes, she stopped and waited a moment then said, I think that's all. So now can we tell it to go?"

"Lord Jesus," Nicole asked, "Is there anything else we need to know before we command this principality to go?" As soon as she asked, she knew that there were two other things Trisha had to do.

She asked, "Is there anyone you have wronged that you need to ask forgiveness from? We have been working from the viewpoint of you extending forgiveness toward those who wronged you; but the other side of that is to consider who you need to seek forgiveness from."

Trisha's face fell in condemnation. "I've hurt more people than I could even begin to count, and there's no way that I could ever even find most of them to ask their forgiveness."

"Look at me Trish," Nicole said. The pain her eyes brought tears of compassion to Nicole's. "There is no condemnation for those who are in Christ Jesus. And in Jesus' name I bind the Spirit of Condemnation and shut the mouth of the accuser of the brethren...in this case the sistern...no that doesn't sound right..." The tension broke as they all laughed and then Nicole continued.

"Trisha, the reason it's important for you to deal with this side of forgiveness is not to cause guilt, but to recognize the ways that you have sinned through the conviction of the Holy Spirit so that you can repent and be forgiven. 2 Corinthians 7:10 says, '*For godly sorrow produces repentance leading to salvation, not to be regretted; but the sorrow of the world produces death.*' This is talking about the two kinds of guilt, conviction and condemnation. Godly sorrow leads to salvation and abundant life because it restores the relationship with God that was broken through sin. Worldly sorrow bogs you down with feelings of guilt, shame, hopelessness, blame and spins you into a downward spiral that eventually ends in death. The first step is to ask Jesus to forgive you for hurting others. Will you do that?"

She didn't even answer, she just began to pray, confessing her sin and humbly asking for forgiveness. She claimed the promise of 1 John 1:9 that says when we confess our sins, He is faithful and just to forgive us our sins and to cleanse us from all unrighteousness.

When Trisha was done praying, Nicole said, "The other reason you need to be willing to ask forgiveness of those you hurt, intentionally or unintentionally, is because God is all about restoration of broken relationships, not just with Him, but with the people in our lives. Romans 12:18 says, '*If it is possible, as much as depends on you, live peaceably with all men.*' And Matthew 5:23-24 that says, '*Therefore if you bring your gift to the altar, and there remember that your brother has something against you, leave your gift there before the altar, and go your way. First be reconciled to your brother, and then come and offer your gift.*'"

Trisha expressed concern. "I know that at least one person hates me so much that even if I went to them and begged them to forgive me, they wouldn't. What can I do about that?"

"Our forgiveness is not dependent on the response of the other person," Nicole shared. "They may not be ready or willing to forgive; however, our act of obedience in asking activates God's forgiveness toward us. Our part is to seek forgiveness and to walk in love toward the other person no matter what their response is. God's part is to forgive us and to begin the process of restoring the relationship, and He will work in all hearts involved. Are you willing to ask God to show you how you can love that person even if they don't forgive you? And even if they act badly towards you?"

"I have to love them?" Trisha asked. "What does that mean? You mean like I have to suck up to them? Boy, this just gets better and better!"

"No, you definitely don't have to do that." Nicole giggled at Trisha's colorful words.

Karen said, "You do have to be willing to let God show you what that looks like with each person in each situation. In Matthew 5:44 Jesus says, *"But I say to you, love your enemies, bless those who curse you, do good to those who hate you, and pray for those who spitefully use you and persecute you."* If you ask Jesus to give you His heart of love for them and to show you how to actively love them, He will. So what do you think?"

Again, Trisha said, "Jesus, I don't know how to do that, but if you'll show me, I'll choose to love these people even if they hate me."

Karen clapped and said, "Woo Hoo! Satan's not happy about that, but the angels are dancing with joy!"

In her dry sense of humor and a small smile on her lips Trisha said, "Well I'm glad somebody's happy about it."

Trisha sat quietly deep in thought. After a bit she said, "I know of a few people I can go to and ask forgiveness from, and I am willing to do that. They all live too far away for me to talk to them in person, but I can even email them right now or call them on the phone. The thing that I'm not sure about is that many of the people I've hurt, I don't even know who they are or where they are."

She went on to talk about her involvement with the occult. As she shared more of her story, Nicole realized that God was giving her the opportunity to extend forgiveness to the woman who had taken her to the ritual so long ago. One of Trisha's jobs had been to target children and teenagers and introduce them into the occult. What an amazing turn of events! They were talking about Trisha asking for forgiveness from people she had targeted and taken to rituals, and here she was, one of those people that had been targeted and who was able to stand in proxy for all those unnamed children in Trisha's past.

The impact of that realization just about knocked Nicole off her feet. She had been standing up pacing the floor, and she suddenly sat down hard on the couch. She had been knocked upside the head with a crisis of belief. Did she believe what she had been teaching Trisha? In her heart, Nicole had chosen to forgive all those involved in the occult that had hurt her long ago. Now here was a real life person, not the same who had targeted her, but who represented that woman, and who was seeking forgiveness. Could she choose to walk and act in love towards the woman that Trisha represented to her? Suddenly Nicole saw that woman and all those at the ritual through different eyes. She saw them as she saw Trisha, through eyes of compassion for those who were broken, who had been taken captive by the enemy and programmed or brain washed into doing terrible things. As Trisha had shared her story, Nicole realized that she had done many of the things she did out of fear of punishment and discipline if she didn't follow orders. She was better able to understand why the people had acted as they did, and in that moment, her heart was filled with love for not only Trisha, but for those who had wronged her so terribly in her own past. She knew that she wanted to stand on behalf of all those Trisha had hurt and offer her forgiveness.

With tears in her eyes, Nicole got up and then knelt down in front of Trisha. She took hold of her hands and said, "Trisha, I was one of those who was targeted by someone like you when I was 4 years old. I understand now that neither of you chose to do that, but were assigned that job. You had no option but to obey. And even if that had been a willing choice, you have repented and Jesus has forgiven you. Trish, I choose to represent each one of those you targeted, and we forgive you. In fact, I love you!"

Trisha's heart seemed to come apart at the seams, and a flood of tears gushed from the very core of her being. This was a good kind of broken heart, for the stitches that had been holding it together had been laced with the poison of bitterness and had been working destruction from the inside out. Karen came over to them and knelt on the floor beside Nicole. She placed one hand on each of them and entered into the restorative work of the Holy Spirit. It was a healing moment as the pain of that part of Trisha's past was released and washed away by the cleansing, healing, salty tears of the Lord Jesus Christ and her two sisters in the Lord.

When they stopped crying, they remained quietly contemplating what had just happened there. Only God could have orchestrated such and amazing thing.

After lunch Nicole announced that it was time for Trisha to forgive herself, who received the news with a groan of reluctance. But there was a faint smile behind the groan. Nicole said, "Lord Jesus, forgiving ourselves is always harder than forgiving others. But the truth is that we must extend that same love toward ourselves that we give to others because You have forgiven us. When we don't, we cut ourselves off from Your love and the power of the cross to forgive and heal. So Jesus, please help Trisha to see herself the way You see her and to be willing to accept herself as You do."

They were silent for a moment and Trisha finally said, "I just can't help it. I don't think that I deserve to forgive myself. I know this isn't right, but I feel like I need to punish myself if no one else is going to."

"Well, several thoughts here, Trish. When Jesus tells us to forgive, that means we are to forgive whoever we are holding anger and bitterness towards, and ourselves are not excluded. If you don't forgive yourself, Bitterness will continue to hold a place in your life from which it will keep on spreading its poison. Guilt, Shame, Self-Pity and Worthlessness who work for Belial will try to hold you in bondage and keep you from forgiving yourself because that kicks them out and sets the Holy Spirit's seal on those holes so they can't get back in…that is unless you choose to reopen that door for them by listening to their lies again.

228

Basically, Jesus set you free when He forgave you. He is telling you to forgive, and that includes yourself. To refuse to obey is rebellion against God."

Trisha responded, "I was just thinking about what you said about the difference between conviction and condemnation. Maybe this is one of those things where my feelings are condemnation. But how do I not feel that way?"

"This is also one of those times where you can't listen to your feelings," Nicole said. "You need to make a choice to obey what Jesus tells you even if you don't feel like it. If you want to continue the deliverance process, you need to repent from unforgiveness toward yourself, then choose to forgive yourself. That will destroy the work of the devil and result in hope, healing and freedom. Over time your feelings will change."

It seemed like the fight had gone out of Trisha. She got down on her knees and said, "I do want to be free. Ok, I'm ready."

The Spirit of God descended and moved through the room as Trisha surrendered this area of her life to the Lord. God allowed Karen to witness the destruction of Bitterness or Wormwood. She saw an angel pouring the blood of Jesus out of a pitcher and onto the defiling spirit. It let go of Trisha's head and heart, and grabbed its own head with both its hands, screaming in pain as it began to shrivel up into nothingness. As it disappeared, the others working under it fled in fear and chaos.

The three ladies spent the next several minutes just worshipping their Great God. As they worshipped, Nicole knew that the spirit of Harlotry had lost its rights and stronghold on Trisha. She got up and motioned for Karen to help her. They laid hands on their sister and when Nicole told her that it was time for Harlotry to go, Trisha told it to leave. And it did.

There was peace in the room and they were all exhausted. They went to bed and Nicole fell right to sleep.

CHAPTER 16
THE STRONGMAN

Is was getting impatient. And frightened. These ladies were getting way to close to him and he was tired of others bungling up the job. Never mind them. He would take care of this himself!

Nicole was awakened a short time later by a hissing noise. It was a snake and she could hear its hissing coming closer to her as it slithered across the floor. It crept up onto her bed and she felt it groping her genitals. In her sleepy state of mind, she seemed to think that is was trying to get into her body. She felt a momentary sexually arousing feeling, but with it was mixed a defilement that made her shudder. Even in this place between slumber and waking, Nicole knew it was evil and immediately rebuked it. It slithered away and was gone as fast as it had come.

She was wide awake now. Had she really heard and experienced this or was it a dream? Even as she pondered this question, she knew it had been real. She began to pray that God would show her exactly what this spirit was and why it had tried to invade her. Was it Leviathan trying to attack her and stop the deliverance? Was it a different demon that was attached to Trisha that was trying to stop her from identifying it and casting it out? But that didn't make complete sense because she had put her armor on and knew that it was sealed tight. Yet this thing had seemed to penetrate that armor and would have gotten to her if she had not woken up and rebuked it. Was there something in her that she was unaware of that had given it the right to touch her that way? The feeling of being attracted and yet repelled seemed vaguely familiar, yet she couldn't quite place it.

Nicole was not afraid. Jesus was so close to her that she could hear Him whispering to her that all would be brought into the light very soon. After praying protection around Trisha, Karen, and herself, she fell back to sleep and slept peacefully the rest of the night.

In the morning as soon as she awoke, the event of the night before came to her mind, and with it came the revelation that this was a sexual spirit. A name that she had heard in her thoughts repeatedly before this meeting, Incubus Succubus, kept nagging her, so after breakfast and devotions, Nicole decided to ask about it.

"Hey, Trish, does the name Incubus Succubus mean anything to you?"

She looked up from her Bible and said, "Yeah, it's a sexual spirit. Why?"

Nicole shared what had happened in the night and then Trisha said, "Now that you mention it, I heard something too. It seemed like it was right by my bed and then it got quiet and a woman came and sat near my head. She was leaning over me breathing into my ear. It was like she was whispering things to me but I couldn't understand them. I couldn't move away or stop it. Then I just fell back to sleep."

"Hum. Have you ever experienced this before?" Nicole asked.

"Actually I have. I'll hear a hissing noise and then this same woman comes and sits by my head while I'm asleep whispering into my ears. I'm usually so sleepy that I ignore it. I don't know what it's all about."

"Can you describe her to me?" Nicole asked.

"Well, she's not super old but she has wrinkled skin. She has long dark hair that she wears down with a red scarf around it. Long fingernails, but not painted. I've tried to look at her eyes, but I can never see them. It's like I know they are there, but they aren't. I know that sounds weird."

"How do you feel when this happens? Afraid?"

"No, like I said, I'm usually asleep and just know that she's there. I can never understand what she is whispering, if she is actually saying words. It's almost like she's whispering breaths into me. I've tried to pull away

231

and can't, so that's a little uncomfortable; but she's never hurt me."

"Is there a pattern, circumstance or trigger you can identify that would help us understand it?"

Trisha thought for a moment. "Not really. Well, it does seem to happen more often when I'm trying to follow God. But another thing that's coming to mind is something that used to happen a lot when I was younger. It's funny because I haven't thought of it in a long time. I don't know if it's important or has anything to do with this or not."

"Well, we're trusting God to show us what we need to know, so Lord Jesus, if this is something You reminded Trisha of, please help us to understand it." Nicole said, "Go ahead and tell us."

"It's just that when I would lay down to take a nap or go to bed at night, my Grandmother would show up. She would sit beside me and stroke my hair and whisper things to me. I never connected these two before because the lady with the red scarf doesn't look like my Grandmother. But they both did whisper in my ear. I could never really understand my Grandma either, but I always felt comforted when she was there."

"Was your Grandma alive?"

"No. But the funny thing is I never thought that it might not really be her until now. I guess I liked her coming to visit me."

Nicole began to pray. "Lord, we need to know if these two are connected. We need your truth and Your Word tells us that You will bring to light the things that are hidden in the darkness. You say that when we call to You, You will answer us and show us great and mighty things that we haven't known. So please tell us if these two women are connected, and tell us what they really are. Thank You for helping us, Jesus."

Immediately Trisha declared, "Oh my *gosh*! I see my Grandma and she's changing! It's not really my Grandma at all! It's a snake! And instead of my Grandma whispering in my ear, it's hissing in my ear! Oooh, gross!"

"Well," Nicole said, "It's interesting that this spirit's true nature is a snake, and that there was a snake here last night along with a woman who was sitting by your head whispering into your ear. We can be pretty sure that both women are demons or evil spirits, right?"

Both ladies agreed. Karen added, "And they are probably familiar spirits."

"Good point," Nicole said. "Let's think about the woman beside you last night and the symbols or clues that she is giving us about herself. She had long hair and long nails, and was wearing a red scarf on her head. I wonder what the scarf and the color red symbolizes?" She pulled out The Prophet's Dictionary[6] and found that red was "the color of royalty in its duty to engage in war to defend its land and peoples." And it was an "insignia of the ascending monarch's qualifying victories."

"Wow. Ok," Karen said. "Before we make any comments about how that might apply, let's look at the significance of breathing or whispering."

"Breath has to do with life; moving air; God's Spirit; it comes from the mouth which is where God's creative power was shown; it can be interchanged with 'mind' which denotes inner thoughts. Whispering has to do with secretly plotting," Nicole read.

"How about scarves?" Trisha asked.

"It doesn't say, but scarves worn on the head can represent submission as in a religious belief system. Long hair and nails as well as scarves usually signify the female gender, and in the past, females have held a submissive position."

Karen conjectured, "So we can assume that this was a female spirit, probably a principality whose purpose is to go to war in order to defend its property, which would be you, Trish. Didn't you say that it comes more often when you are closer to God?"

Trisha nodded. "And I'll bet it was whispering curses into my ear."

"Well I'm sure it wasn't breathing truth and life," Nicole said. "I am also thinking that the scarf didn't just signify a color, but may mean that it is working in submission to another spirit."

Trisha said as she leaned back in her chair. "What about the woman that turned into a snake? Do you think that has anything to do with this?"

"Lord Jesus, we need Your wisdom here because we don't just want to conjecture. We want truth so that Trisha can be set free. We know that's Your heart for her as well, so thank You for answering us," Nicole prayed.

Karen said, "I feel that the answer is staring us in the face."

"The Prophets Dictionary does have the word 'mantle' which is comparable to a scarf. It says that a mantle represents authority and power," Nicole read.

"Interesting!" Trisha said. "Authority and power is usually representative of a male role. So we've got the male role verses the female roll of submission. Well, you brought up Incubus Succubus earlier, Nicole," Trisha said. "That is a male and female spirit."

"Oh my goodness, you're right!" Nicole exclaimed. "Two working together as one, united in purpose and strategy. There was a snake that was trying to sexually molest me last night, which would suggest that it was a male, while a female was whispering to you. Male and female. The woman spirit you thought was your Grandma was changed into a snake. I know that principalities can take on different appearances." Nicole clapped her hands in victory. "Ladies, I believe that the Holy Spirit is revealing who the strongman in your life is, Trisha."

"I think so too, but I think we should pray for confirmation," Karen said.

The ladies began to pray. After a few minutes, Nicole looked over at Trisha and saw tears running down her cheeks. "What's going on Trish?" Nicole asked.

"I don't like what I'm seeing and feeling. I don't want to know this!" She slumped down onto the floor and pulled her feet up under her until she was in a fetal position. Nicole laid hands on her and prayed, "Lord Jesus, if this is a memory that Trisha needs to remember, then we ask for holy protection in her and around her while You minister truth to her. But if this is a false memory, please reveal that. In Jesus' name, we will not engage with the enemy of deceit."

Trisha seemed to relax a little bit even though she stayed huddled in a ball on the floor. After a moment Nicole asked, "Trish, can you tell us what is happening?"

She sniffled. "I'm little and I'm lying on the floor in a circle. I'm wearing a red robe and I see a monster hovering over me. I hear someone saying, 'Who gives this girl to be wed with Incubus Succubus?' and someone else saying, 'I do.' I know that voice. It's my pimp. But I didn't know he knew me when I was little." Trisha stiffened and cried out, "Oh God no! That thing is having sex with me!"

Karen and Nicole sat on the floor close to her, praying quietly. Something within Nicole understood what Trisha was experiencing. She was uncertain exactly how she knew, but she did. After a moment Nicole said, "Trisha, I want you to know that these things are only memories from things in the past. God has brought them to your mind right now for a purpose. You need to know that you are safe and they can't hurt you. Do you understand?"

In a little girl voice, Trisha said, "Yes."

"Ok," Nicole said. "Now, do you know where you are?"

In a more adult, controlled voice, Trisha said, "I'm at a ritual. I think it's a wedding ceremony and I'm being married to that monster. Incubus Succubus! I think God is confirming that he is the strongman."

Because Nicole was unsure what to do next, she started to pray. "Lord Jesus, thank you for confirmation. Please help us to know the next thing You want us to do."

Karen said, "Because we don't want to be ignorant of the devil's schemes, let's talk for a minute about Incubus

Succubus. I don't know anything about it except that is a sexual spirit that's part male and part female."

Trisha sat up and said, "It's a demon that has sex with people in their sleep. I always thought that the male part would have sex with females and the female part with males. But now I'm thinking that there's more to it than that. One was impersonating my grandma and it makes me wonder what influences I allowed her to pour into me. I can't believe that I thought that was my Grandma for all these years! Boy was I blind!"

"We are only responsible for what we know," Nicole said. "There is no condemnation, just conviction that will bring freedom."

Trisha said, "It's obvious that I was holding onto false comfort and now I'm seeing that the whispering and breathing was pouring lies, false strength and even evil purposes into me. That creeps me out and I don't like it."

Karen said, "We know the female's role in your life. What about the male's?"

"Well, knowing its nature, it is probably what has driven me to prostitution. It's what has ruled my life," Trisha said.

"I think that a lot of people can have encounters with an Incubus Succubus spirit and not fall under its bondage. But in ritual sex, there is a merging of the evil spirit with the human. That is why you have been ruled and controlled by this strongman, Trisha. Now that we know the rights it has over you, we can deal with this principality. The truth is, you became the bride of Christ the day you gave your heart to Him, and that trumps the counterfeit marriage of the enemy. Are you ready to confess and then renounce it?" Nicole asked.

"Yes!"

So they began to pray. Immediately the Lord stopped Nicole. He let her know that while He had revealed the strongman to them, it was by no means time to deal with it. He would allow Trisha to confess her sin, but she was not to do any renouncing of it because it wouldn't

236

do any good at this point; but He assured her that the time would come.

The three women stood together in a circle with their arms around each other and heads bowed together while Trisha told Jesus that she was so sorry that she had trusted in something that had brought her false comfort. She asked Him to forgive her for listening and obeying this sexually perverted spirit that she had allowed to control her. She told Him that she needed help to know what to do when the whispering started again. She told Him that she wanted to be free.

Trisha was quiet and Jesus spoke into her heart. He assured her of His love and let her know that He would never abandon her or leave her helpless; that when she called out to Him, He would come and help her.

The ladies felt released from dealing with Incubus Succubus, and put him out of their minds for the time being, knowing that he wasn't out of God's mind and that God would protect them until it was time to deal with him. They went to lunch and spent several hours just enjoying life, freedom and friends.

IS was slithering deeper into the recesses of Trisha's soul. The small ray of Light that had pierced his shield was enough to cause severe pain. Yes, he would go deeper and lay low for awhile. His pride refused to allow him to even contemplate defeat, and he had all confidence in his armor bearer. He was certain that these pitiful women would turn tail and run when they came face to face with him. Yes, let the battle begin!

CHAPTER 17
LEVIATHAN

As soon as they entered Trisha's apartment after lunch, they felt the Holy Spirit calling them to worship. After a bit, Nicole knew that the time had come for them to deal with Leviathan. She began explaining what the Lord had shown her about this enemy so that they could remove its rights of influence over Trisha.

"Leviathan is mentioned several times throughout scripture, but Job 41 gives us the most detailed account of this sea serpent or dragon. The Bible describes Leviathan as a creature that lives in the deep waters of the sea that is rarely seen, but is there none-the-less."

Nicole explained, "We know that what happens in the physical is a reflection of the spiritual, so the application for this spiritual principality or power, is that he makes his home in the deep places of our soul and is a master at hiding himself there. He burrows deep down into our mind, will and emotions; our sense of self. He hopes to go undetected so that he can continue to influence what we think, the choices we make and how we feel. He hides so well that we believe that his thoughts and feelings are our own. Leviathan can even counterfeit emotions, or twist and torment ours, causing them to be much more intense than they really are, creating turmoil, strife and drama."

"Well, I've had more than enough of that in my life," Trisha exclaimed.

"Leviathan is also described as having 'heads' in Psalm 74:14," Nicole continued. "In Revelation 13 and 17, it describes a beast with seven heads rising out of the sea. It doesn't say that this is Leviathan, however, it fits his MO. The Greek word for 'heads' in these passages means anything that is supreme, chief or prominent. In other words, each of his heads would be high ranking, important leaders in Satan's spiritual hierarchy. Proverbs 6:16-19 may give us a clue as to what Leviathan's heads may represent, and there are seven of them. *'There are six things that the* LORD *hates, yes, seven which are an abomination to him: A proud look,, a lying tongue, hands that shed innocent blood, a heart that devises wicked plans, feet that are swift in running to evil, a false witness who speaks lies, and one who sows discord among brethren.'*"

"Hey, that sounds a lot like the spirit of Harlotry," Trisha observed. "I guess it goes back to what you said, Karen, about the powers that work under princes. In this case, Leviathan would be the prince, and Harlotry would be an enforcer of his power. Is that what you meant?"

Karen smiled, "You got it girl!"

Nicole said, "Harlotry may be one of Leviathan's heads. Let's think about the other principalities we have dealt with."

"Python, Jezebel, Wormwood or Bitterness," Trisha recalled.

"And Belial," Karen added. "That's six including Harlotry. I wonder what the seventh would be?"

"I'm sure the Lord will show us if we need to know," Nicole said. "It's amazing that each of these principality's jobs or functions line up with the seven things that God hates."

"What about pride?" Trisha asked. "Could that be the seventh head?"

Nicole thought for a moment. "I don't think so. Pride is actually Satan's nature or character, and his minions adopt his nature and function in it. Remember how all the evil spirits we've dealt with have functioned in pride? In fact, our own sinful nature is so full of pride, that when one of them whispers prideful thoughts, we tend to listen.

"Leviathan's nature is also fully based on pride, and when we function in pride, we are opening the door for him. When we welcome pride, Leviathan sets up a kingdom, takes us captive and then rules over us. Job 41:34 says, *'He beholds every high thing; He is king over all the*

239

children of pride.' Jeremiah 13:15-17 says, *'Hear and give ear: Do not be proud,... Give glory to the* LORD *your God...But if you will not hear it, my soul will weep in secret for your pride...because the* LORD's *flock has been taken captive.' "*

"So his goal is to make us be proud? Like, to make us think we are better than other people?" Trisha asked.

"Actually, his goal is to stop people from having a relationship with Jesus. He'll try to turn our prideful hearts toward idolatry as we choose to trust in and rely on something other than God. Under his rule, relationship with God through Jesus will be hindered, blocked, choked and starved out. He'll do anything to keep us from knowing the truth about God's love in our minds, but if that fails, he'll try to stop us from experiencing it. He'll cause a blockage between our mind and heart to keep God's love from becoming real to us."

"You mean just like he used Belial to whisper lies about how worthless I was so that I couldn't believe and accept God's love for me?" Trisha asked.

"Yep. And just like he uses Python to cause misunderstanding of the truth and the inability to understand the Bible," Nicole said.

"And like he uses Jezebel's false religious front to distract us with religious busyness so that we forget about relationship," Karen added.

"He will use whatever it takes to detour God's people from walking in His love and from spreading it to the world; which is contrary to what God's plan has been from the beginning." Nicole said, "In the Old Testament, God's presence was separated from the people, hidden behind a huge, heavy curtain that no one was able to visit except for one priest, one time a year. Jesus came to tear that curtain down so that anyone who wanted to have a relationship with Him could; and that is exactly what happened when Jesus died on the cross. The curtain was torn in two! God was saying, *'Here I am, My people! Now you can freely come into My presence. All of you. Anyone who seeks Me can now find Me. You don't need a priest anymore;*

you can come directly to Me. I have waited since the fall of man for this moment when you and I could have our relationship restored, and the blood of My Son, Jesus, has now made that possible.'

"Leviathan hates that! He does not want us to get anywhere near to God, but he has to be sneaky in his tactics so that we don't detect him. It's as if he's picked up the temple curtain that God discarded and is holding it up inside our soul, hoping that we won't be able to see past it; and if we happen to realize that there is something not quite right, or want to go deeper in a relationship with Jesus, it just seems as if we hit a wall."

Trisha said, "I've felt that way before; like I would get so far in my relationship with Jesus, then fall back, then go forward again only to be stopped in the same place as before. That's why I'm so thankful that you guys are helping me. I've finally been able to understand the things that have been holding me back."

"Leviathan is a master at deception, and every person has had open doors for him in their life at some point or other," Nicole said. Job 41:18 says, *'His sneezings flash forth light, And his eyes are like the eyelids of the morning.'* Leviathan parades himself as a god, but he is a counterfeit god and all of his light, his appeal, his words or ideas, everything he offers is false.

"When we are under Leviathan's deception, we don't realize that we are missing out on the true air and life of the Holy Spirit. His scales are like that curtain in the temple, keeping people separated from God by using counterfeit breath and fire. In order to be healthy spiritually, we need the breath or wind of the Holy Spirit, but Leviathan offers counterfeit air, or poison, *'smoke [that] goes out of his nostrils,'* as we see in Job 41:20. Verse 21 says, *'His breath kindles coals, And a flame goes out of his mouth.'* This is a counterfeit flame of fire. Fire from the Holy Spirit stirs passion for God and empowers us with abundant life so that we produce the fruit of the Spirit based on love for Him and others. Leviathan's false fire stirs up passion for self and takes us into captivity with the intent to destroy, as over time, this serpent coils himself up and around our soul to the point of spiritual hopelessness and despair. Our spiritual eyes become blinded to the truth, and our spiritual ears become deaf so that we cannot hear God's voice or discern the things of God correctly. Without air, without food, the spirit starves, and relationship with God suffers and dies."

"That sounds so hopeless!" Karen said.

"It is unless we understand how the enemy works and then we can overcome. 2 Corinthians 2:11 tells us not to be ignorant of the devil's schemes, so let's look at how Leviathan functions," Nicole said. "Pride is his weapon of choice that he uses against the souls of men...and women. One of his jobs is to cause suffering of all kinds. Job suffered the sorrow of loosing his children, the hardship of loosing all of his property, and the affliction of physical suffering. In Job 3:8, **the word for** *mourning* **is also translated** *Leviathan.*' In verse 22 it says, '...*sorrow* dances before him.' The reason Leviathan loves to cause pain, sorrow, suffering and hardship is because in those times we are most vulnerable to his lies that will take us captive."

"Wait a minute here," Trisha interrupted. "How in the world is pain and sorrow connected with pride?"

Nicole thought for a moment and said, "When we experience pain, suffering, trauma, abuse, or even as we suffer the consequences of our own sin, the thoughts that Leviathan implants in our mind are things like, '*If God really loved me, He wouldn't have let this happen to me.*' '*I can't depend on anybody, not even God. I better take care of this myself.*' '*I've been through enough and I deserve to have a good time.*' '*I can't help the way I am. I know that the things I want to do may be wrong, but I can't change.*' Whatever his thoughts are that he whispers into our minds, he wants us to believe that our way of doing things is better than God's way, and that there is no other way. That's pride talking.

"Most often we think of pride as the attitude that says, '*I'm better than you;*' but it also says, '*I can't trust anyone else to get me through this. I better take control.*' It is

242

that part of us that rises up to protect ourselves and that thinks we can do it better than anybody else, including God. It is false confidence of self that causes us to shut God out and refuse to trust Him.

"Choosing to take things into our own hands as a response to sorrow or pain is pride, and it opens a door in our soul that Leviathan sneakily slithers into so quietly that we have no clue he is even there. His voice sounds so much like our own thoughts because the lies he utters are a reflection of our own familiar sinful, selfish nature that we were born into. Pride; love of self; wanting our own way; searching for and fulfilling selfish ambitions and desires.

"We usually associate pride with attitudes such as *self importance, superiority, haughtiness or arrogance, boasting, independence, self glory, self confidence, a critical or judgmental spirit, or religiosity.* It can look like obvious rebellion or self-centeredness, but it can also hide behind things *like shyness, low self esteem, ignorance, stubbornness, fear, victimization, busyness, apathy, confusion,* etc. For whatever reason, it is a bypassing of seeking God's way for our own, and ultimately leads to turmoil, trouble, suffering and destruction, the very things we are trying to escape!"

"That makes sense," Trisha said. "I can see how I've believed most of those things you said as a result of suffering. So that was Leviathan giving me those thoughts?"

"Most likely." Nicole said. "Job 41:24 says, '*His heart is as hard as stone.*' Leviathan often gains access or power through broken or wounded hearts, divided hearts or rebellious hearts, and the longer we live under his rule and bondage, our hearts don't get healed, they just get hard like his. The remedy for this is found in 2 Chronicles 7:14. '*If My people who are called by My name will humble themselves, and pray and seek My face, and turn from their wicked ways, then I will hear from heaven, and will forgive their sin and heal their land.*' Ezekiel 11:18-20 says, '*...they will take away all its detestable things and all its abominations from there. Then I will give them one heart, and I will put a new spirit within them, and*

243

take the stony heart out of their flesh, and give them a heart of flesh, that they may walk in My statutes and keep My judgments and do them; and they shall be My people, and I will be their God.'"

Trisha was listening intently. "I think that my heart has probably gotten hard. I don't really feel much of anything anymore, but I know it's not because it's been healed. When you said the word 'blocked,' it reminded me that sometimes I feel like I know things with my head about God, but they just don't get down into my heart where I feel like they really make a difference. Is that because my heart is hard or because it's blocked? Is that what you mean?"

"Yes, that is exactly what I'm talking about," Nicole said. "It could be either or both. Sometimes people become Christians but continue to struggle with the same sins and bondages, thought patterns, etc, as they did before they accepted Jesus. Leviathan knows that if a choice is to be made and there is a battle between the mind and the heart, the heart usually wins.

"One of his tricks is to keep the truth from getting into your heart, from becoming real to you. If truth gets through to your heart, you will be able to draw close to God's heart and will know from experience that you can push him aside and enter into the place where there is real air, real food, real relationship. You will experience God's love, grace, mercy, compassion, truth, faithfulness, deliverance, healing, joy, peace, power and miraculous, supernatural interventions in every aspect of your life. The counterfeit will no longer satisfy.

"Leviathan will do everything he can to stop this from happening, but if it does, he will try to stop or block deliverance. He wants to stop the ministry of the Lord God in your life Trisha, so that you will not spread His ministry of love, hope, healing and freedom to others."

"Wow," Trisha said. "This all makes a lot of sense. I've been a Christian for five years and I still keep struggling with the same things I've struggled with my

244

whole life. I guess Leviathan got to me through all the pain and stuff in my past. I never thought of protecting myself, low self esteem, or being controlling as pride. You think that block between my head and heart is Leviathan? He's the one that's keeping me from getting close to Jesus? Let's kick him out! I don't want him anymore. I probably need to confess my pride first, right? But didn't I already confess pride?"

"Yes you did in relation to Python. God is showing you other areas of pride in your life and those need to be confessed as well."

"Oh, I get it," Trisha said as she knelt down on the floor. "Lord Jesus, Please forgive me for listening to the lies of Leviathan, for listening to my pride and choosing to rely on myself for protection instead of you. I do want a relationship with You, and I don't want anything to come between us. Please take my hard heart and give me a soft one so that I can know Your truth and Your heart. In Jesus' name, Amen."

Nicole was quiet a moment as she waited for direction, then she said, "That's good Trish. I feel like dislodging this principality is going to be different from the others. I don't believe that we can just command it to go. I think that the way to freedom from this monster is through pushing past his lies and embracing the truth. We can boldly enter God's presence in humility and surrender to Him; the very opposite of Leviathan's nature. I'm just not sure what this is going to look like, so let's worship and see what God wants us to do next."

Trisha said, "Ok, but let me go to the bathroom first."

Karen and Nicole heard laughing coming from the bathroom. "Is everything ok in there?" Karen asked.

Trisha came back into the living room with a smile on her face and said, "That was so weird! I heard Leviathan talking to me. He was begging me not to make him leave and was even trying to bribe me if I'd let him stay! I think it's funny because here's this huge, powerful spirit and it's begging me like I have power over it!"

"You do!" Karen said. "Now that you know about it and are choosing to do things God's way, he will have no authority to stay, and you have the authority to strip him of his power in your life."

"Awesome!" Trisha shouted. "Let's do it!"

They got on their knees and began worshipping while the praise music played. The room took on an atmosphere of worship and Nicole knew that the Holy Spirit was there along with angels that were joining them in their worship of God. She quietly thanked the Lord for sending help, wisdom and guidance. A fleeting thought went through her mind. She had no idea what she was doing, and yet she wasn't worried or afraid. She had all confidence that God had placed her here for a reason and that the Holy Spirit would accomplish His work.

Out loud, Nicole asked the Lord if there were any spiritual legal rights left that Leviathan was able to hang onto. Nothing came to her mind, and with her eyes still closed, she asked Trisha if she knew of anything that was a stronghold for Leviathan.

When Trisha didn't answer, Nicole looked over at her. She was sitting on the couch with her arms crossed and her legs crossed and folded up under her. She was peering straight ahead, looking at nothing or something very far away, and she had a prideful, haughty and rebellious look on her face. It reminded Nicole of a painting she had seen once of an old Indian chief.

"Leviathan," Nicole announced. "Since you are out, I am notifying you that you are hereby stripped of your authority and power in Trisha's life. In Jesus' name, I command you to tell me what right you have to remain."

He turned Trisha's head in the other direction, away from her. He was behaving as if he believed she wasn't worthy of his acknowledgment, even with a glance.

"You will look at me, you serpent of hell! In Jesus' name, I command you to look at me!" Nicole ordered.

He turned Trisha's head back towards Nicole and looked into her eyes with an expression of strong defiance.

Nicole said, "Ok, if you will not cooperate, I will not deal with you any further. Let me talk to Trisha."

He moved his head to look off into the distance again and pursed his lips together in defiance as he raised his head even higher in a proud stance.

Nicole said, "That's it! We're done! Karen, get the anointing oil! Thank you Leviathan for telling me what your remaining stronghold is!"

Karen looked confused. "He didn't say anything."

"Not with words," Nicole smiled, "but the Lord just showed me that his stronghold is Trisha's body, right where he's manifesting. His rights to her soul have already been destroyed as the layers of the powers under him have been identified and removed. Leviathan is making his last stand in her body."

Suddenly, a loud growl erupted from Trisha and she lunged toward Nicole with her body. Karen jumped back, but the Spirit within Nicole held her steady and she calmly turned her head and looked at Trisha, or rather the entity that was showing itself. The expression on her face was different from what it had been earlier. It was pure hatred. It was keeping its eyes focused on Nicole, instead of looking away like Leviathan had done earlier. It reminded her of a wild, rabid animal that was ready to attack.

"Hello, who are you?" she asked the unplanned visitor. They watched as Trisha struggled, trying to raise her arms but couldn't. It was as if they were being restrained, and they knew the angels were helping to protect them. The spirit just growled in response and drool began to seep from Trisha's mouth. The more it struggled against the invisible restraints, the more frustrated it got, and the anger began to turn to fear.

Nicole started singing the first song that came to her mind and Karen joined in. "Oh how He loves you and me. Oh how He loves you and me. He gave His life, what more could He give...."

The struggling stopped and at the end of the song, Nicole prayed, "Lord Jesus, please show us what you want us to do. Is this just a distraction that Leviathan is using to avoid deliverance? Or is this something that needs to go?" A name came to Nicole's mind. Legion. She wanted confirmation, so she said, "In Jesus' name, I command you to identify yourself."

Through gritted teeth it answered, "My name is Legion and I hate you!" It spit at Nicole. She wiped her arm off and said, "You will not do that again. Lord Jesus please assign an angel over Trisha's mouth so that this demon will only be able to use it to speak truth."

If it hadn't been such a serious matter it would have been quite funny. Legion was trying so hard to open Trisha's mouth but it wouldn't budge. It had begun struggling once again against the unseen forces, and Nicole prayed, "Lord Jesus, please show us what to do about this demon."

"It's not a demon, you idiot, it's a principality like me!" This outburst surprised Nicole, but the pride in its voice and the look on its face told her that they were once again in the presence of Leviathan.

"Ok, Mr. Principality. Tell me what rights it has to Trisha," Nicole ordered.

"It works for me. I'm its superior, and I commanded it to come," he bragged.

"Perfect," Nicole replied. "So when you are gone, it will have to go too."

Nicole knew that they needed Trisha to renounce Leviathan which would give them permission to remove his rights to her body. "Leviathan, I will speak with Trisha now. I command you to go down and no other principality or demon will be allowed to surface. So go down and let Trisha speak."

Like he had before, Leviathan lifted his head up higher as a show of his arrogance and turned his head away from Nicole in defiance.

"If that's the way you want it," Nicole said, "I'll call upon the angels of God to push you down and hold you under."

In the blink of an eye, Trisha was back. "What do we do?" she asked. "It's like I can hear what is happening, but I can't respond."

"Trish, Leviathan's stronghold is in your body, and he's controlling it. Will you renounce him and tell him out loud that you don't want him any more and that you choose Jesus to be your master?" Nicole asked.

"Yes!" Trisha said. "In Jesus' name, I renounce you Leviathan. I don't want you in my life or body anymore. I choose to surrender my spirit, soul and body to Jesus and I will only obey Him. He is my Master now and you don't belong here any more."

As soon as she had said this, Trisha's body stiffened, and her head was thrown back. Leviathan was holding her eyes shut tightly like he thought that if they couldn't see him, maybe he could hold on.

While the angels held Trisha's body down, Karen began bathing her in anointing oil and Nicole prayed over every part of her body. They began with Trisha's mind and brain. While Nicole prayed prayers of releasing and cleansing from Leviathan's power over her mind and brain, and then dedication of it to the Lord Jesus Christ, Karen was drenching her whole head with anointing oil. They went through this process with her entire physical body, and Leviathan's expression gradually changed from pride to fear.

When they finished, Nicole read Isaiah 27:1 in the Amplified version. "*In that day [the Lord will deliver [Trisha] from her enemies and also from the rebel powers of evil and darkness] His sharp and unrelenting, great, and strong sword will visit and punish Leviathan the swiftly fleeing serpent, Leviathan the twisting and winding serpent; and He will slay the monster that is in the sea.*" And then she read Psalm 74:12-17. "*For God is my King from of old, Working salvation in the midst of the earth. You divided the sea by Your strength; You broke the heads of the sea serpents in the waters. You broke the heads of Leviathan in pieces.*"

Nicole got down on her knees with her face on the floor and prayed, "Lord Jesus, what do You want us to do now? What can we do to free Trisha from the power and grip of this principality?"

Job 41:9 came to her mind, "*Indeed, any hope of overcoming him is false,*" and she cried out, "Jesus! We know You want Trisha free! There is no power greater than Yours, so please help us!"

She had no more than uttered these words when she saw the Lord Jesus come riding in on a white horse with His huge sword drawn and raised toward the sky. He rode right up to the monster and pierced its heart clear through with His sword. As the dragon thrashed its body momentarily in pain and then fell to the ground, Nicole realized that indeed there had been nothing that they could have done. Jesus was the only One who was able to overcome this one in victory.

Still on her knees, Nicole opened her eyes and looked over at Trisha. She was sitting on the edge of the couch looking hopeful, and after a moment she said, "Wow! He's gone! I'm free!" She jumped up off the couch and started to jump up and down, but then got a funny look on her face. She looked down at her arms that were soaked with oil, and then her legs and feet that were also covered. She touched her wet hair and said, "Well, it looks like you girls had a good time sliming the devil!" They all laughed and hugged and cried.

The switch was surprising as again, it let out a scream, and was immediately silenced by the angel holding Trisha's mouth shut, but it continued thrashing against the angels that were restraining her body.

Without warning, Legion, the power of Insanity and Violence asserted itself, and Trisha suddenly lunged at Nicole. Nicole didn't see it coming, but felt herself being moved backwards just as she saw Trisha falling towards her. Trisha landed on the floor at Nicole's feet, and in a split second, Nicole knew this was Legion.

"Stay right where you are, Legion," she commanded. "Your commander and prince has been slain and in Jesus' name we take you captive. I bind your hands and feet and mouth in Jesus' name."

He was once again trying to claw Nicole and to curse or spit at her, but as she declared in Jesus' name that he be bound, it was obvious that the angels were active because Trisha's hands were pulled behind her back and she was unable to open her mouth.

"Legion, you are stripped of your function and assignment in Trisha's life. In Jesus' name I command you to release her. Come out of her right now and go to the feet of Jesus to wait for His judgment of you."

The angel released Trisha's mouth long enough for it to declare, "I can't come out because there aren't any pigs around...except for those people out there in the streets...they are more unclean than the swine. Let me go into those, but please don't make me go to Jesus. I hate Him!" Trisha's mouth was shut tight again before he could spit out his vile words.

Nicole said, "Absolutely not! You will go nowhere other than to kneel before Jesus, the King of Kings." Then she prayed, "Lord Jesus, I don't trust this spirit, so please send escorting angels to remove it from Trisha without harming her and carry it to wherever You send it. Thank you."

Trisha's body which was still lying on the floor, tensed up and then relaxed. Her arms were released and fell to the floor beside her. After a few seconds, Karen called out, "Trisha?"

She lifted her head up and smiled such a peaceful, beautiful smile. "I'm so relaxed, I think I could fall asleep right here."

Karen and Nicole laughed in relief. Trisha sat up and said, "I saw four angels come and pick it up and carry it off into the sky. It was kicking and screaming like crazy!" Then she looked at Nicole and said, "I'm so sorry about trying to attack you, Nicole. I could feel it, but couldn't stop it."

Nicole hugged her. "No worries. I knew that wasn't you. Wasn't that amazing though how the angels pulled me backwards?"

"Well, I think it was amazing how they didn't let me scratch you to pieces because I could feel Legion's hatred and he really wanted to kill you!" Trisha said.

"Hey," Karen exclaimed. "I think we just discovered Leviathan's seventh head!"

"I think you're right!" Trisha agreed.

The girls were all very tired, so they agreed to take a short nap before Karen and Nicole headed home. Nicole rested, but felt that there was one more thing that they needed to do. When they got up, Nicole said, "Trisha, I would like to pray for healing over you." Karen agreed that that was important.

So they worshipped the Lord and thanked Him for His mighty hand of victory and deliverance. They prayed that the Holy Spirit would fill all the places in Trisha's spirit, soul and body that had been vacated by the enemy, and that seal of the Holy Spirit would cover all of the places that had been open doors for him in the past. They asked Jesus, the healer to bind up and to heal any wounded places in Trisha's heart and to heal her broken heart and damaged emotions. They asked Him to take her heart of stone and make it flesh, moldable so she could become like Him. They asked the Spirit of Truth to renew Trisha's mind as she searched the Word of God daily. They asked Jesus the healer to destroy any seeds of infirmity from her physical body, along with any seeds of insanity that had been planted in her mind. And then they asked for an anointing of the Holy Spirit to come upon Trisha and to give her the gifts of the Spirit as she acted in obedience to His voice. They asked especially for the gift of spiritual discernment so that she would know the voice of the enemy from that of her Savior. They placed the armor of God on her and asked that Jesus would remind her every day and night to make sure it was tightly in place. They asked the Holy Spirit to help her learn to use the weapons, keys and tools of His Kingdom. They asked God to help Trisha's will to be conformed to His, and that she would choose to walk in humility, to crucify her flesh and to die to her own desires in exchange for God's.

It was time for Karen and Nicole to head home. As they hugged Trisha, she asked, "Hey, what about Incubus Succubus? The strongman."

"We'll wait until the Holy Spirit tells us it's time to deal with him," Nicole said. "In the meantime, seek the Lord with all your heart and learn to love Him with all your heart, soul, mind and strength. And as Paul said in Philippians 4:9 '*Practice what you've learned and received from me, what you heard and saw me do. Then the God who gives this peace will be with you.*' I'm confident that He who began the good work in you will bring it to completion."

CHAPTER 18
REFLECTIONS

Several days later, it was still dark as Nicole was sipping her morning coffee in her window seat that she shared with Jesus every morning. She was reflecting on the wild adventure she, Karen and Trisha had experienced. Had it been real? She was very glad that Karen had been with her as a witness, because if she had been alone, she might have really wondered. It almost felt as if she had been a bystander watching what was happening because it didn't seem like her. Not one time had she been afraid! It was then that she realized two things. She wasn't the same person because Jesus had healed her and given her a new identity that was based in His Spirit and power. Second, it had been the Lord who was doing His work. She had only been His instrument. What a trip!

It seemed like God was saying, "Ok, kiddo. Let's review the lessons you've been learning." As she thought about the principalities and powers she had encountered, a few things stood out to her. The keys to overcoming were fasting and praying, humility and surrender to God. The weapons of warfare were trust in God and relying on Him, His Word and His Spirit, step by step obedience to God, forgiveness, claiming and acting on the truth of God's Word regardless of feelings, renouncing the old and announcing the new. The tools for cultivation would be living in the presence of God, so close to Him that His heart and mind became hers; crucifying the flesh, dying to self and living for God. The results were hope, healing and freedom.

Nicole had learned so much and wondered what God had in store for her in the future. She wondered if she would encounter these same principalities again. How common were they? She didn't really know much about spiritual warfare, but she imagined that she could relate to how the disciples must have felt when Jesus sent them out into the world telling them to do what He did; and who, in Luke 10, came back saying, *"Lord, even the demons are subject to us in Your name!"* Jesus had replied, *"I saw Satan fall like lightning from heaven. Behold, I give you the authority to trample on serpents and scorpions, and over all the power of the enemy, and nothing shall by any means hurt you. Nevertheless do not rejoice in this, that the spirits are subject to you, but rather rejoice because your names are written in heaven."*

"Nicole," Jesus whispered. "There are millions of demons and principalities. Don't worry about which ones you will encounter, for I will always reveal who they are and their functions to you as needed. I allowed you to deal with these specifically so that you could learn important principles of spiritual warfare. It had nothing to do with who they are. It has everything to do with who you are as you are in Me and I am in you."

It was clear that Jesus intended her to be involved in spiritual warfare, to use the authority and power over the enemy when He directed her to. And suddenly she knew that the greatest and most important key, weapon and tool was her relationship with Jesus through intercessory prayer. She realized that while there were common principles, there were no formulas for warfare or healing or deliverance or love, or anything else in God's Kingdom. It all had to be done under the direction of the Holy Spirit through obedience to the Word of God and the gift of spiritual discernment through her connection with Jesus. There it was again.... intercessory prayer.

Day was just dawning when Nicole finished her devotions and reflections. She looked up and saw that the sky was illuminated with intense colors that were welcoming in the morning. Jake noticed it too and both stepped out the front door to take in the magnificent beauty. To their surprise, the color surrounded them, all 360 degrees! Nicole had never seen a sunrise with such brilliant color that covered the entire sky before. She happened to think of the scripture in Psalm 74:16. Right after saying that God had broken the heads of Leviathan in

255

pieces, it said, '*The day is Yours, the night also is Yours; You have prepared the light and the sun.*' Through the beauty, she knew that Jesus was telling her that He was pleased with them; that He would surround them completely with His presence, power and magnificence as they followed Him.

Jo came lumbering sleepily out the door, clearly not ready to be awoken, but taking his job of protector seriously as always, he couldn't let them go out of the house without him. He looked at them, then around the yard, barked once to let anyone out there know that he was on guard, then backed his body into a sitting position and sat down. He yawned, then lowered the rest of his 180 pounds down onto the deck with a "humph," and closed his eyes.

Nicole smiled at her dog, her constant shadow, then reached over and linked her arm through her husbands as she turned her attention back to the sky. She was content. And something else. Nicole suddenly realized that God had fulfilled the prophetic word for their marriage that Karen had recorded so long ago. God had indeed brought them both from their opposite spectrums of belief concerning Ramoth Ranch, and as each of their hearts had met God's heart, their own hearts had been knit together in unity and a deeper love than she had ever known. Since Nicole had submitted herself to God's plans and her husband's leadership, the ranch had housed several ladies for certain periods of time; some on weekend visits; some for a week or a month, and God always did His amazing work of hope, healing and freedom in their lives when they surrendered to Him.

"Thank you for my husband, Jesus. You have blessed me abundantly with a man who is rich in love, wise in understanding and compassionate for those who are hurting," Nicole blessed the Lord with her praise.

As she rested her head on Jake's shoulder and watched the color in the sky recede, she knew that no matter what lay ahead for them, they would be walking in the true Light of the World and that there was no safer or more beautiful place to be. God had given wings to Nicole's vision, and even though it wasn't happening the way she thought that it would, she realized that she had been learning to fly.

They had no idea that this was but a quiet moment before the storm.

IS was roaring in outrage against the Soul Redeemer, and vowed to relentlessly pursue Nicole and to fulfill his desire to reclaim that which had been stolen from him.

Suddenly the sound of thunder ripped through the sky and dark storm clouds blocked the rays of the rising sun. Nicole jumped as a warning in her spirit responded to the physical manifestation of the fury erupting in the spiritual realm.

EXCERPT FROM BOOK TWO:
"THE SOUL REDEEMER: From Victim to Victory"

Nicole asked, "How long before I can go home?"

He responded, "Look lady, like I told you before, just call me Sam. And I wish I could tell you when you could go home, but it'll depend on a lot of things. We're working on it, so have some patience here."

Nicole impatiently replied, "By 'we' I assume you mean the good people who are on your side that hired you." He nodded, and she asked, "What is the plan, Sam? Are you going to let me in on it? I want to help."

He studied her a moment as if measuring her strength, and she looked steadily back at him. Then he asked, "Don't you think you've taken in enough information for now?"

She was disappointed and frustrated. "Sam, I want to go home. There's a woman in my house and in my bed and my husband believes she's me! You won't let me just go home and kick her out. You say that there's a plan in place to fix this situation. I want to know what is being done about this and what I can do to help!"

Sam sighed, "Ok lady. The bottom line is that I believe we are in the last days and Satan is pulling a trump card even as we speak. With new technology, heightened spiritual knowledge and enhanced physical capabilities through interaction with demons, the Illuminati have come up with what they believe is a better, more effective way to attain their goals…"

Dear Reader, FYI, the situation Nicole finds herself in at the beginning of Book 1 is resumed and continued in Book 2 as well as the excerpt above.

[1] *"Sweet Jesus Peace," Words and music by Reba Rambo, 1977, Heart Warming Music.*

[2] *ROMANS ROAD OF SALVATION explained by David Jeremiah:*
www.davidjeremiah.org/site/about/becoming_a_christian.aspx
> **A. Because of our sin, we are separated from God.**
> *For all have sinned and fall short of the glory of God. (Romans 3:23)*
> **B. The penalty for our sin is death.**
> *For the wages of sin is death, but the gift of God is eternal life in Jesus Christ our Lord. (Romans 6:23)*
> **C. The penalty for our sin was paid by Jesus Christ!**
> *But God demonstrates His own love toward us, in that while we were yet sinners, Christ died for us. (Romans 5:8)*
> **D. If we repent of our sin, then confess and trust Jesus Christ as our Lord and Savior, we will be saved from our sins!**
> *For whoever calls on the name of the Lord shall be saved. (Romans 10:13)...if you confess with your mouth the Lord Jesus and believe in your heart that God has raised Him from the dead, you will be saved. For with the heart one believes unto righteousness, and with the mouth confession is made unto salvation. (Romans 10:9,10)*

[3] *Thayer's Greek Lexicon, Strong's Concordance, Sin: G266*

[4] *Strong's Concordance, Repent: G3340*

[5] *Neil T. Anderson, "The Steps to Freedom in Christ," (Gospel Light), 2001.*

[6] *Paula A. Price, PhD., "The Prophets Dictionary," (Whitaker House), New Kensington,   PA, 2006.*

Made in the USA
Middletown, DE
01 July 2015